BEYOND MIDNIGHT

ALSO BY IAN K. SMITH

FICTION

Eagle Rock: An Ashe Cayne Novel
The Overnights: An Ashe Cayne Novel
Wolf Point: An Ashe Cayne Novel
The Unspoken: An Ashe Cayne Novel
The Ancient Nine
The Blackbird Papers

NONFICTION

Eat Your Age
The Met Flex Diet
Plant Power
Burn Melt Shred
Fast Burn
Mind over Weight
Clean & Lean
The Clean 20
Blast the Sugar Out!
The SHRED Power Cleanse
The SHRED Diet Cookbook
SUPER SHRED
SHRED
The Truth About Men
Eat
Happy
The 4 Day Diet
Extreme Fat Smash Diet
The Fat Smash Diet
The Take-Control Diet
Dr. Ian Smith's Guide to Medical Websites

BEYOND MIDNIGHT

An Ashe Cayne Novel

IAN K. SMITH

AMISTAD

An Imprint of HarperCollinsPublishers

Without limiting the exclusive rights of any author, contributor or the publisher of this publication, any unauthorized use of this publication to train generative artificial intelligence (AI) technologies is expressly prohibited. HarperCollins also exercise their rights under Article 4(3) of the Digital Single Market Directive 2019/790 and expressly reserve this publication from the text and data mining exception.

This is a work of fiction. Names, characters, places, and incidents are products of the author's imagination or are used fictitiously and are not to be construed as real. Any resemblance to actual events, locales, organizations, or persons, living or dead, is entirely coincidental.

BEYOND MIDNIGHT. Copyright © 2025 by Ian K. Smith. All rights reserved. Printed in the United States of America. No part of this book may be used or reproduced in any manner whatsoever without written permission except in the case of brief quotations embodied in critical articles and reviews. For information, address HarperCollins Publishers, 195 Broadway, New York, NY 10007. In Europe, HarperCollins Publishers, Macken House, 39/40 Mayor Street Upper, Dublin 1, D01 C9W8, Ireland.

HarperCollins books may be purchased for educational, business, or sales promotional use. For information, please email the Special Markets Department at SPsales@harpercollins.com.

harpercollins.com

FIRST EDITION

Designed by Michele Cameron

Library of Congress Cataloging-in-Publication Data
Names: Smith, Ian K., author.
Title: Beyond midnight / Ian K. Smith.
Description: First edition. | New York, NY: Amistad, 2025. | Series: An Ashe Cayne novel; 5
Identifiers: LCCN 2025005785 (print) | LCCN 2025005786 (ebook) | ISBN 9780063459229 (trade paperback) | ISBN 9780063459236 (epub)
Subjects: LCGFT: Detective and mystery fiction. | Novels.
Classification: LCC PS3619.M588 B49 2025 (print) | LCC PS3619.M588 (ebook) | DDC 813/.6—dc23/eng/20250325
LC record available at https://lccn.loc.gov/2025005785
LC ebook record available at https://lccn.loc.gov/2025005786

25 26 27 28 29 LBC 5 4 3 2 1

To Chicago legend Jim Reynolds, who always eagerly awaits the delivery of the next Ashe Cayne installment and stays up into the dark wee hours of the morning finishing the story then texting me his approval.

1

"My uncle is dead," Ivan Ramirez said, sitting across from my desk in a loose golf shirt and black Titleist cap that he wore slightly tilted to the side. An even tan made his swarthy skin glisten under the sun coming through the large window behind me.

"So are Shakespeare, Mandela, and Van Gogh," I said.

"What's that supposed to mean?" he said.

"Your uncle is in elite company," I said.

"Will you help me find out what really happened to him?"

"Very unlikely."

"Why?"

"Because last week I decided to take the rest of the year off."

"But it's only the second week of September. How can you make money taking off four months of the year?"

"When I do make money, I'm very miserly. And I have a kid about your age named Balzac who takes my money and doubles then triples it while I'm on the golf course."

"You like to play golf?"

"Wrong word choice."

Ivan looked at me quizzically.

"The correct word would be 'love.' I'm obsessed with golf."

"So am I."

"How good are you?"

"Better than good. Half a season from being great."

I liked this kid.

"Maybe you should talk to the uniforms about your uncle," I said. "I have a friend named Burke who's a pain in the ass, but he's kind of a big shot in the department. I can get the two of you face-to-face. He owes me a favor."

"I already talked to the cops," Ivan said. "And they weren't any help."

"What did they say?"

"My uncle was drinking, fell into the lake, and drowned."

"That's not a fun way to go," I said.

"That's not how he went."

"How can you be so sure?"

"Because my uncle didn't drink and he couldn't swim, so he never went near water. You had to almost medicate him just to drive over a bridge. My uncle never would've gone near the lake and definitely not close enough to fall into it."

"So what do you think happened to him?" I said.

"I think someone killed him."

"Why?"

"I have no idea. That's why I want to hire you."

"Unfortunately, as I said a few minutes ago, I'm not available. You're off by four months. But I have a couple friends who are pretty good at sleuthing."

"You like big words," he said.

"Only when I can't think of any small words to say."

He smiled.

"I don't want anyone else," he said. "I want you. I was told you were the best."

"I know you're still young, but you shouldn't believe everything you hear."

"I believe everything Ms. Packer says."

That sat me up.

"Penny Packer?" I said.

He nodded. "She was the one who told me about you."

Penny Packer was the richest woman in the city, more connected in Chicago than the pope is in Vatican City, and she was as much of a golf junkie as I was. The one difference being that she could just hop on her jet anytime and go play the world's greatest golf courses without blinking an eye.

"You buried the lede," I said.

"What does that mean?" he said.

"You should've opened with Penny. That brings a different hue to the conversation. How do you know her?"

"I caddied for her at Butler National last week."

"How did she shoot?"

"Five over."

I shook my head.

"And that was from the men's tees," he said.

"Sounds like Penny," I said. "So what's a kid like you doing caddying at Butler?"

"Just did it for the summer," he said. "They let the caddies play for free after the members are off the course. I'm trying to make it on the Korn Ferry Tour; then once that happens, hopefully I will make it to the PGA."

"You have to qualify for the Korn Ferry first."

"I have my first tournament in two weeks in Texas."

"Why are you here about your uncle and not his wife or kids?"

"Because they're back in Colombia. That's where we're from. I'm his only family here."

"Did he live alone?"

"No, he had two roommates. They do the same kind of work."

"Did you talk to them?"

"I did. They said he left one morning to go find work, and he just never came home. They tried calling his phone the next day, but it kept going to voicemail. The following night, when they hadn't heard from him, they called me. I tried calling him also, but his phone wasn't ringing. It was off. I tried leaving a message, but his box was full. I called his wife, and she said she hadn't heard from him in two days, which concerned her, because she talked to him twice a day—once in the morning and once at night."

"How many kids did he have?"

"Three boys."

"Ages?"

"I'm not exactly sure, but they're all under the age of ten or eleven."

"How did you find out he had died?"

"A detective showed up at my uncle's apartment building and told the guy who lived next door to him that my uncle had been found in the lake near the Point on the South Side. The detective asked him a few questions, gave him his card, then left. The neighbor called me."

"Have you talked to the detective?"

"Briefly. He seemed busy. He said he had a lot of cases. He said my uncle was drunk and fell into the lake."

"That was it?"

"I tried to tell him that it wasn't possible and that my uncle would never put himself in that situation. He said that sometimes people do things you don't expect them to do that don't make sense. This was one of those situations."

I nodded. I wasn't surprised. A poor Colombian immigrant had no chance of getting any real attention from CPD unless they walked into the mayor's office with five pounds of dynamite strapped to their waist.

"When did all of this happen?"

"They found his body last Tuesday," Ivan said. "I talked to the detective last Friday. So it's been about a week."

"You remember the name of the detective?"

Ivan reached into his golf pants and pulled out a business card.

Detective Seamus O'Halloran. I didn't recognize the name. He worked out of the Second District.

"You said your uncle was heading off to work," I said. "Where did he work?"

"Anywhere he could get a job."

"What does that mean?"

"He worked heating and cooling his whole life back in Colombia. He got a job here with a company over in Englewood, but he quit about six months ago. He said he didn't get along with a couple guys. So he started going to the Home Depot in Back of the Yards to stand out with the other guys and pick up jobs with contractors who needed help."

"When was he last seen?"

"All I could figure out was that his roommates saw him leaving for Home Depot, the guys saw him at Home Depot, and then he got into a van with some man to go do work. No one saw or heard from him until his body was found in the lake."

"Interesting," I said.

"Does that mean you'll take the case?" Ivan said.

"It means I'll dig around a little unofficially and see if there's anything here."

"I don't have much money," he said. "But I'm willing to give you what I have, and the rest I can make up in golf lessons."

"I won't take your money, Ivan. The golf lessons are fine by me. I'm hovering at a ten handicap. Been stuck there for the last five years. I need to get down to single digits."

"I can help you get there in three months."

I liked the kid's confidence. I also liked that if he was right, I'd finally get to the other side of the mountain.

"Do I need to sign some kind of contract?" he said.

I extended my hand, and he shook it firmly.

"You just did," I said.

THE NEXT MORNING, I GOT up early, ran a couple miles along the lake with Stryker off his leash, then headed over to the Home Depot in Back of the Yards. I didn't get to this neighborhood often.

Several men in overalls and sweatshirts stood near the entrance of the parking lot, drinking coffee and talking among themselves. All of them looked to be Latino. I sat in my car and watched the flow of traffic. Contractors in a wide array of vans and trucks pulled into the enormous parking lot, mostly men in oversized work pants and boots still wiping sleep from the corners of their eyes. Vans would pull up to the day laborers standing near the entrance. There would be a short exchange—I assumed a description of the job and a negotiation on the price—then the men would climb into the van and be on their way. As time moved on, the traffic increased and the activity became more frenzied. After an hour of watching, I felt as though I had an understanding of the rhythm.

I got out of my car and walked over to the handful of men who remained. They stared at me skeptically as I approached.

"Morning, guys," I said. "How's it going?"

All of them nodded without speaking.

"Can I ask you guys a few questions?" I said.

They all looked to a short guy with an ample belly and thick mustache.

"Who are you?" the man said in perfect English.

"My name is Ashe Cayne," I said. "I'm a private detective."

"You're a cop?" the man said.

"Used to be," I said. "Now I do investigations to help people who have problems and need answers."

The other men looked at the short guy, and he quickly said something to them in Spanish that seemed to calm them.

"Do you have identification?" the man said.

"I have my business card," I said, pulling one out and handing it to him.

He inspected the card carefully, then said, "What questions do you have for us?"

I took my phone out, pulled up a photo of Joaquin Escobar, and showed it to him. The men gathered around him to see the image for themselves.

"Do you know this man?" I said.

"Joaquin," the man said.

"You know he's dead?"

The man nodded somberly.

"Do you remember when he was here last?"

"Monday. Last week."

"Did he seem normal?"

"Claro que sí. Just like always. He was happy. He got picked up for a job."

"Do you remember who picked him up?"

"First time I saw this van. Big black van with a ladder on top."

"Did you see the driver?"

"Not really. White guy. Thirties or forties. He wore glasses."

"Do you know what happened to him after that?"

"No," the man said. "They drove away. We never saw Joaquin again."

"Can you ask your friends for me if they know anything?"

He turned to the other men and spoke several sentences in Spanish. A few of them responded, and there were a couple of animated exchanges.

"They don't know what happened," the man said. "But one of them said Joaquin was in trouble."

"What kind of trouble?"

The man turned to a slim guy wearing white painter's pants and a ripped sweatshirt. He had a mess of curly dark hair that fell down his forehead and almost over his eyes. They had a brief exchange.

"He says Joaquin had a problem because of a woman. He messed around with a lady, and her boyfriend found out and wasn't happy."

"Does he know the name of the lady?"

The two men conferred quickly, then the short guy said, "He doesn't know the lady's name, but he knows where she works."

"Where?"

"In a restaurant called Atotonilco Taqueria over on Forty-Seventh Street. She's the manager."

"What does she look like?"

He asked the guy for a description, then turned back to me and said, "You can't miss her. She's one of the prettiest women in Chicago. And she has green eyes the color of emeralds."

2

I walked into Home Depot and after several minutes found a manager. Luis Cabrera sat on a forklift, helping move refrigerators from the ground up to a shelf about twenty feet in the air. The other workers laughed at how poorly he was working the controls. He told them it had been a while since he'd used one of these machines, but he could still get the job done faster than they could. When he stepped out of the driver's seat, I approached him.

"Can you give me a couple minutes?" I asked.

"Is it going to cost me?" he joked.

"A lot less than an auto mechanic or psychiatrist."

"In that case, I don't mind."

"My name is Ashe Cayne," I said.

"Luis Cabrera," he said.

We shook hands.

"I'm a private detective," I said, "and I'm looking into a situation that happened with a man who picks up work in your parking lot."

"One of the laborers?" he said.

"A guy named Joaquin Escobar."

"Something bad happen?"

"The worst kind of bad that can happen," I said. "He's dead."

"He died in our parking lot? I didn't hear anything about that."

"No, he died in the lake, but the last he was seen was in your parking lot."

"We have a group of guys who pick up work," Cabrera said. "We used to chase them away, but then they would just stand on the street, and a guy almost got hit one day, so we figured, what the hell, they aren't hurting anyone standing out there. They're just trying to make an honest living."

I took out my phone and the photograph of Escobar and showed it to him. He looked at it, tightened his lips as he thought for a moment, then said, "Sorry, I don't really pay much attention to who's out there. But I know one guy is there all the time. Short guy, big stomach, heavy mustache. They call him El Gordo. He seems to be the leader. You talk to him?"

"I did. He said Escobar showed up that morning and got in a black van with a ladder on top, and that was the last time they saw him."

Cabrera shook his head. "A man can't even make a living these days without some psycho doing something crazy."

"Well, we don't know for sure if the man did anything," I said. "We just know that was the last anyone who knows him actually saw him. But I need to find the man. That's why I was hoping I could take a look at your video."

Cabrera scratched his head. "I want to, but I really can't," he said. "Corporate policy."

"Understood. How about you take a look and just let me know if you can see the van and Escobar getting into it?"

"It would be a lot easier for me if the cops asked for it. I have to follow the rules. Corporate gets really uptight about these things."

"Not a problem," I said. "I'll be back in about fifteen minutes."

I walked out the store and dialed the number for Commander Rory Burke, my mentor and former boss when I was a detective working in Area Three. He was big and gruff and always in a hurry.

"What the hell you want now?" Burke said, as a way of greeting. He was a man who saw little use for pleasantries.

"I'm at the Home Depot in Back of the Yards," I said.

"You at Home Depot?" he said, laughing. "Talk about a fish out of water. Why the hell aren't you walking on a golf course with some kid holding your bag?"

"Because I'm trying to help the kid who would be holding my bag," I said. "His uncle was found off the Point, and the kid wants to know what happened to him. He was last seen getting into a van in this parking lot. I need to see the make and license plate of the van."

"Thus the call to me to get the video."

"Or at least talk to the manager to let me see the video."

"Is the manager there?"

I walked back into the store. Cabrera was helping some woman use the automated key cutting machine.

"The cops, as you requested," I said to him, handing him the phone.

The conversation was quick, and all I heard Cabrera say was "No problem, Commander." He returned my phone and said, "Let's go."

I followed him to the back of the store, behind the lumber section, through a door that led into a narrow hallway, and up a long flight of steps.

"Not for the uninitiated," I said after reaching the top step.

"When you do it thirty times a day like I do, you get used to it," he said. "Those steps are my gym."

I followed him into a small, sparse office with two computer monitors and an old metal desk and a tall filing cabinet. A brown lunch bag sat next to a thermos on the desk. He pulled a chair around for me to sit next to him as he booted the computer. Once it was up and running and he had logged into the system, he opened the log of video recordings.

"Which day are you looking for?" he said.

"They found his body last Tuesday, so let's start there," I said.

Cabrera tapped on the keyboard, scrolled through several downloads, then finally got the recordings from that day to pop up on the screen. The cameras were motion activated, so they only recorded when there was activity in the parking lot. He found the camera that gave the best view of the area where the laborers were standing and pushed play. We watched through the entire morning of recordings, and while several trucks and work vans had pulled up to the laborers, none of them were black with a ladder on top.

"Let's look at Monday," I said.

Cabrera found the recordings, then hit the play button. The employees started showing up a little after five o'clock. Those who drove parked their cars toward the back of the lot. Cabrera explained this was store policy. Customers always first.

About a quarter to six, the first laborer walked onto the lot, sipping from a coffee mug. He stood at the entrance, looking at his phone. Ten minutes later, several guys were dropped off in a pickup truck, and they joined the first guy, exchanging greetings and handshakes. El Gordo arrived a few minutes later carrying a Dunkin' bag. He pulled out a doughnut and passed the bag around. At six o'clock, the store opened, and all the contractors who had been queued at the door lumbered inside.

At 6:35, a small white car pulled into the parking lot and stopped in front of the men. Joaquin Escobar got out of the car, bent down, and said something through the window to the driver, then joined the other men. I asked Cabrera to pause the video for a second as I opened a blank page in the Notes app on my phone and typed in the time Escobar had arrived.

Once the video resumed playing, I asked Cabrera to speed it up a little so we could get through the tape faster but still clearly see what was happening. Over the next few minutes, two of the guys were hired for work. The pattern was the same. A truck or van would pull over. El Gordo would step up to the passenger side of the vehicle and lead the conversation. Once it was done, he'd point to one of the guys, talk to them briefly, and then they would get in the truck and head off to work. Ten minutes after the first two guys had departed, a black transit van with a ladder affixed to the roof pulled into the parking lot.

"Stop it right there," I said. "I need to get the time stamp."

I wrote *6:53 a.m.* in my notes, then told Cabrera to continue. Same process. El Gordo walked to the van, spoke to the driver, and pointed at Joaquin, who came over and had a brief conversation with the driver before jumping into the passenger seat. The camera's angle was not right to capture the driver. The van started to pull off.

"Pause it," I said. "I want to see if we can read the words on the side."

"These cameras aren't the greatest," Cabrera said. "I'm embarrassed to say how old they are. Let me see what I can do."

He played with a couple buttons and zoomed in on the van. The picture grew increasingly grainy the more he pushed in.

"That's about the best I can do," he said.

We couldn't read all the words, but we were able to catch two of them. *THERMAL* and *WINDY*. I wrote them in my notes. Cabrera continued the video, but this time in slow motion. The van did a U-turn to leave the parking lot, and when its license plate faced the camera, I told him to pause.

"Never gonna get it," he said, playing with the zoom and contrast. "Too far away."

"Can you print that image for me?" I said.

"Sure."

Within seconds, the small printer on the counter behind his desk came to life and delivered the image of the rear of the van. He handed the printout to me. He was right. You could barely see that there was even a license plate, let alone be able to read what it said. He pushed play on the video, and the van pulled out of the lot, onto Western, and joined the stream of cars heading north.

I stood up. "Better than nothing," I said.

"Wish I could've helped more," he said.

I gave him one of my business cards. "If you hear anything, give me a call," I said.

"Will do," he said. "You think whoever hired him killed him?"

"No idea," I said. "But I sure as hell plan on finding the driver. He might not have done it, but he can definitely help fill in the timeline."

I SAT STARING AT CAROLINA Espinoza, who was staring at an apple pancake the size of a wedding cake that could feed a party of a hundred. We were having breakfast at the Original Pancake House down in the Gold Coast. It was our last breakfast before she and a group of friends headed over to Belize for their annual girls' trip.

"Why do you always order that thing and only take two bites of it?" I said.

"Because two bites satisfy me, but just looking at it does, also."

I had made quick work of my buckwheat pancakes and thick-cut bacon.

"Besides," she said, "I need to fit into my bikini in forty-eight hours, and no matter how much I love this apple pancake, I'm not going to let it ruin my vacation."

"You could eat two of those a day for an entire month, and your weight wouldn't budge," I said. "You've been the same weight since I met you."

"Not true," she said.

"Which part?"

"Both. If I ate just one of these things, I'd gain five pounds. And I'm not the same weight as when we first met. I'm actually a pound and a half heavier."

She smiled.

"I'm going to miss you," I said.

"You always say that," she said. "Then I leave, and you play two rounds of golf every day and totally forget I'm not here."

"Well, that's not gonna happen this time," I said. "I've gotta figure out what happened to this kid's uncle."

I brought her up to speed on the little I had gleaned thus far.

"But I thought you were taking the rest of the year off," she said. "You were adamant."

"I was. But then Ivan walked into my office and told me his story."

"And you couldn't say no."

"I did at first, but then he told me he was a scratch golfer, and Penny had made the referral."

"Did anyone from CPD investigate his uncle's death?" Carolina said.

"If they did, it was cursory at best. He's an immigrant from Colombia found floating in Lake Michigan. You think he's at the top of the priority list?"

"He's probably not even on the list."

"My point exactly."

"You think the girlfriend's boyfriend did it?"

"Relationship issues. One of the top three causes for homicide."

"What about the black van?"

"That's where you come in," I said.

"Moi?"

"Oui, toi. I need you to do a search on what we were able to read on the side of the van. Maybe you can find the company, then cross-reference it with the van in the motor vehicle database."

"But you don't have any part of the license plate number. You just have two words and the vehicle description."

"And you."

"Flattery will get you everywhere," she said, leaning over and kissing me softly.

"Can you do it before you leave for Belize?"

"Sure, in between my last-minute shopping, hair appointment, waxing, and pedicure."

"See, outrageous beauty can be a blessing and a curse. Setting the bar that high is the easy part. The difficult part is keeping it there."

Carolina shook her head. "Don't turn on the charm now," she said. "Save it for later tonight at your apartment."

"I didn't know I would need it," I said.

"You might not if you choose the right bottle of wine."

"I'll keep that in mind."

"Where are you going next?" she said.

"To find a woman who some are calling one of the prettiest women in Chicago. Present company excluded, of course."

"And who's that?"

"Emerald Eyes."

3

Atotonilco Taqueria was squeezed into a long line of low-rent storefronts near the intersection of Forty-Seventh Street and South Paulina Street in the Back of the Yards neighborhood. Its loud green, white, and red banner screamed from several blocks away, wanting to let you know the Mexican food at this joint was not only authentic but good and affordable. I stepped into the busy restaurant full of people grabbing takeout on their way home. A few diners sat at the rectangular orange tables with matching vinyl chairs. I looked around but didn't see Emerald Eyes. Maybe she was back in the kitchen. I waited in line patiently until I reached the register. A short, no-nonsense middle-aged woman wearing an apron and hairnet looked up at me.

"Your order?" she said.

"I'm looking for someone who works here with ojos verdes," I said.

"Julieta?"

"¿Tiene ojos verdes?"

"Sí."

"¿Muy bonita?"

"Sí."

"Can I talk to her?"

"No. She don't work here anymore."

"When did she leave?"

"I have people who want food," she said, pointing to the increasingly more impatient line of customers behind me. "Do you want to order?"

"I need to talk to Julieta," I said.

The woman shook her head. "I can't help you," she said.

"Can you give me her phone number?"

The woman shook her head.

"Can you tell me her last name?"

The woman shook her head again.

"How can I reach her?"

A man about the same size as the woman and wearing a stained black apron stepped up to the counter.

"Is there a problem, mi amigo?" he said.

The woman said something to him in Spanish, much too fast for me to understand, but I did catch *Julieta* in what she said.

"She doesn't work here," the man said.

"Where does she work?" I said.

"Step aside, please, so my customers can order," he said.

He moved over to the other side of the woman, and I followed.

"I just need to ask her a couple questions," I said. "Can you tell me where I can find her?"

"Who sent you?" the man said.

"No one," I said. "She knows someone who I know, and I want to ask her a question about him."

"Mi amigo, I can't help you," he said. "Julieta doesn't work here, and I can't say anything else."

He turned away from the counter and went back to the stove in the kitchen. I looked at the woman at the register, but she wouldn't look at me, so I turned and left. When I was about to open my car door, I heard a girl call, "Mister?"

I turned to find a short girl, somewhere in her late teens, with long, red-streaked hair and tight jeans and a T-shirt with the restaurant's name emblazoned across it in bright letters.

"You are looking for Julieta," she said.

"I am."

"Why do you want her?" she said.

"I need to ask her questions about someone who died."

"Who died?"

"A man named Joaquin Escobar."

A hint of recognition registered on her face.

"Is Julieta in trouble?" she said.

"Not with me," I said.

"Are you a policeman?"

"No, I'm a private investigator."

"Julieta is hiding," the girl said.

"Hiding?"

"She left last week. She's scared."

"Why?"

"I really can't say. She doesn't want anyone to find her."

"Do you know who she's hiding from?"

"I do, but I can't say nothing."

"I need to talk to her," I said. "I think she might be able to help me figure out what happened to Joaquin."

"What is your name?" she said.

"Ashe Cayne."

"You promise she isn't in trouble and you're not going to do anything to her?"

"Would a face like this cause anyone any trouble?" I smiled.

She smiled back. "Well, you are kinda cute," she said. "Give me your number, and I will give it to her. If she wants to talk to you, she'll call you."

I gave the short girl one of my business cards. She started to leave, then turned back around. "What happened to Joaquin?" she said.

"They found him against the rocks on the lake."

She winced, then walked away.

MY FATHER SUMMONED ME TO dinner at his town house in Bronzeville. He phrased it as an invitation, but it was clear by the way he said it that I had no option but to accept. He informed me that Pearline, his part-time cook/housekeeper, was cooking clam chowder to start, followed by braised lamb chops, candied Brussels sprouts, and mashed potatoes. Dessert would be my favorite: sweet potato pie. My father always had a planned menu when I came to what he called a *proper* dinner. I couldn't remember Dr. Wendell Cayne ever inviting me over to watch a football game over pizza and cold beer.

"I'm glad you could fit me into your busy schedule," he said as I took a seat across from him in the library. My father always liked to have a drink before dinner. He was sipping a cognac that had probably been made back during the French Revolution. He had an old-fashioned waiting for me next to my chair. There was a happiness in his eyes that I hadn't seen in a while. He was in total control. As always.

"Why do you always make it seem like I never have time for you?" I said. "I always answer your calls, and I always come for dinner or lunch when you ask me to."

"That's exactly my point," he said. "When I ask you to. I shouldn't have to always ask my son to come home and have dinner. Sometimes *you* should just pick up the phone and ask *me* if I want to grab a bite or something."

"'Or something'?" I laughed. "You are not an or-something type of person. And you know that."

My father nodded slightly. "Well, I'm at least a grab-a-bite type of person," he said.

"Fine," I said. "Next time, I'll be the one who makes the invitation and the menu."

He took a sip of his cognac and stared across the room at the hundreds of rare and first edition books lining the walls. The fireplace was all aglow, the logs in a perfect cross pattern. It wasn't cold enough yet to have the fireplace on, but he loved how fire roared in this room and the way a flame's shadows flickered across the dark-paneled walls. He nodded approvingly at his vast collection.

"Fifty long years to assemble this," he said. "I don't know what I'd do if I didn't have books. Marcus Tullius Cicero once said, 'A room without books is like a body without a soul.' All of these will be yours one day," he said. "You're my only son. You will get everything I have."

"You know I don't like talking about things like this," I said. "It's creepy. I don't want to discuss your mortality."

"Death is part of life," he said, waving me off. "Properly planning for it is something most people don't do, and that's a mistake. Especially in this country. The government will rob you blind if you're not prepared for those robber barons down in Washington. They'll suck you dry before my body is cold in the ground."

I took a sip of the old-fashioned. It was perfect as always. Had my father not been a renowned psychiatrist, he could've been an all-world-caliber mixologist.

"I prefer to focus on the things we can share while we're both alive," I said. "Experiences are more meaningful to me than material things. 'All my possessions for a moment of time.'"

"I don't know that one," my father said.

"The Virgin Queen," I said. "Elizabeth the First."

"Your mother would've been so proud to hear you say that," he said. "It's a blessing you took after her in that regard." He placed his drink down and stood, which signaled it was time to eat. "Let's eat in the sunroom tonight."

My father rarely ate in the kitchen, and depending on his mood or the purpose of the dinner meeting, he chose the room accordingly. The sunroom was always his choice for more relaxed conversations. It had an entire wall of windows that overlooked the small park behind his house and the western portion of the downtown skyline. He'd had the wall torn down and turned into windows for my mother. This had been her favorite place to eat.

Pearline had everything set up and waiting for us upstairs. The food sat in several silver warming trays on top of a bureau against the wall opposite the windows. A pitcher of ice water and a pitcher of fresh raspberry lemonade sat between two ornate candelabras stationed at the ends of the dining table. We served ourselves quietly, my father blessed the food, and then we dug in. The Sears Tower—never "Willis Tower"—glistened in the distance. Its antennas stood washed in burgundy, a color I had never seen there before. When I was a boy, my parents and I would sit here as a family and look at the tower and guess what the color represented. My father noticed my gaze.

"Burgundy," he said.

"I've never seen it that color before," I said.

"First time," he said. "It was like moving heaven and earth, but after all these years, we got them to agree to give us a week this month. Sickle Cell Awareness Month."

"I never hear anything about it," I said.

"Of course not," he said. "Because it's *our* disease. We own eighty-five percent of the country's cases. Awful, torturous disease. My cousin died from it when he was a child. With the treatments now available, if he had been born today, he'd have lived to be an old man. No one talks about it because it kills *us*, not them."

I continued looking at the Sears, thinking about how towering a figure my father really had been in his career and our community. I found it difficult to express the awe I held for his accomplishments. I figured it would only be a reminder to him of how much I hadn't accomplished by not following his plans for me.

"What will you do with all your time the rest of the year since you're not taking any cases?" he said between bites of his chops.

"Working on a case," I said.

He looked up, surprised. "What do you mean?" he said.

"I decided to help a kid whose immigrant uncle was probably killed."

"Probably?"

I filled him in on the investigation. When I finished, he said, "I really hope you can help the kid and his family. The way this country has treated and continues to treat immigrants is deplorable. What those coward governors did in Florida and Texas a couple years ago was criminal. Imagine shipping humans across the country just to send a message and score cheap political points. These damn politicians have lost their minds. Don't they realize immigrants are real human beings, not some pawns in a political chess match?"

"And don't forget, the voters in those states keep reelecting them," I said. "What does that tell you?"

"That no matter how much progress we've made to unify this country and treat people with equality, there's still a large contingent of Americans who simply want us to return to pre–Emancipation Proclamation days."

"Never gonna happen," I said. "Too many people are determined not to let them tear this country in half. And these young people are different today than in the past. They won't just protest. They'll fight in the streets and die if they have to."

"Let's hope it doesn't come to that," my father said. "There really aren't any unblemished winners in situations like this. Bad damage on both sides."

We finished dinner, then started in on dessert, the homemade sweet potato pie.

"There's something I need to talk to you about," my father said.

I knew he had summoned me for a reason.

"I'm not getting any younger," he said.

"No one is," I said.

"This house is kind of big for one person," he said. "It gets lonely being here alone. Pearline is here to help out most days, but other than her, it's just me."

"Maybe you need man's best friend," I said.

"I do," he said. "But not the animal variety. I need a human. A woman in my life."

"Are you saying what I think you're saying?"

"I am."

"This is why you wanted to have dinner? To tell me this?"

"I thought it was important for us to talk about it face-to-face," he said. "Some conversations shouldn't be held over the phone."

"Mom has been gone for almost ten years," I said. "It's not surprising that you would like to have female companionship."

"How do you feel about it?" he said.

"I'm happy for you," I said. "I think you're lonely. I've thought this for some time, but I didn't say anything."

"Why?"

"Because I didn't want to have an argument with you. If I said you were lonely, then you'd say you weren't, and we'd go back and forth and get nothing accomplished."

"Well, I'm not lonely," he said. "Anymore. I have a friend."

"For how long?"

"Just over a year."

"Does she make you happy?"

"So far."

"Do I know her?"

"I don't think so. I met her playing tennis. She lost her husband about the same time we lost your mother. She's a retired federal appeals court judge. She moved here a few years ago to be closer to her grandchildren."

"What's her name?"

"Constance M. Baker. Everyone calls her Connie. She's a golfer. Very good, from what I hear. She'd like to meet you."

I wasn't expecting him to say that. And I knew my response was important. So I took a moment, then said, "How soon?"

"She's having a birthday party in a few weeks. Her sixtieth. She'd like you to come along. I told her I'd ask."

"I'll be there," I said. I regretted the words as soon as they left my mouth.

4

The next morning, I got up early, took a quick run along the lake, then went to my office in the South Loop just because I figured I might be more productive there than sitting at home, watching the Golf Channel. I sat back in my chair, watching Buckingham Fountain in Grant Park send just a smidge over fourteen thousand gallons of water into the air through a mind-boggling 134 jets. In about a month, when the weather turned, it would be shut off for the winter. I looked at the boats docked at the Yacht Club. The numbers were already dwindling: yet another reminder that our winter punishment was not in the too-distant future. My phone buzzed. It was Carolina.

"Let me guess," she said. "You're about to tee off."

"Nope."

"You and Stryker are on the lake."

"Nope."

"You're sitting at home, thinking about last night and how much you already miss me."

"Halfway there?"

"Which half?"

"The missing-you part. But I'm at my office."

"You never go to the office this early."

"Figured I'd practice occupying all my free time so I'll be prepared when you leave for Belize tomorrow."

"You always know the right thing to say."

"'If we are not ashamed to think it, we should not be ashamed to say it.'"

"Shakespeare?"

"About fifteen hundred years before his time. The Roman writer and orator Cicero."

"What made you think of him?"

"Sitting in my father's library of ancient tomes last night."

"He owns a book written by Cicero?"

"No, but it might be the only collectible he doesn't own."

"Speaking of own," she said, "I found out who owns that black van your client's uncle got into that morning. Windy Cooling & Thermal Dynamics. It's a small business over on Fifty-Eighth Street, near the corner of South Laflin, owned by a guy named Matis Klukas."

"Is it clean?"

"Seems to be. No city violations. Paperwork is in order. Just a small mom-and-pop."

"Anything on Klukas?"

"Charged for an aggravated assault three years ago. Got into a fight at a bar with another man over a soccer bet. Fight spilled out onto the street. Klukas went to his truck and grabbed his gun, came back, and pistol-whipped the guy unconscious."

"So we got a tough guy on our hands," I said.

"Are you going to talk to him?"

"That's my intention."

"Please be careful."

"I won't need to be."

"Why?"

"Mechanic is coming for the ride."

I PUT IN A CALL to Detective Seamus O'Halloran and left a message on his machine. If his voice was any indication of his attitude, this guy was going to be a piece of work. Then I called the Second District and left a message with the desk.

I picked up Dmitri Kowalski, otherwise known as Mechanic, after his sparring session at Hammer's gym. Mechanic had long been officially my unofficial partner, and he was absolutely fearless. The son of Lithuanian immigrants, he had grown up on some of the city's toughest streets and had seen things no adult, let alone a child, should see. They started calling him Mechanic as a teenager because he had an unrivaled knack for fixing people's problems. Everyone in the neighborhood knew that if you had a problem, you took it to Kowalski. He could fix anything. Guns and violence were his specialties, and his legend had only grown as he became an adult.

We headed south to Fifty-Ninth Street, then turned and drove west. The luxury high-rises of downtown and the South Loop gave way to squat storefronts and dilapidated row houses with old cars propped up by cinder blocks in the small side yards. This was one of those neighborhoods where you could only survive on grit and a healthy dose of good luck. We pulled up to a small, single-floor building squeezed between a car wash and barbershop that looked like it hadn't been in business since a Democrat had lost a mayoral election. No signage on the building indicated what business was conducted behind the crumbling brick façade, but a black Windy Cooling & Thermal Dynamics van sat parked against the curb. I pulled in behind it, and we found our way to the front door. A young woman sat behind an old metal desk covered in a mess of papers. An infant sat in a baby seat next to the desk, playing with a small plastic toy. The woman looked up, as if surprised she had visitors.

"Can I help you?" she said.

"We're here to see Matis Klukas," I said.

"Are you a customer?" she said.

"No, I'm a private investigator."

"Does Matis know you?"

"Not yet."

"What does that mean?"

"Once we have a chat with him, then he'll know us."

She looked back and forth between Mechanic and me, then said, "Matis isn't here right now. I can take a message for him."

"How about you tell us where we can find him," I said.

"He's on a jobsite. He won't be back until later this afternoon."

"Do you own a cell phone?" I said.

"Of course," she said. "Who doesn't have a cell phone?"

"Then how about you pick it up, dial his number, and let him know we'd like to have a little talk with him."

"I'm sorry, but Matis is very busy. He doesn't like to be disturbed while he's at a job unless it's important."

I looked at Mechanic, who then opened his shirt a little to show the grip of his .500 Magnum. The woman jumped back in her chair.

"Is that important enough?" I said.

She picked up the phone and quickly dialed a number. She had a brief conversation in Lithuanian, then turned to me and said, "1217 West Fifty-First Street. Corner of Fifty-First and South Elizabeth."

"Cute baby," I said before turning and walking out of the office.

It only took a few minutes before we arrived at a narrow two-story brick building with a large piece of white-painted plywood covering the front window. It sat alone between two empty lots. Matis had parked his van out front. Some guy was carrying tools inside when we pulled up. We opened the door and heard several voices coming from the other end of a short hallway. We walked toward them but were intercepted by a guy just barely six feet tall and one varškės spurgos away from tipping the scale to three hundred pounds. He had a big forehead and a flat nose and hands the size of a waffle iron. He didn't seem too pleased to see us.

"What the hell do you want?" he said by way of a friendly greeting. His accent was thick, but his English well adapted.

"Are you Matis Klukas?" I said.

"Who the hell wants to know?" he growled.

"Santa Claus," I said. "Just checking if you've been naughty or nice."

"What the fuck?" he said.

"You've said three sentences to me, and each one of them has contained a curse word. This is my fifth sentence, and I haven't used an ounce of profanity."

"Fuck you," he said.

"Your streak continues. Are you gonna tell me if you're Matis or not?"

"Are you gonna tell me what the fuck you want?"

I took out my phone and pulled up the photo of Joaquin Escobar and showed it to him. He looked down at it, then back at me, and said, "And?"

"Progress," I said to Mechanic. "A one-word sentence without vulgarity."

Mechanic kept his eyes on Klukas. He hadn't blinked since we'd been standing there.

"This guy worked for you last Monday morning," I said.

"You got a problem with that?" Matis said.

"Other than the fact the guy is now dead and you might've been the last person to see him alive, I don't have a problem."

"You saying I killed that guy?"

"That guy's name is Joaquin Escobar. And what I'm saying is, someone killed him the same day he worked for you, and I'm just trying to find out what happened."

"Let me see your badge," he said.

"We're not CPD," I said. "You think police officers look as handsome as us?" I smiled. Mechanic had a slight twitch in his right cheek.

"You're a real comedian," Matis said. "If you're not police, then who the hell are you?"

"I'm a private investigator," I said. "I'm trying to help his family figure out what happened to him."

He nodded his head at Mechanic. "And who is he?" Matis said.

"An associate."

"He don't speak?"

"He speaks softly and carries a big gun."

Matis eyed Mechanic, then said, "What do you want me to say?"

"Whatever happened the day you picked Joaquin up for work."

"Simple. I went to the store parking lot. I asked the little fat guy if anyone could do HVAC work. They told me Joaquin could do it. We agreed on a price, and I drove him here to work with us."

"That's it?"

"That's it."

"Did he work here all day?"

"He worked til we finished. Four o'clock. He asked for a ride to the train station over on Forty-Ninth Street. One of the guys dropped him off. That was it. He was supposed to come back the next day. He was a good worker. He knew everything we do. But he never showed up. I figured he got a job somewhere else. Those guys aren't reliable. They go with the highest offer."

"You mind if I talk to the guy who dropped him off?" I said.

"He's gonna tell you the same thing I told you," Matis said.

"He might remember something he didn't before," I said.

Matis shrugged, then yelled down the hall, "Nikolai!"

Seconds later, a thin, short man with a heavy dark beard and arms almost as long as his legs made his way toward us. Matis said something to him in Lithuanian, then Nikolai turned to me, ready for questioning.

"Do you remember about what time you dropped him off?" I said.

"About a quarter after four," he said.

"Did he tell you where he was going?"

"No. He just said he needed a ride to the train."

"Did he talk on the phone when he was with you?"

"Someone called him."

"Do you remember what they were talking about?"

"Not sure. Something about a meeting. He was upset. He was talking fast. And he was talking in Spanish and English. I only understood some of the English."

"Did he say any names?"

"I don't remember."

"Did he say where the meeting was?"

"No. I told him I would drive him home, but he said he wasn't going home. He thanked me for the ride, told me he would see me tomorrow, then left the car and walked into the train station. That was the last I saw him."

Mechanic and I got back into the car and headed over to the Orange Line train station on Western and Forty-Ninth Street. I wasn't sure what we would learn there that could help us understand what happened, but in the early stages of an investigation like this, anything was worth a try and nothing should be ruled out too early.

I parked a few yards down from the entrance of the train station. A steady stream of passengers entered and exited the station as the trains arrived and departed. I noticed two cameras on the exterior that were probably wide-angled and able to catch anything from the street to the station's physical structure. Mechanic and I sat there in silence, something we did often that bothered neither one of us. My phone rang. I didn't recognize the number, but I answered it anyway.

"This is Carmen," the caller said. "You came to the restaurant yesterday looking for Julieta."

"Yup, that would be me," I said.

"Well, I have a message to give you from Julieta."

"My ears are tingling."

"What?"

"Never mind. I'm ready to hear what you have to say."

"She wants to talk to you," Carmen said. "But she doesn't want to talk on the phone. She thinks her ex might have a way of listening."

"Say how we'll talk," I said.

"She wants to meet you in person. At my parents' house. She will be safe there."

"When?"

"Saturday night at eight o'clock."

"Where do you live?"

"4791A South Winchester Avenue. Do you like Mexican food?"

"I like any food that's good."

"My mother will insist that you eat something. She feeds everyone who comes to our house."

"I'll be sure to bring my appetite."

5

"You guys gonna make love out there or box, for Chrissake?" Hammer yelled from outside the ring.

Seventy-three-year-old Arnold "Hammer" Scazzi had not only been the youngest Golden Gloves champion, but he might have become one of the greatest professional fighters ever, pound for pound, had he not been in a freak car accident and lost the peripheral vision in his right eye. He'd hung up his gloves and opened up his own gym in the basement of Johnny's Icehouse, a large skating rink in the West Loop.

Mechanic and I pounded each other for another three rounds before agreeing to call it quits. We stepped out of the ring to make way for two hotshot fighters Hammer was hoping would be the next great Chicago boxing hopes. As we sat on the bench and started chugging a gallon of water, my phone rang. I didn't recognize the number.

"This Ashe Cayne?" the guy said.

"I go by no other name," I said.

"This is Seamus O'Halloran from the Second," he said. "How can I help you?"

"Thanks for calling me back," I said. "I was interested in the Joaquin Escobar case you're working on."

"I'm not working on that case," he said. "It's closed."

"Closed how?"

"Closed as in there's nothing more to investigate. The man got drunk, fell into the lake, and drowned."

"Have you talked to his nephew?" I said.

"I did."

"The nephew doesn't think that's how he died."

"From what I remember, the nephew wasn't there when it happened. So how the hell does he know how the man died?"

"Well, with all due respect, the kid isn't saying he knows how his uncle died. He's just saying his uncle didn't die that way."

"How long has it been since you left the department?" O'Halloran said. "About eight years, right?"

"Give or take a few months," I said.

"Well, things are a little different around here. Crime is through the roof, which means caseloads are too. I've got fifteen cases on my desk, and my sergeant is up my ass to get them cleared. So excuse me if I don't pull a bunch of all-nighters investigating some guy who had one too many and made the stupid mistake of going to the lake instead of going home and sleeping it off."

"Did you even look at the possibility that someone might've been involved in his fall?" I said.

"I did."

"Did you have a chance to talk to the guys he hustled for jobs with at the Home Depot in Back of the Yards?"

"I did not."

"Did you talk to the girl he was messing around with?"

"I was not aware he was messing around with some woman. I thought he had a wife down in Colombia."

"He does. And three young kids. Which is why taking a second look at his case seems to be the right thing to do. They deserve to know the truth about what happened to their husband and father."

"The guy comes to our country to make money to send back home to family in another country, then he starts fuckin' around with some chick while his wife is down there raising the kids. Sometimes karma's a bitch."

"'We should be rigorous in judging ourselves and gracious in judging others,'" I said.

"They warned me that you like to quote a lot of Shakespeare," he said.

"Only when I want to be a little tricky," I said. "That was the great English theologian John Wesley. Founder of Methodism."

"Jesus Christ. Now you wanna give me a religious lecture."

"Better than one on how to conduct a proper investigation."

"Are you trying to tell me how to do my job?"

"Never. I'm just reminding you that you have a job to do."

CLARINDA GRAVES HAD BEEN A friend of my mother's as long as I could remember. They'd sung in the choir together in the soprano section and talked at least once a day. My mother's passing had been as hard on her as it had been for my father and me. Given how distant my relationship was with my father, having her support helped keep us together. She had been working in the medical examiner's office for the last forty years. Whenever she was questioned about her retirement, her answer was always the same: "When I can figure out something better to do with my time."

I dialed her cell phone. She picked up just before her voicemail kicked in.

"This is a pleasant surprise," she said. "I was thinking about you the other day. It's been a while since I made a peach cobbler."

"Which means it's been a while since I've been happy," I said.

"Don't let your lady friend hear you say that," Mrs. Graves said. She chuckled softly.

"She's on her way to Belize, so I'm all alone. I could use the company of some of your peach cobbler."

"Consider it done," she said.

"I need to ask you a question about a body you have there," I said. "Can you talk?"

"I can."

"His name is Joaquin Escobar. He should've arrived last Tuesday or Wednesday."

"Give me a minute."

I could hear her tapping her keyboard, then reading names to herself. She finally said, "Thirty-seven-year-old Hispanic male. Found in the lake at the Point. Family has been notified, identification confirmed. Awaiting pickup."

"No autopsy was performed?"

"No. And he's not scheduled for one either."

"There should be," I said. "That man's death is suspicious at best and murder at worst."

"It says here that he fell into the lake and drowned."

"A convenient determination made at the scene," I said. "No one was willing to dig deeper."

"Well, if it was an accident, he really should've made it to the table. Accidents, homicides, suicides, sudden and unexpected natural deaths—we're obligated by county ordinance to perform autopsies. But to tell you the truth, we have so many bodies in here, they've had to prioritize which cases they decide to do."

"What's the fastest way to get him on the list?"

"Next of kin. Have them call and ask for an autopsy due to suspicious circumstances. Once they make the request, I'll see what I can do on my end to cut down the wait time."

6

The Delarosa family lived in a tiny bungalow-style house on a block full of working-class families with dreams for their children. The small-front A-frame façade had been divided into laminate attempting to resemble brick, and the bottom level was plastered with some type of faux stone that looked like a strong wind might rip completely off. I climbed the small flight of wooden steps and knocked on the wrought iron screen door. Seconds later, a tiny woman with long black hair tied behind her head and sharp, petite features on a face that looked like it had gotten stuck in adolescence opened a series of locks before pushing the door open and greeting me with a wide smile.

Carmen stood a couple feet behind her with a relieved smile on her face. She and her mother could pass for twins.

"Welcome," the mother said. "Let's get something to eat."

They led me into the next room, which was fully occupied by a table that could cram six people around it as long as the chairs were turned at a certain angle. Plates and silverware had been neatly arranged, along with plastic drinking glasses with some type of ornamental design that was the manufacturer's attempt at distracting from the fact that the material was plastic and not bone china. A man about an inch taller than the mother squeezed his way into the room carrying two cervezas. He quickly handed one to me after introducing himself as Fernando. A figure suddenly appeared in the doorway behind the father. Emerald Eyes. She was every bit of five-ten and not one ounce of beauty less than how she had been described. Her olive skin and dark hair made her green eyes glow like polished gems in a crown. She smiled with a perfect set of teeth that only made her raw beauty underscore how unfair it was that God would compile so much of it in one person. She was no more than early twenties, but she had a maturity about her that went well beyond her age. She introduced herself, and then we all found seats around the table while the mother went to the kitchen and returned with several plates of food.

Once dinner was over and the father excused himself to go upstairs to watch a soccer match, Carmen led Julieta and me down a short hall and into a bedroom in the back of the house. Carmen closed the door behind her as she went to help her mother clear the table.

"So here we are," I said.

"Here we are," Julieta said.

"Is it easier for you to tell me your story, or do you want me to ask you a few questions?" I said.

"I think it's easier for you to ask questions," she said.

"Not a problem. How about we start with you telling me why you're in hiding?"

"Rio," she said.

"That would be a great place to hide, especially during Carnival. No one would ever recognize you with all those colors and costumes."

She laughed softly. "You're kinda funny," she said. "It's hard to believe you're a real detective."

"I can show you my gun if that would make you feel better."

"I don't like guns," she said. "They scare me."

"Me too, but I don't let the bad guys know that. I just pull it out when I need to even the score."

"Rio has lots of guns," she said. "And that scares me."

"Having lots of guns doesn't mean anything," I said. "It's how well you can shoot them that matters most. I have an associate who only has two guns in rotation. I'd take him over an entire army any day of the week."

"Rio is very violent," she said.

"Violence is my friend's oxygen."

"What's your friend's name?"

"Mechanic."

"Who names their kid after a car repairman?"

"No one. His parents named him Dmitri, but the neighborhood named him Mechanic because he's a fixer."

"What does he fix?"

"People's problems."

"You both fix people's problems?"

"I tend to be more charming and less violent," I said. "Back to Rio. Who exactly is Rio?"

"His real name is Dario, but everyone calls him Rio," she said. "He's my boyfriend. Well, ex-boyfriend."

"Does he know he's your ex-boyfriend?"

"He knows, but I don't think he accepts it."

"Then that's a bit of a problem. You're afraid of him, I take it?"

"He's not a good person. I never should've dated him in the first place. And like I said, he's violent. I was stupid to think he'd changed."

"Changed from what?"

"Being such a hothead. He has the worst temper I've ever seen. The smallest thing makes him snap. Someone comes into his lane without using a blinker. A guy looks at me too long. He just loses it and can't stop going off until he's done something bad."

"How bad does it get?"

"Real bad. He thinks the answer to everything is hurting someone."

Unfortunately, I had interviewed many women like Julieta who had husbands or boyfriends like Rio. The playbook was all too familiar. It was difficult looking at such a beautiful girl and hearing her pain. The two just didn't match.

"Did he ever hit you?" I said.

She shook her head. I knew she was lying. But when someone was a victim of domestic violence, the last thing you wanted to do was press them right away. You would never earn their trust and thus their honesty. I moved on.

"Why exactly are you hiding from him?" I said.

"Because I think he's going to hurt me for what I did."

She lowered her head and worked her hands softly.

"I was wrong," she continued. "I should've just told him I didn't want to be with him anymore. But I was afraid. If I told him that, he would have gone crazy, like he always does. So I just pretended like we were over, because we were in my mind. And then I met Joaquin. He was how I wanted Rio to be. We met at the restaurant. Just a friendly conversation. He was nice, funny, calm. Also very handsome. But Rio is handsome too. But all he has is his looks. Nothing else about him is any good."

"You have a picture of this dashing Rio?"

Julieta opened her phone, tapped the display a few times, then turned the screen toward me. Rio was definitely handsome. And he was definitely cocky. He had a tat on the right side of his neck and diamond studs in both ears. A player. At least, that's what he considered himself to be. I returned the phone.

"So you and Joaquin started off as being just friends to eventually being more than friends?" I said.

"Yes. We met last summer, but we didn't start really hanging out in that way til this spring. He took me out for dinner on my birthday in April. I can count on one hand how many times Rio has taken me out to a real sit-down dinner in these last three years."

"Joaquin knew about Rio?"

She nodded.

"You know about his wife?"

She nodded.

"Did Rio find out about Joaquin?"

More nodding.

"Not the most ideal situation," I said. "That's what kids these days are calling an entanglement."

"Rio is very jealous."

"I can imagine. You're an extremely beautiful girl."

She lowered her eyes and sighed deeply.

"How did Rio find out about Joaquin?"

"I was on my phone, talking to my girlfriend. When I hung up, I put the phone down on the table and went to use the bathroom. Rio picked it up and opened my phone before the screen locked. He went through my call log and saw Joaquin's number."

"You had it saved under Joaquin's name?"

"Of course not. I didn't have it saved at all. He saw that Joaquin had called me several times. So he got suspicious."

"Then he confronted you when you came out of the bathroom?"

"Yes. And he made me call the number while he was standing there in front of me. Joaquin answered, and Rio grabbed the phone from me."

"Then what happened?"

"Rio did what Rio always does. He lost his mind and started screaming at Joaquin, at me, at everything. It was crazy."

"Did he do anything to you?"

"Like what?"

"Become violent."

"No, because I ran into my bedroom and locked my door. I was afraid he was going to kick it in, but he didn't."

"What did he do instead?"

"Threw my cell phone against the door, then stepped on it and smashed it. Then he said he was gonna kill Joaquin when he found him."

"A proclamation that doesn't surprise me, given his previously stated proclivity toward violence."

"Proclivity?"

"Tendency."

"I've never met a cop who uses SAT words like that," she said.

"That's because you've never met a cop whose father drinks nineteenth-century cognac from Waterford Crystal."

She laughed. I laughed with her.

When the mood had stiffened back up, I said, "Do you know what really happened to Joaquin?"

She shrugged. "Not for sure, but it's easy to guess."

"Rio?"

"When I found out Joaquin was dead, that's all I could think of. I figured that Rio must've done what he said he was going to do."

"Has Rio killed anyone before?"

"I don't know if he's killed anyone, but I know he shot a couple people and got shot himself. I could see the scar on his side whenever he took his shirt off."

"Where do you think I can find Rio?" I said.

"Are you sure you want to do that?" she said.

"Extremely sure."

"Rio is not going to be happy."

"I'm accustomed to dealing with unhappy people. Part of the job description."

"Are you going to tell him that I told you about all this?"

"I know he's not the brightest bulb on the tree, but he's probably gonna figure it out one way or another. This information can't come from too many other sources."

"Then he'll come looking for me for sure."

I had tried to avoid looking into her emerald eyes for most of the conversation to avoid distraction, but this time, I couldn't, and they caused me to take a moment. What kind of fool would throw this away?

I finally gathered myself and said, "You have nothing to worry about. After my visit, he won't even dare speak to you again."

"How can you be so sure?"

"Because remember Mechanic, my associate I told you about?" She nodded. "The one who fixes problems with his two guns?"

"I'm bringing him along for the ride."

7

TNL Heating & Cooling occupied a large, refurbished warehouse on the eastern border of Englewood, one of the deadliest zip codes in the city. Gangs mixed with poverty and political apathy had taken what was once a thriving middle-class neighborhood and allowed it to be overrun by senseless, savage criminality. There was only one set of laws in Englewood, and that was the laws of the streets. After some heinous crime occurred in the neighborhood, mayors and aldermen would pop up on television and vow more financial and law enforcement resources, but once the camera lights turned off, everything went back to how it always was. I pulled into the empty lot adjacent to the warehouse, then walked through a raised garage door. Several work trucks sat along the far wall, with various heavy-duty equipment scattered about the floor. A couple guys were loading gear into the back of one of the trucks. They stopped when they heard me approach.

"Hey, fellas," I said. "There a manager here I can talk to?"

"What kind of manager?" the older man said. He had close-cut gray hair and a Sox baseball cap that was seemingly too large for his head.

"Supervisor?" I said. "A boss?"

"Closest we got to a boss right now is Mrs. McCarley."

"Where can I find her?"

"Through that door," the old man said, pointing to a glass door in the corner of the warehouse. "Better go now, because she takes a lunch exactly at noon and she doesn't like anybody messin' with her lunch hour."

I took out my phone, pulled up Joaquin's photo, and showed it to them.

"You guys know Joaquin Escobar?" I said.

The old guy pulled out a pair of readers from the front pocket of his work overalls, then scrunched up his face as if he smelled something bad. He looked at the younger guy, who was about a foot taller and fifty pounds lighter than him. There was some nonverbal thing happening between them.

"I don't know anybody called Joaquin," the old man said. "But I know that man right there in that picture."

I looked down at my phone just to make sure I had pulled up the correct photo. It was Joaquin.

"This is Joaquin Escobar," I said. "He worked here for about six months."

"No, that's Santana," the old man said. "His name is Diego, but everyone here goes by their last name."

"Are you sure?"

He looked up at the young guy, who nodded his agreement.

"Sure as my momma six feet in the ground," the old man said. "That man is Diego Santana. Now, you can call him Juwan or Juakom or Juan or whatever you called him, but that muthafucka right there is Santana."

In this line of work there's an old axiom: *Expect anything, be surprised by nothing.* I was doing my best to stay true to it, but I was struggling right now. I'd never seen this coming.

"Did you work with him?" I asked.

"We both did," the old man said. "Did plenty of jobs together. Quiet guy. Hard worker. Knew his shit for such a young guy."

"He ever talk about his girlfriend?" I said.

"Didn't know he had one," the old man said. Then he turned to the young guy. "He say anything to you, Newsome?"

"Nah," Newsome said. "Never had that kind of personal conversation. Like you said. He was quiet. Minded his own business."

"Other guys like him?" I asked.

"Everybody round here liked Santana," the old man said. "Good man to work with. Never caused no problems."

"Why did he quit?" I said.

"Quit?" the old man said. He looked up at Newsome, who shrugged. "Santana didn't quit. There was some kind of misunderstanding in the office, and Blackwell let him go."

"Who's Blackwell?"

"The man who owns this company."

"Is he in there with Mrs. McCarley?"

The old man shook his head. "I think we done said enough. You best go into the office and talk to Mrs. McCarley."

I walked to the corner of the garage and through the glass door as they had instructed. This led me down a short hallway with a couple empty rooms off it. The end of the hall opened up into a large room with three desks arranged in no particular order. A large woman sat behind the desk closer to the back wall, with a full view of the office. She sat in front of a large computer monitor and a stack of multicolored folders. She looked up as I walked in.

"How did you get in here?" she said.

"Through the garage. Two guys directed me here."

"They let you walk through the garage?"

"Well, I couldn't exactly fit my private jet in here; otherwise, I would've flown."

She pushed back from the desk, the chair under her squealing in pain. "No need to get smart with me," she said. "We can't have regular people walking through the garage. Insurance liability. Something happens to you, and it's a big mess for us. We have a front door that customers can use."

"I'll be sure to use it next time," I said. "But I'm not a customer."

"What are you?"

"A private investigator."

"I don't think I've ever seen a private investigator before," she said.

"Voila," I said, spreading my hands in the air.

"You're not what I thought one would look like," she said.

"What did you expect?"

"Nothing as handsome as you."

"You've been watching too many TV shows," I said. "We're not all slovenly with disheveled hair, drinking problems, and personal demons."

"Slovenly?" she said. "Now, don't come in my office using those downtown words. You're in Englewood, honey. Talk real to me."

"Okay," I said. "I can talk real. Why is it you had an employee named Diego Santana whose real name was Joaquin Escobar?"

"What's your name?" she said.

"Ashe Cayne," I said.

"Well, Ashe Cayne, I don't know what the hell you're talking about."

I pulled out my phone and turned it so she could see Joaquin's photo.

"You think I got Superman vision?" she said. "Come over here and let me see that."

I walked over to her desk and handed her my phone. She examined the photo carefully.

"Have a seat," she said, returning my phone and pointing to a vinyl-padded folding chair across from her desk.

Once I got as comfortable as possible, she moved the pile of folders that was in our eyeline and said, "Let's start from the beginning, Cayne. We call everyone here by their last names. I'm Mrs. McCarley. What exactly are you trying to do?"

"I'm trying to find out why the man in the photograph I just showed you was going by two names," I said.

"Who says he has two names?" she said.

"His family knows him as Joaquin Escobar. You all know him as Santana. Those sound like two different names to me."

"There you go getting smart again," she said. "We can't get nothing accomplished if you gonna insist on running at the mouth like that."

"It's just my nature," I said. "Accept my apologies."

"Apologies accepted," she said. "Now tell me what's going on."

"The man in this photo worked for your company for about six months," I said. "His name—or at least the name his family calls him—is Joaquin Escobar. I haven't seen his birth certificate, but I talked to his nephew, so I have every reason to believe that's his real name. He worked here up until about six months ago. Last week, his body was found in Lake Michigan."

Mrs. McCarley's eyes widened. "Dear Mother of God," she whispered. "Santana is dead?"

"I'm afraid so."

"But how?"

"They're saying he drowned."

"Healthy young man like that just up and drowned in the lake?"

"I don't believe it, which is why I agreed to help the family figure out what the police are too lazy or too discriminating to do."

"Well, what can I do to help you?" she said. "Santana was a nice young man. I want to do whatever I can to help."

"Let's start with his name," I said. "That's the name he gave you?"

"That's the name he filled out on his paperwork."

"He provided a Social Security number?"

"How else would he have gotten paid?"

"Did your payroll service match the number with his name?"

"Honey, you're looking at the payroll service. Me and a checkbook in my drawer. Do you see all the work on this desk? I don't have time to do all kinds of extra work. The man gave me a name and a Social Security number. I filled out the papers on my end and paid him like everyone else."

"Can you give me his Social Security number?" I said.

"He dead now, so I guess it don't matter," she said.

Mrs. McCarley pulled open the bottom drawer, bent over with great effort, rummaged through several folders, and then said, "Here we go." She produced a W-2 filled out and signed by Diego Santana.

I took a picture of it with my phone.

"Who hired him?" I said.

"Blackwell."

"He's the owner? And you call him by his last name too?"

"What part of 'everyone' did you not understand?"

I nodded. I had an answer for that, but things had been going much better these last several minutes, so I stayed focused.

"Who here didn't like Santana?" I said.

"Why do you assume someone didn't like him?" she said.

"Because his nephew told me he quit because he didn't get along with a few people here."

"That's news to me. Everyone around here liked him. He didn't quit."

"What happened?"

"Blackwell let him go."

"He say why?"

"Nope, and I didn't ask. I got enough on my plate without being worried about personnel issues. One day, Blackwell came in and said Santana didn't work here anymore. I knew enough to leave it at that and mind my own business."

"Any way I could talk to Blackwell?"

"You can when he gets back from vacation. He always takes his vacation after summer, when we're not as busy."

"When will he be back?"

"Sometime next week, hopefully. He's down visiting family in North Carolina."

—◇—

IVAN RAMIREZ STEPPED UP TO the golf ball he had just placed on the tee, took a calm and measured practice swing, and then placed his club behind the ball and took a real crack at it. The ball exploded into the air and traveled well beyond the three-hundred-yard marker before hitting the ground and rolling another twenty-five yards.

"Jesus Christ!" I said.

"I'm just getting loose," Ivan said.

"How far do you hit when you're loose?"

"Another fifty yards if I really get ahold of it."

We were standing on the practice driving range of Olympic Golf & Tennis Club in the south suburbs. I had finally joined my first club thanks to a bonus I had earned solving a case for the Kantor family and discovering what happened to their billionaire father. Ivan was already making good on our retainer agreement and giving me my first lesson.

I took another twenty swings under his supervision, making small tweaks to my new stance and putting a little more flex in my knees.

"We need to talk about your uncle," I said, grabbing my water bottle and taking a long sip. The temperature was unusually hot for a September day. "Couple of things have come up that aren't matching."

"Like what?" Ivan said.

"Let's start with his name," I said. "Did you know he had two names?"

"He had three," Ivan said. "Joaquin Luis Escobar."

"I mean two names as in he had a name different from Joaquin. He also went by the name Diego Santana."

Ivan was about to swing his driver but stepped back from the ball and looked at me like I had just grown a second head.

"Who is Diego Santana?" he said.

"That's what I was hoping you would tell me."

"Never heard of the name in my life. My uncle's name was Joaquin. Always has been. I don't know where you're getting this other name from."

"I looked at the W-2 he filled out and signed when he worked for TNL Heating & Cooling. He used the name Diego Santana, Social Security number and all."

"I don't think my uncle had a Social Security number," Ivan said. "He didn't even have his papers yet. He was working on getting them."

"Well, that's what the company knew him as. Which leads to the second discrepancy: You said your uncle quit."

"He did," Ivan said. "He told me a couple guys were giving him a hard time, so he decided to leave."

"Your uncle was fired, and everyone at the company liked working with him," I said. "There wasn't any bad blood at all. No one conspired against him. They said he was a good worker and knew his shit."

"This doesn't make sense," Ivan said after taking a long swallow of water. I could hear traces of defeat in his voice. "Why would Joaquin lie to me?"

I let his question hang in the air for a moment. "Sometimes life doesn't make sense," I said. "Sometimes people do things that we're not meant to understand."

"But why would he not confide in me? I was his nephew. I was his only family here. He could have told me anything."

"He could have, but he didn't. There must've been a reason."

"What the hell was he up to?"

"'We dance round in a ring and suppose, but the Secret sits in the middle and knows,'" I said.

"You think Joaquin was leading a double life?"

"I think Joaquin might've gotten himself caught up in something that didn't work out so well."

"Like what?"

"The girl he was seeing for a while."

Ivan didn't appear surprised by the revelation of his uncle's infidelity.

"Did you know?" I asked.

"I had my suspicions, but I never said anything. It wasn't my place to bring it up."

"Her name is Julieta, and she had a boyfriend named Rio who doesn't possess a lot of charming character traits but does possess a lot of guns and a penchant for violence. Rio found out about their affair a few weeks ago. Calling him unhappy about it would be putting it extremely mildly."

"You think he killed Joaquin?"

"Men have killed over a lot less."

"What will you do now?"

"Brush up on my Portuguese just in case and go talk to Rio."

"You're not worried about stepping up to a guy like that?"

"About as worried as knowing one of those birds flying around out there plans on taking a rest in a tree."

8

Lieutenant Hector Delgado and I had been upstart patrolmen together in the Third District, fresh out of the academy. He'd wanted to work closer to where most of his family lived, so after a few years, he got transferred up to the Seventeenth, in the far north reaches of the city. We had stayed in touch sporadically through the years and both made detective six months apart. He navigated and survived the vicious political jungle of CPD and stayed on the upward track, becoming one of the youngest lieutenants in the department's history. He now worked in the Fourteenth District but had spent several years before that as a detective in the Second.

"Cayne," he said, picking up his phone. "What the hell have you been up to, my man?"

"Spending too much time solving crimes you guys won't, and not enough time working on my swing."

"I see not much has changed."

"I lost three-tenths of a second off my mile the last couple years."

"What a slacker," he said, laughing. "You still boxing?"

"Gotta stay tougher than the tough guys," I said.

"And these streets are getting tougher by the day," he said. "So what have you been up to lately?"

"I'm calling to pick your brain a little."

"Whatever's left of it," he said. "I've been cutting back on my coffee, so by this time of day, my brain is fried."

"I'm calling about a guy named O'Halloran," I said.

"Out of the Second?"

"That's him."

"Bad guy," Delgado said.

"How's that?"

"How do you think? Big chip on his shoulder. He's young, but he's a throwback. Not the biggest fan of diversity. You look or talk a certain way, you're already guilty. When I was there, he had several complaints against him. Excessive force. Profiling. Verbally abusive. Most of the time, he was a real asshole."

I wasn't surprised to hear this. "Is he any good at his job?"

"He's competent," Delgado said, "when he sticks to the evidence and doesn't let his extra baggage get in his way."

"I'm working one of his cases from the outside."

"You talk to him yet?"

"Couple of days ago."

"Then you already got a feel for him."

"I did, which is why I'm calling to make sure my feelings are correct."

"The best advice I can give you is to be careful with him," Delgado said. "He actually plays the politics much better than you'd expect."

I told Delgado about Joaquin Escobar—what Ivan had told me and how O'Halloran was determined not to consider any other possibilities in regard to how Joaquin had died.

"He seemed so determined to close the case," I said. "Almost as if he didn't want to find anything that would go against the narrative he had accepted. I'm just trying to figure out if the reason he's being so obtuse is because the guy was a poor immigrant or because there's something else going on that no one else knows about."

"I'll dig around a little myself," Delgado said. "I still have a few friends over in the Second. Don't press him too hard right now. Let me see what I can find out, then I'll let you know."

MECHANIC AND I SAT IN my truck in Washington Park, looking out the window at a softball game with not much interest in the game but a lot of interest in the spectators watching the game. One of those spectators was Dario Vazquez. He was standing near the team that was wearing black uniforms. He spent most of his time chatting up a stocky guy badly in need of a haircut. The black team was getting the better of the white team, which greatly pleased Rio and his friend. Once the game was over, Rio and the stocky guy headed over to a gleaming, tricked-out red Ford F-150 Lightning Platinum truck. The tires looked big enough to stick under an eighteen-wheeler.

"That's a hundred-thousand-dollar truck," I said to Mechanic, who had as much interest in the truck as he had in the game. He didn't bother with a response. I pulled in a few cars behind them and followed. Rio jumped on the Dan Ryan Expressway, then minutes later pulled into the Pilsen neighborhood. He parked in front of a two-story building with a black façade that had a colorful mural painted on it. Several high-top wooden tables were arranged on the sidewalk adjacent to a long seating area underneath a row of blue tents. I parked behind him. The bar's name had been quietly painted in the window. *SIMONE'S.*

"Let's keep it outside," I said to Mechanic. "Just in case it gets messy."

Mechanic and I got out of my truck before Rio's door opened. I was waiting for him when he stepped out. Mechanic took a position behind the truck in full sight of the stocky guy, who was also climbing down from his seat.

"Nice truck," I said to Rio. "What's under the hood?"

"Two electric batteries," Rio said.

"About five hundred horse, right?" I said.

"I got the extended-range batteries. I can get five hundred and eighty horse on a full charge."

The stocky guy walked in front of the hood of the truck and stood by Rio's side. He seemed inpatient.

"Mind if I ask you about Joaquin?" I said.

"Joaquin?" Rio asked.

"Joaquin Escobar," I said.

Rio looked at the stocky guy, confused.

"The guy who was spending time with Julieta," I said.

"Who the fuck are you?" Rio said. Our friendly conversation had just taken a different turn.

"I'm a friend of Joaquin's nephew."

"Man, fuck him, his nephew, and fuck you too."

"That's a whole lotta fuckin'," I said. "You sure you got enough stamina for all that?"

The stocky guy took a couple steps in my direction, but we were still a good five feet apart. He wasn't a threat yet. It was a mock charge, sort of like what elephants do when you get too close to their calves. Mechanic made his way to this side of the truck, just enough for them to see he was there.

"Get back in your old truck and go back the hell where you came from while you can," Rio said.

"I was hoping we might get a drink first, maybe a couple of tacos," I said. "I haven't been down here in Pilsen in a while."

"This ain't the place for you," Rio said. "Or your mute friend over there."

"Best if you keep him out of this," I said. "Just a little friendly advice."

"Fuck you," the stocky guy said. "Both of you."

I looked at Mechanic. He had his hands still crossed in front of him. He could draw Black Betty faster than the stocky guy could take his next step.

"What did you do to Joaquin?" I asked Rio. "I know you weren't happy he was being more of a man to Julieta than you had ever been."

That was enough to get things started. As I expected, the stocky guy was the one to make the first move. He came charging, low and fast. I knew he would need to get in close to hit me, given the difference in our reach. I also knew that it was an amateur's mistake to wait to defend yourself against a charging bull. The first strike is always important in any street fight. I sprung toward him as fast as I could, and just when he was within reach, I quickly swung a right jab to his nose. Amateurs always think you hit a guy on the jawline. That's shit for TV and movies. The nose is the softest part of the face; thus, you're less likely to break your fingers or wrist by landing a punch there. Hit a guy hard enough in the jaw, you might break it, but you'll end up breaking something in your hand too. My jab landed right on the button, and his nose immediately splintered. He stumbled back a couple steps and collapsed to the ground. The blood was pouring out of his busted nose like a garden hose someone forgot to turn off.

Rio quickly turned and opened the truck's door, reached in, and came out with a gun. But before he could pull it up, Mechanic said, "Lift it an inch, and I'll put the first one between your eyes and the next one in your left ventricle and blow your aorta out."

Rio's hand trembled, and he dropped the gun onto the street. The stocky guy was still on the ground, trying to staunch the river of blood with his white sweatshirt that was now a shade of pink.

"Now we can finish our conversation," I said. "What did you do to Joaquin?"

"I ain't did shit, man," Rio said. "Swear on my momma."

"You threatened to kill him for being with Julieta."

"I was talking shit, man. I was mad. You'd be too. Besides, I ain't gonna kill nobody for a bitch who was just my girlfriend. My wife, that's a different story. But just a piece of ass, nope. Most I'm gonna do is beat the shit outta him, but I ain't gettin' locked up for a piece. I don't care how fine she is."

I believed him.

"You ever get a chance to fuck him up?" I said.

"I tried, but that bitch gave me the wrong address so I couldn't find him. And I haven't been able to find her either. You know where she is?"

"That's the other part of this conversation," I said. "You come within a mile of her, we will hunt you down, and I will personally rip your heart out of your chest."

The stocky guy finally stood, his crisp Air Jordans in a pool of blood.

"I make myself clear?" I said.

Rio nodded.

"A phone call, a text, talking to any of her friends—you try to contact her in any way, and I'll kill you with my own two hands."

Mechanic and I backed up to my truck and opened our doors. "Might wanna get your friend over to the county," I said. "They'll do the work and not ask a lot of questions. We send a lotta business through their doors."

We got in the truck, backed up, and headed east on Eighteenth.

"Left ventricle?" I said to Mechanic. "Getting all anatomical on me."

"Been hanging around your fancy-talking ass too much," Mechanic said. "That shit is contagious."

9

The next couple days were painfully quiet. I was waiting to hear from Blackwell, but it was still early in his vacation. Carolina called me from Belize to let me know how attentive the male staff had been to their group of five single women. I checked in with Julieta, who confirmed that Rio hadn't tried to communicate with her in any way. My father reminded me twice about his girlfriend's birthday party and how excited she was to finally meet me. The feeling was far from mutual, but I couldn't tell him that.

I sat in my office with the lights off, looking out the window at the quiet water. In just a couple months, it would turn choppy and a drab gray. The lakefront would be all but deserted except for the few of us still willing to run against the violent wind gusts blowing hard off the water.

My cell phone buzzed on my desk. It was Mrs. Graves.

"Hope I didn't catch you at a bad time," she said.

"No, that would be if I were putting for a birdie on a long par four. Right now, I'm just looking at the lake, dreading the idea of winter."

"Please don't remind me," she said. "I was in my closet the other day and saw my winter coat hanging in there. All I could think of was the snow and the wind and how for months we'll be stuck inside trying to stay warm."

A chill ran through me just hearing her say that.

"Anyway, let's live in the moment," she said. "We have a few more weeks of decent weather, so let's be grateful and take full advantage of it. The reason why I called is because they're putting your case on the table tomorrow."

"Who's doing it?" I said.

"Dr. Melody Farmer," she said.

"I don't know her," I said.

"She's young but good. Very meticulous. Takes her time. Goes through everything twice."

"How long before the report will be in the system?"

"Usually forty-eight hours after the exam, but with Farmer, she takes a little longer. Usually three days."

"Okay, let me know when it's there."

"Something else," she said. "You didn't make any friends at CPD with this?"

"What do you mean?"

"There's a detective with some Irish name who's not very happy," she said.

"O'Halloran?" I said.

"Give me a sec," she said before putting down the phone. She returned a few seconds later. "Yup, Seamus O'Halloran."

"What did he say?"

"One of the other girls took his call. She said he pitched a fit. They had to have him talk to the chief. For some reason he didn't think an autopsy was necessary."

"He actually complained that an autopsy was being done?" I said.

"That's what Regina said."

"Have you ever heard of that before?"

"A detective on a case not wanting an autopsy?"

"Yes."

"Only once before."

"What was the reason?"

"It was a young kid who supposedly died in his sleep. The detective claimed he didn't want the family to go through what he called 'the ordeal of an autopsy.' He said they had gone through enough. But we had to do it by law because the kid had been healthy and died suddenly of what seemed like natural causes."

"So what happened?"

"They did the autopsy and found the kid had massive bleeding in the brain. Shaken baby syndrome. Come to find out the father was upset the child was crying so much and kept shaking him to make him stop. He killed that poor child. The detective's wife was friends with the child's mother. They knew what had happened the entire time. The detective knew what the autopsy would show. He wanted to keep it all hidden."

When I got off the phone, I called Burke. He picked up right away.

"Make it fast," he growled. "I didn't have anything to eat for breakfast, and I'm about to sit down and have my lunch."

"I need a favor," I said.

"And I need a couple million dollars for my retirement," he said. "Tell me something I don't already know."

"The sea is gonna swallow up a lot of land."

"What the hell?"

"By 2050, thirty-four billion dollars' worth of real estate along the nation's coasts will be flooded because of global warming."

"Big shit. I'm a Midwesterner. Won't touch us."

"And that's exactly the attitude that's destroying Earth," I said.

"What does this have to do with the favor you wanted to ask me?" he said.

"Nothing, but you told me to tell you something you didn't know."

"Thank God that fuckin' retirement also means not having to deal with your bullshit anymore."

"You've been threatening retirement for the last five years," I said.

"Every time I put my paperwork in, they find a new reason why I should stay," he said.

"What does the missus say?"

"That she'll divorce me if I retire. No way we can spend that amount of time together and not kill each other."

"Ever think about taking up a hobby other than eating?"

"Fuck you, Cayne. I've lost six pounds since you last saw me."

"That was six months ago. Congrats. At the rate you're going, you'll crack two hundred pounds by the time you're ninety."

"You called me to lecture me on my weight?"

"I called you because I need to see the case file on Joaquin Escobar."

"That the Colombian guy who fell into the lake drunk?"

"He didn't fall into the lake, and I doubt he was drunk. But the autopsy will determine that. I want to see what's been reported on him."

"What's your theory?"

"Someone killed him, threw him in the lake, and made it seem like he drowned. I also think the detective on the case doesn't want it to be a case."

"How's that?"

"He doesn't want the ME to do an autopsy."

"Why the hell not?"

"That's a question only he can answer."

"Doesn't make any sense to me, unless..." Burke's voice trailed off.

"He wants the case to stay closed," I said.

"No disrespect, but it's not like the guy worked for the Colombian Consulate and there are some diplomatic high stakes," Burke said. "What did the guy do for a living?"

"Fixed heating and cooling units."

"Well, you got me on this one," he said. "I don't know what to tell you."

I was about to tell him that Escobar had also been using a second name, but I wanted to close the loop on that before I made any assumptions or passed along bad information.

"Can you get me his general case file?"

"Sure, give me a couple days."

"What are you having for lunch?"

"Italian beef from Al's."

"In one of those big Styrofoam containers?"

"Al's sure as hell doesn't serve sandwiches on fine china."

"It will take over five hundred years for that Styrofoam to decompose."

"And only one second for me to find some peace."

The line went dead.

I JUMPED INTO MY TRUCK, turned onto Lake Shore Drive, and drove the seven minutes it took to reach Promontory Point, which everyone simply called the Point. It wasn't accessible by car, so I parked on the other side of Lake Shore Drive and walked through the tunnel that had been built underneath it and opened into the meadow. Cyclists pedaled freely along the paved bike path, mothers and nannies sat on blankets playing with toddlers, and a group of seniors stood off in a circle practicing tai chi. I first walked around the entire field house to see if there were any surveillance cameras. There weren't any. I then stood along the northern edge of the peninsula and faced the rocks below and the downtown skyline and Navy Pier in the distance. I slowly scanned the landscape in a semicircle. I couldn't see where there would be any video surveillance that could've captured what had happened when Joaquin arrived on the Point or when his body had been found.

I walked down the gigantic revetment and sat on one of the rocks just a few feet away from the water. I was there alone, and all other noises had been drowned out by the loudness of the waves and the various other sounds that can be heard on open water. A family of seagulls quietly flew circles in the far distance, diving to the water's surface occasionally, then returning to the air. My phone buzzed and sang in my pocket. I didn't recognize the number.

"This is Mrs. McCarley," the caller said. "Remember me from TNL?"

"How could I ever forget?" I said.

"Are you busy right now?"

"I could be busier."

"Can you come and talk to me? It's very important."

"Are you propositioning me, Mrs. McCarley?"

"Honey, you fine, but you ain't that fine. I got grandchildren almost your age."

"I'll be there in thirty."

By the time I made it to TNL Heating & Cooling, it had taken me closer to thirty-five minutes with traffic instead of thirty, and Mrs. McCarley had already called again to confirm I was still coming. Her voice sounded more urgent than it had during our last conversation. I pulled up outside of the office, and instead of going through the garage like I had last time, I made sure to enter through the nondescript door that looked more like it led to a house than an office. Mrs. McCarley was seated prominently behind her large desk. She was alone. She didn't bother getting up but waved me over.

"Have a seat," she said when I approached. Her eyes were red and glassy. She had been crying.

I sat down in the same folding chair I'd sat in last time.

"Everything alright?" I said.

"No, it's not," she said. "Blackwell is missing."

"What do you mean?"

"I got a call this morning from his daughter. She was all upset. Some sheriff in North Carolina got a call from some man who said there was an empty boat on the lake, and they realized it was Blackwell's boat, and he wasn't in it, and they couldn't find him in the cabin, and his car is still there, and his phone is turned off."

"Hold on for a minute," I said. "Let's take this slowly."

Mrs. McCarley closed her eyes, took a deep breath, and leaned back in her chair.

"Where does Blackwell own a cabin?" I said once she had opened her eyes.

"Down in Greenville, North Carolina. That's where his people come from. He's owned that cabin for years."

"Is Blackwell married?" I said.

She shook her head. "Never been married."

"Any other kids?"

"Just the one daughter who lives in Dallas. Her name is Holly. She just got married last year to a young man she met in Peru."

"Who does Blackwell live with?"

"Here or in North Carolina?"

"Both."

"He lives alone over in the Gap."

The Gap, so named because it was nothing more than a sliver of houses on the South Side occupying only a hundred acres between King Drive and State Street, running only four blocks between Thirty-First and Thirty-Fifth Street.

"What about the cabin?" I said.

"No one lives there," Mrs. McCarley said. "Blackwell goes there about four or five times a year. I don't know if he takes anyone there with him or if he meets people there. I don't know that side of things. I just know he loves to get away and go down there and he plans on building a house there for his retirement."

"Is it possible Blackwell just decided to go somewhere else and not tell anyone?" I said. "Maybe he went to visit a friend and just didn't come home yet."

"I guess it's possible, but then why was his boat out on the water, floating around by itself? I don't know anything about boats, but wouldn't you tie it up to a dock before leaving? And why were his suitcase and clothes still in the house? Where would he have gone without clean clothes?"

I knew the likelihood that he had spontaneously decided to travel to a different destination was extremely low. But I also didn't want to agitate Mrs. McCarley any more than she already was.

"Can you get the daughter on the phone?" I said.

Mrs. McCarley lifted the handset of the large phone on her desk and quickly punched in a number she seemed to have memorized. When the line started ringing, she hit a button to turn on the speakerphone.

"Holly, I have that young detective I told you about," Mrs. McCarley said. "He's sitting here in the office."

"Ashe Cayne?" Holly said.

"I'm here," I said.

"Thank you for talking to us," she said. "I don't know what's going on, but Mrs. McCarley said you might be able to help."

"I'm not sure what exactly I can do," I said. "But I will help any way I can. Where are you now?"

"On my way to the airport to fly to North Carolina."

"Who have you been in touch with?"

"The local sheriff over there. A man named Simpson. He's the one who called me and said that my father was missing. He seems like a very nice man."

Holly repeated everything Mrs. McCarley had already said to me, just a little slower and with more detail.

"Does your father have family down there?" I said.

"He has a couple cousins and a great-aunt who still live in Greenville. I spoke to them. They heard from him when he got there. He was supposed to drive over and get some barbecue, but he never showed up. They called his number several times, but he didn't answer. They thought he might've gone back to Chicago early. Then I got the call from Sheriff Simpson early this morning."

"What are they going to do next?"

"He said they already had divers out there in the lake. I've never been there, but he said it's a pretty big lake. So far they haven't found anything."

"What did they say about the cabin? Had someone broken into it? What condition was it in?"

"He said everything appeared normal. Nothing seemed out of

place. His car was in the driveway. There was lots of food in the refrigerator and cabinets. They don't know what's happened to him."

"When was the last time you spoke with your father?"

"Three days ago. He was normal. He was happy. He said it felt good getting away from work and Chicago. The summer had been very busy. He was talking about how nice it would be to retire down there."

"Busiest summer we ever had," Mrs. McCarley said. "All that heat had people's systems working overtime. We had so many service calls, the men were working well into the night sometimes."

"Was there anything he said, Holly, that gave you reason to believe something might be wrong?" I said.

"Nothing. He was very relaxed and positive."

"Did he have a girlfriend or anyone who might've been visiting him at the cabin?" I said.

"I'm not sure. Dad always went there alone to get away. I don't know if he ever had any company, but if he did, he never mentioned it to me."

"Have you been there?"

"Several times. I usually make it out there once a year. But I didn't go this past year. I was so busy with the wedding and getting settled into my new house."

I gave Holly my number, then told her to give me a call once she was on the ground in North Carolina. I didn't have high hopes for her father, but there had been plenty of instances in other investigations when I had been wrong. I was hoping this was one of those times.

10

Later that night, I grabbed a deep-dish from Malnati's for my date with my TV and Thursday Night Football. The Bears were playing the Vikings in Minnesota, and as usual, the local sports guys were repeating their annual mantra: "This could be the season." I put Stryker on his leash, then headed out into the unseasonably warm night. We stopped at the dog park, which was mostly empty. Stryker immediately started chasing a black Labrador. At first, I thought it was Rex, a dog we had met a year ago, but the woman called him Barry, and she looked nothing like Rex's owner, Karla Coe. That put a thought in my head. I dialed Karla's number.

"The dashing Ashe," she said, answering the phone. "I haven't heard from you in several months."

"Last time I checked, the phone works both ways," I said.

"It does," she said. "But I didn't want my call to get lost with all the others blowing up your phone. A self-respecting girl doesn't like to be one of many."

"If only my life were as exciting as you've imagined it," I said. "I wouldn't be grabbing pizza by myself and about to sit down in front of my TV for the rest of the night, where I'll fall asleep only to be awakened by Stryker's snoring."

"I'm about to head out and watch the game with a couple friends," she said. "Why don't you join us? I'm pretty sure we'll make better company than a snoring cockapoo."

I thought about it for a moment. Didn't sound like a bad offer. I could always stick the pizza in the fridge and have it for lunch tomorrow.

"Where are you going?" I said.

"Clover in River North," she said.

"Where is it?"

"Grand, just west of Union. They have cheap beer, all-you-can-eat free popcorn, and dartboards."

"Sounds like a lot more fun than sitting home alone," I said.

"C'mon, Ashe," she said. "You'll have a good time. My friends are chill and funny. You'll like them."

"Well, since you're twisting my arm," I said, "what time?"

"We'll be there in about an hour, but come whenever you want. We'll have a seat waiting for you."

I almost hung up before asking her about the Social Security number issue, which was why I had called in the first place. "Have you worked with a lot of immigrants as a public defender?" I asked.

"Definitely," she said. "They almost always have to rely on our office for representation. They don't exactly have a six-hundred-dollar-per-hour budget."

"What do you know about fake Social Security numbers?"

"I'm not exactly an expert, but I've had to deal a lot with that issue when it comes to my clients. A lot of them haven't gotten their citizenship yet, but they want to work, and if they want to work in a place that doesn't want to pay cash, then they need a number. They can't get a number unless they're a US citizen, permanent resident, or eligible nonimmigrant worker. So they go outside of the system to get a number."

"Illegally."

"Unfortunately, yes. The other options are limited and, if I'm being honest, a real pain in the ass."

"You mind if I pick your brain a little more when I see you tonight?"

"I'm all yours."

"That's a very dangerous thing to say to me once the sun has set," I said.

She laughed.

"Danger isn't always a bad thing," she said. "Life would be a total bore if you didn't live a little on the edge."

I typically wasn't one who liked to go to a sports bar to watch a game. The patrons were either buzzed or falling down drunk. I could deal with the buzz phase, but when it moved too far beyond that, things often went south quickly. People tended to say things they shouldn't say and feel ways they shouldn't feel; then all of a sudden, people were in each other's faces, and no longer was it about the game but about proving manhood. I preferred the calm, controlled environment of my apartment or a friend's place with good food and a remote control so I could hit the rewind button and watch the plays I liked several times before moving on. But Carolina was down in Belize getting pampered and ogled at in her small bikini, and Stryker would be snoring before the first quarter was over, so meeting Karla and her friends seemed like it wasn't too bad an option.

I arrived at Clover just before the game's opening kickoff. It was a medium-sized bar living underneath two floors of apartments. The design had been kept purposely sparse, unlike the bars in Fulton Market, where the owners spent exorbitant amounts of money, as if they were competing for the cover of *Architectural Digest*. Clover was a lot more low-key, which I liked, and more about the atmosphere. A single long L-shaped bar sat against the wall when you walked in, with a row of TVs hanging both above it and on the opposing wall. The requisite pool table and a table shuffleboard game filled out the rest of the main area. A side room had been cleared out, and a sizeable dart range had been set up with three adjacent boards and a popcorn machine that customers were free to use.

The crowd was on the younger side, energetic but not obnoxious. The business at the bar was brisk. I spotted Karla sitting with two other women at a high-top table across from the bar. One was a tall Asian woman in a black motorcycle jacket and high heels. The other was a Black woman with straightened hair that flipped at her shoulder. She had large eyes and high cheekbones, and her nails were painted a vibrant red. Karla sat across from them, her blond hair pulled back into a ponytail. She wore a tapered women's Bears jersey and tight black jeans with an assortment of silver zippers and buckles. All three of them were nursing beers and drawing lots of attention, especially from the table of guys sitting next to them. I delighted in cutting off their interest. The Black girl noticed me first as I approached the table. She smiled with a set of perfect teeth. Her face and eyelashes and hair were all natural, a rare commodity these days. That scored extra points in my book.

"This seat empty?" I said.

"These are my friends," Karla said. "This is Chloe." She pointed to the Asian woman. We shook hands. Chloe's fingers were long and delicate. "And this is Marisol." Marisol eagerly took my hand and continued to blind me with her smile.

"Short for Maria de la Soledad," I said.

"You know that?" Marisol said, giggling. "Almost no one ever knows that unless they went to Catholic school."

"Mary of the Solitude," I said. "The title given to the Virgin Mary. I slept through most of my religion classes, but I remember that."

"Virgin?" Chloe said, widening her eyes and laughing. "Marisol?" Marisol playfully tapped her shoulder.

"We were just placing bets on if you'd show up or not," Karla said.

"Who won?" I said.

"Marisol."

"You doubted me?" I said to Karla.

"You didn't sound overly committed on the phone."

"I was standing there with Malnati's in one hand and Stryker's leash in the other," I said. "Was just doing some quick calculations when you asked me."

"Well, I'm glad I won over a box of deep-dish," she said. "I don't know if my ego could've taken a defeat like that."

"I didn't mean it that way," I said. "You know how it is when you have it made up in your mind what you're going to do after a long day, and even if it's not the most exciting thing, you're looking forward to it. That's all it was. Had nothing to do with you." Karla smirked playfully. I turned to Chloe and Marisol. "And nothing to do with your beautiful friends either," I said.

"We've heard all about your charm," Marisol said, rolling her eyes. "Not working this time."

"'Now my charms are all o'erthrown, and what strength I have's mine own, which is most faint,'" I said.

"Shakespeare in a sports bar?" Chloe said incredulously.

"If you don't like that, I can do several songs from Queen's *News of the World* album."

"Five bucks you can't," Marisol said. "I know every Queen song ever recorded, even before the movie came out and everyone found them again."

"'Buddy, you're a young man, hard man, shouting in the street, gonna take on the world someday.'"

Marisol said, "'You got blood on your face, you big disgrace, waving your banner all over the place.'"

We sang the chorus together with Karla and Chloe joining in. "'We will, we will rock you!'"

When we finished, Marisol turned to Karla and said, "You were right, girl. He is fun."

And then, as if I weren't sitting there, Karla said, "And like I told you, not bad to look at either."

Chloe and Marisol sounded their agreement with closed mouths.

"If you're trying to see me blush, it's not gonna work," I said, rubbing my cheeks. "I've developed melanin superpowers that completely hide it."

A loud cheer erupted. The Bears' kick returner caught the opening kickoff and took it all the way back to the Vikings' forty-yard line. Glasses were tipped throughout the bar and high fives abounded. I was empty-handed, so I made my way through the cluster of bodies, copped a Guinness, and headed back to the three ladies, who were in the midst of whispering conspiratorially but stopped as I approached.

We watched the game sporadically when the Bears had the ball on offense, talked about random topics, and ate popcorn for the better part of an hour. Marisol was also a lawyer, who worked in one of the titled law firms in a skyscraper on Wacker. Chloe ran her own PR company in Lincoln Park. They had been friends since college.

Halftime arrived with the Bears up by a field goal. Marisol and Chloe excused themselves for a bathroom break. Karla was several beers in at this point and feeling very comfortable. She put her hand high up on my leg and leaned into me, close enough that I worried our lips were going to touch. Her eyes shimmered.

"So what do you think about my friends?" she said.

"Very pretty and a lot of fun," I said. "And they know a lot more about football than I expected."

"They think you're really hot," Karla said.

"Even without my charm?" I said.

"You're charming even when you're not trying to be," she said. "Every girl in here has looked at you at least twice since you walked in."

"And every guy has been waiting for me to go to the bathroom to have a free shot at you," I said.

"They'd be wasting their time," she said. She took another sip of beer, then came back to me and said, "So why do you want to know about Social Security numbers? Sort of a strange thing to ask."

"It's about a case I'm working on," I said.

"Can I hear about it?"

"A guy was found in the lake. They thought he was drunk, fell in, and drowned. The guy's nephew disagrees. I'm trying to figure out what really happened. He was an undocumented immigrant from Colombia. As I was looking into what happened, I found out he was using a different name with a Social Security number."

"That's not uncommon," she said.

"Is it hard to get a number these days?"

"The hardest part is getting the money together," she said. "The rest is a piece of cake."

Halftime had ended and the game had resumed. The bar suddenly ignited with a roar. The Bears had just gotten an interception and ran it back to the Vikings' ten-yard line.

"Where do you go to get a number?" I said, once the noise had quieted.

"There are several ways to get one. First, you can steal someone's number. Let's say you know someone who dies, and they don't have much. Could be an old person living in a nursing home. You could steal their name and Social and could probably get away with it for a while, especially if the person doesn't have a family or someone looking after their affairs. With the bureaucracy in our government, it can take a long time before one hand knows what the other is doing. That number remains active with the Social Security Administration until all the paperwork is completed and entered into the system."

"That doesn't seem too difficult," I said. "What's another way?"

"Just make one up," she said. "When you fill out a W-2, put whatever name you want on it and whatever number. Submit the paperwork, and the company pays you. But that won't last too long. Once the company pays into your Social Security account with the government under that false number, SSA will eventually realize it's a fraudulent number, then contact the business and let them know. You can probably get away with that for three to six months, but not much longer."

"And the third way?" I said.

"Rent a number," she said.

"What the hell?"

"Exactly. And there's a huge market out there for this. It's simple. People have young children with Social Security numbers. They will rent you the number for a certain fee, and since the child isn't using the number for anything official, SSA doesn't really have any reason to look into your use of the number. The only way they will know something is wrong is if the number is reported stolen. Other than that, it's pretty much clear sailing."

"So you basically take the kid's name and Social Security number and use that when you need it for something like employment papers or a bank account or anything official?"

"Exactly."

"I never even knew people were doing that."

"It's a billion-dollar business."

"How much do they charge for renting a number?"

"All depends," she said. "There's no set charge. Every situation is different."

"Have any of your clients done it?"

"Absolutely."

"What have they paid?"

"A range, but some as high as ten thousand dollars."

"All at once?"

"Usually not. They will break it up into payments. Most people don't have enough money to make a lump-sum payment like that. They need to work it off. But eventually they're able to do it."

"How do you think I can find out if my guy did something like that?"

"I'm not exactly sure," she said. "I'd have to think about that. The easiest thing to do is to figure out if it's a real number or not. That's the first place to start. If it's fake, then you have your answer. If it's real, then either he stole it or he rented it. If that turns out to be the situation, I'm not sure how you would figure out what he did."

THE NEXT MORNING, I WAS just about to sit down to a plate full of pancakes that I had made using my grandmother's recipe when my phone rang out from the bedroom. I thought it was Carolina, but when I picked up the phone, I noticed a Texas area code. It was Holly Blackwell.

"I'm sorry I didn't call you yesterday," she said. "There was just so much going on, and I was talking to so many people. By the time I got back to my hotel, I could barely keep my eyes open."

"I completely understand," I said. "I know this is difficult."

"I'm just scared to death," she said, "and confused. This isn't like my father."

"What isn't?"

"Any of it."

"Explain."

"First of all, my father and I never go more than a few days without checking in with each other. Even if he decided to go somewhere else, which I don't believe he did, my father would've called me to let me know. For him to change his plans and not tell me isn't typical behavior for him."

"These are important details to know," I said. "This is why it's critical that you're there. You would notice things that no one else could."

"The boat," she said. "My father has owned a boat for my entire life. He has fished since he was a little boy. His father taught him how to drive a boat when he was a teenager. Why would he leave his boat undocked in the middle of the lake with the motor off?"

"Unless he fell into the water," I said.

"Which is another problem," she said. "Dad's an excellent swimmer. He was in the navy for fifteen years. He's one of the few Black people who would go up north and swim laps in the lanes up near Oak Street Beach. If my father, for some reason, fell into the water, he more than anyone would be able to swim back to the boat or to shore. But to think he fell over and just drowned? That doesn't make any sense."

"Does your father have any health problems?"

"He had just developed a little high blood pressure, but it wasn't a problem. He didn't even need medication. He was controlling it through diet and exercise. My father is extremely fit."

"I've never seen him before," I said. "Can you send me a photo?"

"I will as soon as I get off the phone."

"What did the cabin look like when you got inside?"

"Very neat. My father has always been meticulous when it comes to his living spaces. But there was something that bothered me, and I didn't realize it until I got back to my hotel room."

"What was that?"

"Well, there are three bedrooms in the cabin. There's a master and two much smaller guest rooms. It looked like he had been using the master bedroom. His suitcase was in there and his hats, but the bed wasn't made up. That's just strange."

"Why?"

"First of all, my father never used the master," she said. "Even when he was there by himself. He used the bedroom at the back of the cabin because that room has the best view of the lake. Whenever I went to the cabin with him, he always insisted I stay in the master. Second, his bed wasn't made up. I don't care where he was; whether we were home or staying in a hotel on vacation, the first thing my father did when his feet hit the floor was make up his bed. When I was a little girl, I couldn't even go to the bathroom in the morning before I made up my bed. It's his military training, and it never left him, even after all these years. I don't know what else to say other than I got a weird feeling seeing that. It just wasn't the way my father does things."

Wrong bedroom used and a bed that wasn't made up. These were definitely clues, and they were talking, but what were they saying?

11

"How's it going down there?" I asked Carolina. She called me just as I was getting out of the shower. I was trying to dry off and talk at the same time without getting my phone wet.

"This is our best trip ever," she said. "Why can't my life be Belize and Chicago be my vacation?"

"Because then your vacation would be a lot worse than your normal life, and you would never want to come to Chicago for vacation, since vacations are meant to be a reprieve from your daily life, and thus I would never see the apple of my eye."

"You could always visit me in Belize," she said. "The dollar is very strong. We could live like a king and queen."

"Sure, but that would mean having to fly all the way there," I said, "which would probably work out to seeing you two or three times a year."

"I was thinking more like once a month."

"If they had twelve world-class golf courses down there, I might consider that arrangement."

"Do you miss me?"

"Like Romeo missed Juliet."

"I'm worth dying for?"

"Ten times over."

"Are you keeping yourself busy?"

"I went to a sports bar in River North last night to watch the game. When are you coming home?"

"Obviously not soon enough if you've been reduced to sports bars. How is your case going?"

"A couple unexpected turns."

"Such as?"

I filled her in on Joaquin and his two names and mysterious Social Security number, as well as the discrepancy between his getting fired from the heating and cooling company when he had told his nephew that he'd quit. I told her about O'Halloran's rush to close the case and keep it closed. She also found it strange that Blackwell was suddenly missing down in North Carolina.

"Do you know if the Social Security number is real or fake?" she said.

"Not yet," I said. "Someone is trying to run that down for me."

"If I wasn't here, I could find that out for you. Wait, why don't you call Burke? He has access to Accurint."

Accurint was a special, subscription-only service available to police officers that used cutting-edge investigative technology to expedite finding people's identification. A quick search in the database could bring back an enormous amount of information about a person's assets, where they've lived, who their direct family members are, cars they've owned, and even the names of their previous and current neighbors. It was like Google but only accessible to government, commercial, and law enforcement agencies.

"I don't know where my head is," I said. "I didn't even think to ask Burke, and I just talked to him yesterday."

"I'm not around, and suddenly that genius brain of yours can't think clearly," she said. "It's good to know my absence has that effect on you."

"And several others I can tell you about when I get in bed alone tonight."

"I gotta go," she said, laughing. "The girls are calling me for our spa appointment, then we're going to have lunch in the rainforest."

As soon as I disconnected the line, I called Burke.

"Two calls in two days," he said. "You lonely or something?"

"Carolina is down in Belize on a girls' trip," I said.

"Which explains why you were at Clover last night entertaining a table of women," he said.

I didn't even bother asking him how he knew that information. Burke had eyes everywhere, and everyone knew he and I were close.

"Who did you watch the game with?" I said.

"Watch the game? Why the hell would I do that? Set myself up for another heartbreak at the end of the season? I've put enough holes in the wall behind that damn team. I don't care how much the local sports guys like to hype them up. Until we get new owners, we're never gonna win. Period."

"But that family has owned the team for over a hundred years."

"And that's about ninety years too long."

"Well, they beat the Vikings last night," I said. "And their season is off to a four-to-one start. They're tied with the Packers. You gotta admit that's pretty damn good."

"Don't hold your breath," he said. "We'll have this same conversation in mid-December, and they'll be fighting and praying just to make the playoffs. Different year, same story. Think about it. We have more players in the Hall of Fame than any team, yet we've only won one Super Bowl. People can sell false hope and tell lies all they want, but the numbers always tell the truth."

"Speaking of numbers," I said. "I need you to run a name and Social through Accurint."

"What am I, your damn office clerk now?"

"I like my clerks a little prettier," I said.

"Fuck you, Cayne. What do you need?"

"It's Joaquin Escobar. I found out he was using a different name with a Social Security number."

"Big shit," he said. "That's as common as diarrhea."

"A lot of fecal references," I said. "Everything okay at home?"

"Jesus Christ," Burke said. "Sometimes having a conversation with you is worse than going to a damn dentist. At least the dentist gives me numbing medication. You're just a raw pain in the ass."

I gave him Joaquin's alias and the Social Security number he used.

"I'll run it in about an hour," Burke said. "I have my own damn work to do."

"If that's what you call sitting behind a big, shiny desk and going to city hall for photo ops with Bailey."

A dead phone line was his only response.

I SPENT THE NEXT HOUR sitting at my office computer, searching for anything I could find on Hank Blackwell and his company, TNL Heating & Cooling. Blackwell had a quite impressive history for someone who many probably thought was just a guy who could fix boilers and furnaces. He had been a graduate of the University of Illinois before he entered the navy as an officer. He had done two tours of duty in the Persian Gulf, for which he was awarded both a Distinguished Service Medal and a Silver Star. He spent several years teaching at the Naval Academy before retiring and moving back to Chicago, where he joined the civilian workforce and started working for a commercial HVAC company. Five years later, he opened his own company on the South Side.

A few minutes later, I found several images of Blackwell at a construction site in the West Loop with several dignitaries at the groundbreaking of the Old Post Office building on Van Buren. This was a long-awaited, multiyear project that had poured eight hundred million dollars into renovating the 1920s building into an office and events complex with dining and a roof garden. Blackwell must've scored one of the contracts to work on the project, because not only was he one of the contractors at the groundbreaking, but he also was in several photos with Bailey at the ribbon-cutting ceremony. I remember there had been a large fight in city council about how the contracts were to be awarded and what type of transparency would exist, so the public clearly understood the criteria that were used in the competitive bidding process. Blackwell was one of a few African American contractors in the photos, but he obviously had done something right to make it through the political gauntlet.

I clicked the images tab and found more photos of Blackwell, either at official functions or with a group of kids handing out coats at a clothing drive. Then, at the bottom of the page, I saw a photo of him standing next to Penny Packer at a jobsite. They were both wearing hard hats and pointing at something in the distance. This was just confirmation of the adage that the world really is small. I never would've thought the two of them had ever crossed paths.

I was just about to do another search on his cabin in North Carolina when Burke called back.

"I got a hit on your Diego Santana," he said. "He's got absolutely no connection with Joaquin Escobar. Diego is a three-year-old boy who lives in Pilsen with his mother, Guadalupe Rivera. There's no record of the father, but I'm assuming the father's last name must've been Santana. Diego has an older brother, Raphael Santana, who's eight."

"What about the Social Security number?" I said.

"That number belongs to Diego. The mother lived in Hammond, Indiana, with her paternal grandparents before moving to Chicago about five years ago. The mother works at the Burlington Coat Factory over on Canal Street. Before that, she worked at the Panera right across the street from Burlington. She has a sister and brother who live in Hammond and have the same last name."

"Any arrests or citations?" I said.

"Nothing," Burke said. "She comes back completely clean."

Joaquin had been either using a stolen number or renting it. There was only one way to find out: talk to Guadalupe Rivera.

I CLOSED MY OFFICE EARLY and decided to meet Mechanic at Hammer's for a few rounds in the ring. I was growing a little frustrated with the case. While I hadn't found myself coming to a lot of dead ends, I did feel as though every time I got an answer cleared, two more questions popped up in its place. I needed a physical release, and nothing would be more physical than standing in the ring across from Mechanic.

As I pulled into the alley behind Hammer's to look for a parking spot, my cell phone rang. It was Mrs. Graves. The fact that she was calling me from her cell phone and not her office line during work hours was a clear sign that whatever she wanted to discuss needed to be kept discreet.

"You have a couple minutes?" she said.

"As much time as you need," I said. "Just about to jump into the boxing ring and release some tension."

"Please be careful," she said. "Boxing is so dangerous. Look what all those punches did to poor Muhammad Ali. Most beautiful man I've ever seen, and he was nothing but a shell of himself at the end of his life. Anyway, something is going on with your case. I don't have the specifics right now, but I just wanted you to know that something's not right."

"What happened?"

"That detective who put up a fit earlier in the week when he was notified an autopsy was being done just left here not looking very happy."

"Is this autopsy over?"

"Yes, but I don't have the results. Remember, it's Farmer. She won't have that report in the system for another few days."

"Why do you think O'Halloran was so upset?"

"Regina said she's not a hundred percent sure, but she thinks the detective and Farmer had a disagreement over her findings."

"Does she know which findings were in dispute?"

"She overheard Farmer talking to the chief, but she didn't hear the full conversation. But whatever it was, the chief told her she backed her up and did the right thing."

"As soon as you find out something, let me know," I said.

"Don't worry, I got you," she said.

No sooner had I hung up the phone than I got a text message from Karla Coe. **Can you talk?**

I dialed her number.

"That was fast," she said.

"I was about to go a few rounds in the boxing ring," I said. "So I figured I'd call you first while my head is still clear."

"I didn't know you were a boxer," she said.

"Which would've been handy last night if any of those guys decided to act on what they were thinking."

"You felt like someone wanted to fight you?"

"To get to you."

"Not hardly. I feel like guys can easily read that I'm unavailable."

"Now you tell me?"

"I don't say 'unavailable' to everyone."

"Ego stroking is so underrated," I said. "We need to talk more often."

"Did you have fun last night?"

"I did. The free popcorn was my favorite part."

"Excuse me?"

"After your company, of course."

"The girls really liked you. They've both sent me several messages today, and you were in half of them."

"Let's do it again soon," I said.

"Be careful what you wish for," she said. "Speaking of wishes, I got some information on that name and Social Security number. Both are real, and they match."

"One of my sources confirmed that earlier," I said. "What's your guess, stolen identity or rent?"

"I don't have a guess," she said. "I know what it is. Rental."

"How are you so sure?"

"Because the mother did the same thing with her older son and got caught doing it. She could've gotten jail time, but the judge was lenient, and she had a good public defender who got her probation."

"So much for learning your lesson."

"Ten thousand dollars is a lot of money to a single mom selling sneakers and winter coats."

"People gotta do what they gotta do."

"What are you gonna do next?"

"I'm not sure," I said. "I was going to talk to her, but I don't know what good that would do other than scare her and add more stress to her life. I already know he rented the number and why he likely did it. What I don't know is who was so upset with him that they wanted him to sleep with the fishes."

12

Penny Packer and I sat at her kitchen table in her Lincoln Park mansion, talking about our two favorite topics: golf and my cases. Barzan, her private chef who she had stolen from a downtown Michelin-starred restaurant, went about his work quietly, putting the finishing touches on what was never less than a four-course meal. We sipped a Bordeaux the president of France had given Penny on her last trip to Paris. This was our last dinner of the year. We met here for our private meal every month, except for October, November, and December, when she was wintering at her ranch in Palm Springs.

"How did August play?" I said.

"It didn't feel as long as the last time," she said.

"Maybe because you're driving the ball twenty-five yards longer."

"Possible, but I also felt like the tee boxes were moved up a little."

"Was the course in good condition?"

"Pristine. You could eat off the fairways."

"Who did you play with?"

"Some old codger who runs a private bank in New York. His wife came along and couldn't hit the ball in the fairway if her life depended on it. I think she really came to make sure he behaved himself. He can get a little handsy when he's had a couple drinks."

Penny was somewhere in her late fifties, but she looked as good, if not better than, most women half her age, and without any dermatologic enhancements. She was a lifelong athlete and, despite her family's wealth, had played almost every sport growing up, including rugby. She never ate before ten or after nine, and she worked out four times a week without a trainer.

"You need to come down and play the course," she said.

"How am I gonna do that? With my good looks?" I said. "An invitation might help."

"I'm truly embarrassed it's taken me this long to invite you," she said. "I promise we'll do it next year, and you'll be my first guest of the season."

Barzan walked the half mile from the other side of the kitchen to deposit our first course, and he explained it was a Lancaster Farm early squash salad made with squash shipped in from an organic farmer's co-op in Pennsylvania Amish country, complemented with smoked ricotta, pickled barberries, tender greens, Concord grapes, and a maple-walnut vinaigrette.

"So what's going on with your latest case?" Penny said. "You know I want all the details."

"I'm working on a case you actually referred to me," I said.

"Which one?"

"The Colombian kid whose uncle was found in the lake."

"Ivan really did reach out to you," she said. "I didn't think he was going to go through with it. He's an amazing golfer. If only all caddies could also play the game as well as he can."

"He's determined to make the tour," I said.

"I have no doubt he will. I'm going to see if I can make some calls for him and get a couple wild cards."

"I was with him on the range the other day. He hit the ball so far, I lost track of it."

"Can you just imagine if we had even half the stuff he's got? We'd win the club member-guest tournaments from coast to coast."

"I like the kid," I said, "and I feel bad about his uncle. But a lot of things just aren't adding up."

"Like what?"

I brought Penny up to speed on all that I had learned about Joaquin and his second name. Penny was captivated by the details of his affair with Julieta and my physical encounter with Rio and his friend in Pilsen. Then I told her about Blackwell.

"He's a navy veteran who runs an HVAC company out of Englewood," Penny said. "I've met him a couple times."

"I know you have," I said. "I saw a couple pictures online where you both were at a groundbreaking."

"That was at the University of Chicago a few years ago. I donated some money in memory of my father. They were looking to build a new residential hall for the students. The president called and asked if I'd help out."

"How well do you know Blackwell?" I said.

"Not that well," she said. "But I know he's extremely knowledgeable and a very interesting man. He told me about his tours in the Persian Gulf War and his work at the Naval Academy. I also remember how connected he was. He knew a lot of people down in city hall."

"His daughter is in North Carolina right now trying to figure out what happened," I said. "In my experience, most of these cases don't turn out well."

"You think he's at the bottom of that lake?"

"If he is, I don't think it was by any fault of his own."

"As in someone might've killed him?"

Barzan brought over our second course on a tray. He cleared our first plates, then explained we were going to have a North Carolina swordfish with green-shoot bok choy, gingered carrots, and a miso pink-peppercorn sauce.

"North Carolina," I said, after Barzan had journeyed back to the other side of the kitchen. "Ironic."

Penny shrugged. "His poor daughter must be beside herself," she said. "It must be downright agonizing waiting to find out if he's dead or alive."

"What makes it worse is that he might've died in the very arena where he earned those prestigious medals—in the water."

"I just can't see how a navy man who is still fit could have an accident like that on a still lake and drown."

"Neither can I. Doesn't add up for me, but stranger things have happened."

"Like that entire tragedy with Elliott last year. What a mess that was."

Elliott Kantor was one of Chicago's richest billionaires, who was found tied up to a four-poster bed in his secret apartment in Lincoln Park. His son had hired me to find out what had happened.

"The Kantor case taught me a lot and confirmed many things I already knew," I said.

"'Expect anything, be surprised by nothing,'" Penny said. "Those are great words for anyone to live by."

Our appetizers had been quickly tucked away, and Barzan returned to clear our plates and serve up our entrée of Wagyu beef striploin with braised red cabbage, herbed corzetti, and honey-glazed Brussels sprouts, all in a creamy béchamel sauce. He informed us that our dessert choices would be either a warm chocolate ganache cake with vanilla bean ice cream or something he called Le Président gâteau that came with a complicated explanation of which I only understood the word *chocolate*. We decided to get both choices so we could share. Penny insisted she would only take a single bite of each and not an ounce more.

"Do you think Blackwell's disappearance has anything to do with the death of Ivan's uncle?" Penny asked.

"If it does, I can't see any reasonable connection," I said. "Other than Joaquin working for Blackwell for a short time, I can't imagine any other ways their lives might've intersected."

"This isn't the first time I've heard you say that," Penny said. "You said it during the Gerrigan case, if I remember correctly."

"Sure enough, and looked how that turned out. Twists and turns to the very end."

A COUPLE DAYS LATER, I got two calls I had been waiting for. The first was from Mrs. Graves.

"Farmer uploaded the report on Escobar," Mrs. Graves said. "You need to take a look at it right away."

"How soon can I get it?"

"When I take my lunch break."

"Usual place?"

"Yup."

"I'll have your matcha latte waiting for you."

An hour later, Holly Blackwell called in.

"The lake is empty," she said. There were traces of hope in her otherwise tired voice.

"What happened?" I said.

"They sent divers and sonar equipment and all kinds of machinery down there," she said. "They didn't find anything."

"How confident are they in their search?"

"Sheriff Simpson said that if he was down there with all they used, they would've found him."

"And his cell phone is still turned off?"

"I call it every hour. Nothing."

"Do you know what kind of phone he had? Android or iPhone?"

"I don't, but Mrs. McCarley will probably know. It's likely he has it listed in his business account."

"Did your father keep a car down there, or did he drive a rental?"

"Both. He always picks up a rental to get him from the airport to the cabin. He doesn't like taking taxis, and he definitely isn't a fan of rideshares. He has an old Jeep he keeps in a small garage. He uses that when he's driving in the mountains because the terrain can be pretty difficult, especially when it rains and the dirt roads turn to mud."

"You wouldn't know what rental company he used?"

"I don't, but I can find out when I go to the cabin. The car is still there, so I assume the keys are in the house."

"When are you planning on going back to Texas?"

"I'm not going anywhere until my father is okay."

"Is the sheriff keeping you updated regularly?"

"He is, but I don't understand what he's saying when he starts talking the police lingo. Do you think I could hire you to help?"

"I'm not sure how much help I can be up here when everything is happening a thousand miles away down there."

"I'm desperate," she said. "Even if you could just talk to the sheriff and ask questions I don't know how to ask or understand the information that doesn't mean much to me. I'm by myself, and someone with your experience could make a difference. I'll pay whatever your fee is."

As a general rule, I never took on two cases at the same time. It wasn't like I had a team of investigators. I had Mechanic to back me up when I was in a tight situation or people didn't want to cooperate, but that was it.

"Please, Mr. Cayne," she said. "My father is a good man. He's all I've got next to my husband. I'm scared. Anything you can do would be a big help."

"I don't want to take your money," I said.

"I don't want you to work for free."

"Let's find your father first, then go from there."

"I can't tell you how much this means to me," she said, crying. "You are a blessing from God."

"That's not exactly what my mother said when I was coming out the womb, but I'll take it now."

"You're also very funny," she said, laughing between her tears.

"Text me Simpson's number, and I'll start working with him,"

I said. "Let him know I have your permission to inquire about the investigation and receive all information."

"I'll get on that right away," she said. "One more thing before you go. I had a conversation with my father's neighbor down here, Mr. Crawford. Well, I guess they're neighbors, but not like neighbors are in a city. He lives farther up the hill, about a quarter of a mile. He and Dad get along because they both were in the military. Mr. Crawford was in the army. And they both like to be up here alone. He said he hadn't heard from my father at all since he'd been here."

"Does your father always call him when he goes there?" I said.

"He said he doesn't remember a time when my father hasn't called him and stopped by to talk or eat something."

"Did he drive by your father's property at all?"

"Several times, but he wouldn't have been able to see my father's car or the cabin, because the driveway is long and winds between the trees. You can't see the main road from any part of the cabin. My father liked the seclusion after living in the city for so many years, where your neighbors see every time you leave your house or take the garbage out."

"What does Crawford think happened to him?" I said.

"Unfortunately, he thinks everything is a conspiracy," she said. "Even before they searched the lake, he was convinced my father wouldn't be there."

"Text me his number. I want to talk to him now."

I was in the midst of eating spicy tuna sushi rolls, so I quickly dipped a couple rolls in some This Little Goat Everything Sauce, devoured them in a millisecond, then opened Holly's text and dialed Crawford's number. I could tell it was a landline because it rang six times and didn't go to voicemail. He answered on the seventh ring.

"Holly told me you'd be calling," Crawford said. "Honorable thing of you to help the family out."

"I hear you're a vet," I said.

"Thirty years in, twenty out," he said.

"Thank you for your service."

"You're welcome, but I wish others felt the same way. The way some of our fellow Americans are attacking our own democracy makes me wonder sometimes what the hell we were fighting for. Lost six buddies defending our people's rights to be free and enjoy the opportunities of our great country, and now we don't have to worry about foreigners attacking our institutions—our very own people are doing it. This country is upside down, and we're all going to be in hell if it doesn't change fast."

"I can understand how pissed you and other vets must be, given all your sacrifices. Was Blackwell disappointed too?"

"Hell yeah, he was. He served two tough tours against a country that wanted to wipe us off the face of the Earth. Damn right he's upset about all this madness."

"Holly said you hadn't heard from him since he'd been there."

"Not a peep. And that's not like Black. He always rang me up to let me know he was coming down here, and he would let me know when he arrived. Not a word from him."

"Why do you think?"

"It's a mystery to me," Crawford said.

"Do a lot of people live in the area?" I said.

"Not many at all," Crawford said. "Maybe six or seven of us year-round. Another five or so have cabins they come to now and again."

"Blackwell have any problems you know of?"

"Not recently, but when he first got here, a couple boys were trying to get something started."

"Like what?"

"Leave messages with a bunch of slurs on his door, in his mailbox. Shit that wasn't right and that Black didn't deserve. Listen, my people come from deep in these mountains, backward as shit 'cause they never got a chance to see the bigger world. Well, the army gave me a chance to see not only how great our country is but how a man ain't the color of his skin. He's what's on the inside. I knew who was leaving those messages, so I paid them a little visit and had a talk. They stopped."

"Nothing since?"

"Not a peep."

"Have you talked to Sheriff Simpson?" I said.

"I haven't talked to Cole himself, but I talked to one of his deputies. Young guy, still wet behind the ears. He came up here asking questions like he wrote them down from watching some TV show. It was pretty much a waste of time."

"Holly just told me the lake is clean."

"They didn't have to do all that to find that out. I knew he wasn't down there in the first place."

"Why were you so certain?"

"All kinds of reasons."

"I'll take whatever you wanna give me first."

"Well, let's start with the obvious," Crawford said. "Black was a squid. The man was as used to the water as an Arab is to the sand. One summer, he was up here, and we got to talkin' shit together. I bet him a steak dinner from a restaurant in town he couldn't swim across the lake without stopping. That lake must be damn near three football fields or thereabouts. Black stripped to his drawers and jumped in without a second thought. Not only did he swim all the way across without stopping, but once he got to the other side, he stood onshore and waved at me and swam right back. When he got out of the water, he was breathing so easy, I had to look at his chest real good just to make sure he was breathing at all. And you want me to believe a man like that is at the bottom of that lake? Hell naw. Not unless someone tied him up and put him down there. Black ain't at the bottom of nobody's lake."

"Did you tell this to the deputy?" I said.

"I tried, but he wasn't really listening to me," Crawford said. "He had his own agenda, and that was it."

"What do you think happened to Blackwell?"

"Well, I didn't want to say this to the daughter on account of her already being so upset, but I don't think he ever came here."

"Why would you think that?" I said. "His car is in the driveway, his suitcase and clothes are in the bedroom, and the refrigerator is full of food."

"Don't none of that impress me," Crawford said. "What ain't up there are the flags."

"What flags?"

"Black has a flagpole at the beginning of the driveway, next to the main road. Every time he comes here, *first* thing he does before he even takes a shit is hoist up two flags—the navy veteran flag and the Chicago city flag with the four stars on it. Both of them. Not one or the other. Both of them. I drive by his property every day to go down the hill to do what I need to do in town. None of his flags were hanging, and if you go up there now, they're still not hanging. Let me be as clear as I can to you. Black *never* came here and didn't fly those flags. Somebody might've been in his cabin, but it sure as hell wasn't Black. I'll bet my damn life on that."

13

I walked into the Chipotle at Ogden and Damen, just a block away from the medical examiner's office. Mrs. Graves was sitting at a table, working on a burrito bowl with rice, chicken, guacamole, and cheese. I set the iced matcha latte I had brought onto the table in front of her, then took a seat.

"Are you going to eat?" she said.

"Nope. I'm saving up my appetite. Carolina is coming home tonight, so we're having a big dinner downtown."

"Where did she go?"

"Girls' trip to Belize."

"Times are so different now. We didn't have anything like that when I was that age. Girls didn't travel together like that, and if we did, we barely had enough money to pay for gas to drive down south. Now you kids pick up and fly to other countries just like you're going from the South Side to the North Side. I guess it's nice to be able to see the world. I know people who've been living their whole lives on the South Side and have never stepped one foot across Madison to enter the North Side."

"Old habits die hard," I said.

"Speaking of die hard," Mrs. Graves said, reaching into her handbag sitting on the chair next to her and pulling out a large manila envelope. She slid it across the table and went back to work on her burrito bowl.

"Did you read it?" I asked.

"Just skimmed it," she said. "But there's something in there that detective isn't happy about. He really put up a fit."

"Have you ever seen him before?"

"First time. And hopefully the last. His attitude was terrible. Most officers are respectful when they come into the office to conduct their business. He was pushy. Arrogant. I didn't like the looks of him. Farmer called him in so he could see what she found."

"Do you know what she listed as cause of death?"

"I was too busy trying to get out of the office to look," Mrs. Graves said. "But Regina heard her clearly say that the man may have been in the water, but he didn't die from drowning."

I left Mrs. Graves to finish her lunch, then jumped in my car and opened the envelope. I skipped through the details of the exam, which I would go through later, and went right to the cause of death.

Pericardial tamponade and cardiac arrest, secondary to right atrial laceration consistent with stabbing.

I IMMEDIATELY CALLED DR. BARRY Ellison, a retired pathologist and medical school classmate of my father's who now spent most of his time trying to lower his handicap on the golf course and teaching science a couple days a week to underserved high school students on the South Side. He had helped me decipher these reports in several of my previous cases. A couple times, he provided critical information that led to my solving the case.

"You packing up for Florida?" I said.

"Usually I would be," he said, "but I'm going down much later this year. Both of my daughters and their husbands and my five grandchildren are coming to celebrate my birthday on November 24. But as soon as they leave, I'll be on the first flight out."

"Since you still have some time before you leave, you mind helping me on a case I'm working on?"

"Not a problem," he said. "I could use a little excitement. What do you have going on this time?"

I brought him up to speed on Joaquin Escobar but didn't say anything about Blackwell's disappearance, because it wasn't relevant to the medical examiner's findings.

"You say this young man was otherwise healthy?" Dr. Ellison said.

"According to his nephew, he didn't have any history of medical problems," I said. "Still played soccer every weekend in the park. Drank occasionally but wasn't a big drinker."

"And the initial thought was that he was drunk, fell in from above the revetment, and drowned in the lake?"

"Exactly."

"Now an exam has been done, and that's changed. So what's listed as the cause of death?"

"It says, 'Pericardial tamponade and cardiac arrest, secondary to right atrial laceration consistent with stabbing.' What does that mean to you?"

"He was stabbed in the upper right chamber of the heart, which caused him to bleed into the sac that the heart sits in. When fluid builds up to a certain point, it starts restricting the heart's ability to expand. It's like trying to blow up a balloon inside of a bottle. The balloon will inflate to some degree, but it will be heavily restricted and never reach its full expansion. When the heart is in that situation, it can be deadly, because this pressure prevents the heart chambers from filling completely with blood. Thus, the flow of blood to the rest of the body is greatly diminished, and this means not enough oxygen is getting to the rest of the body. This is a medical emergency. If it's not treated, a person will die."

"How long would it take to die from it?" I said.

"Depends on how fast the blood accumulates in the sac," Dr. Ellison said. "In some cases, the accumulation is slow, so it can take days before enough fluid is in the sac to cause problems. In other cases, it can be minutes or hours, depending on how much blood and how fast it's accumulating. Send me the report, and I'll take a look at it to see what else is there."

I hung up my call with Dr. Ellison and pulled my car onto Damen, then was about to turn onto the Eisenhower to head east toward downtown before thinking better of it. Just as I was entering the Loop, my phone buzzed with a text message. It was from Holly Blackwell.

He rented the car from Alamo at Pitt-Greenville Airport on September 15.

Crawford's words were still in my head. *Black* never *came here and didn't fly those flags. Somebody might've been in his cabin, but it sure as hell wasn't Black.* I parked my car in the garage, went straight to my office, found the number for the Alamo at the airport, and dialed. A man answered right away.

"I rented a car from you on September 15," I said. "I don't remember if I put on any additional drivers in my contract."

"Name or rental agreement number?" the man said.

"Hank Blackwell."

"One moment."

I heard him tapping his keyboard and saying something to someone nearby. He then got back on the phone and said, "You already have one additional driver," the man said. "If you want to add another, you can do it through our app or come back in. The app is a lot more convenient."

"We're a long way away, so I'll do it through the app," I said. "There are three of us driving, but I forgot which one of the other two I added."

"Lawrence Godwin," he said.

"That's right. Larry was with me at the counter. Dave was still getting his bags at baggage claim. I'll just add him through the app."

"Anything else I can help you with?"

"Nope, this was perfect. Thanks for your time."

I called Holly Blackwell right away.

"You know anyone named Lawrence Godwin or Larry Godwin?" I said.

"Never heard of him," she said. "Why?"

"Your father added him as an additional driver on his rental agreement."

"Larry Godwin," she repeated slowly. "Only Godwin I know was an econ professor I had in college. His name was Cyrus Godwin. I've never heard of a Larry Godwin."

"Give it some thought," I said. "If anything comes to mind, let me know."

I called Mrs. McCarley next, who told me she had never heard of a Larry Godwin. She said she would ask around the office to see if any of the men had ever heard of him.

I spent the next hour at my computer, trying different combinations in a Google search. Old, young, Black, white, alive, dead—there were Lawrence and Larry Godwins everywhere. There was no way I was going to narrow down who it was on that contract just by doing this kind of search. I pushed back from my computer and stared out the window at the lake. It was meditatively calm out there. A few undulations, but no waves and very little movement. This happened a lot during this time of the year, and in just a few weeks, there would be white caps the height of a single-story building, rolling to shore like a runaway freight train.

I picked up the phone and dialed Sheriff Simpson. It was time to have a little chat.

"This is Ashe Cayne from Chicago," I said when he picked up the phone. His voice was soft and his Southern drawl thick like hot syrup.

"Ms. Blackwell told me you might be calling in at some point," he said. "Y'all get snow up there yet?"

I laughed. "Winters are tough," I said, "but we do get a bit of a fall season before the cold clamps down."

"Only been up there once in my life," he said. "Made the mistake of going in January. Took me about three months to thaw out when I got back down here."

"Someone give you bad advice?" I said. "You need to come back during the spring or early summer, when we're waking up from winter and the lake comes back to life and the parks are full of fresh blooms and restless people excited to step outside without three layers."

"Maybe I'll give that a try," he said. "It's a beautiful city—just didn't get to enjoy any of it."

"How's it going down there?" I said.

"Bit of a mystery," he said. "We're covering our bases, but not a lot is making sense right now. You know how that is early in an investigation. Ya got bits of information, but nothing is fitting together."

"I know it all too well," I said. "You can be looking at all the evidence and not even realize the answer is staring right back atcha."

"That's the problem," Simpson said. "We don't have a lot of evidence. Hank was here, and then he wasn't."

I noticed him calling Blackwell by his first name. I wondered if he knew him to be so familiar.

"You sure he was there?" I said.

"Well, his rental car, his keys, his old Jeep, his suitcase, his clothes, and a fridge full of food. I think it's fair to say he made it in okay."

"But no one saw him there, right?"

Simpson chuckled softly. I imagined a big man with a big belly and a soft touch.

"You been talking to Kip Crawford, haven't ya?" he said.

"I have."

"Well, let me tell you about Kip. He was one helluva military man. Damn near thirty years of service. Tough as a box of roofer's nails. But unfortunately, Kip ain't always in his right mind."

"What do you mean?"

"All that fighting and stuff he saw on the battlefield—his brain is a little scrambled. He don't think as clearly as he used to. It's common for a lot of vets. PTSD."

He said the letters slowly, like a reservationist patiently repeating a flight confirmation number.

"Crawford and I had a nice conversation," I said. "To be honest, he seemed quite with it when we talked."

"Don't get me wrong. Kip has his moments when he can make a helluva lot of sense, but he's one of those vets who thinks there's always a war and the bad guys are always out there plotting against him and the rest of the country."

"I'm no psychiatrist, but that sounds more like a little paranoia than it does PTSD," I said. "And with all that's going on out there in the Middle East and Russia, I'm not sure he's too far off the mark."

"I ain't no doctor either," Simpson said. "But I know crazy when I see and hear it. Kip Crawford ain't all there upstairs."

"Did you have a chance to speak to him?" I said.

"I sent one of my deputies up there. He came back with a report. Wasn't much there to chew on."

"Have you talked to other people who live in the area?"

Simpson chuckled softly. "Of course we have," he said. "We might not be in a big, fancy city like Chicago with thousands of police officers, but we know how to conduct an investigation too."

"I didn't mean any offense," I said. "Just wondering if anyone else had seen or talked to Blackwell or seen anything the slightest bit off."

"No offense taken," Simpson said. "We canvassed the area. No one reported seeing him or being in contact with him."

"What are you thinking happened?"

"Right now, your guess is as good as mine. I know he's not in that lake; that's for sure. If he was, my men would've found him. We covered every inch of it with divers and machines. He didn't fall off that boat. And if he did, he managed to get out of the water."

"Have you ever heard of a Lawrence or Larry Godwin?" I said.

"Name doesn't ring a bell," Simpson said.

"Blackwell put his name on the rental agreement contract as an additional driver. I figured maybe it was someone who lived down there."

"I see you've been doing a little digging of your own," Simpson said.

"Just trying to help where I can," I said. "His daughter is trying to hold it together, but she's under a lot of pressure."

"Understood, given the circumstances. She's a nice girl. We're doing our best to find her daddy. I'll have one of my men see if he can find anything on that Lawrence Godwin you mentioned. Do you have any other information? Age? Physical description?"

"All I got was the name. I've been trying to search for him online and not getting anywhere, seeing how common a name it is."

"That's how it goes with that damn internet," Simpson said. "It can be a help, but sometimes it's a big waste of time."

"What are you going to do next?"

"Bite into a hot pulled pork sandwich my wife just dropped off."

"Hearing that makes me want to fly down and get some myself."

"You're more than welcome. We got as much barbecue as you want. Slow cooked outside in a big smoker."

"What's the plan after the pulled pork sandwich?"

"I have a call with SBI in about an hour or so, see what resources they might be able to contribute to the investigation."

"SBI?"

"North Carolina State Bureau of Investigation. Around here we just call it SBI. They've got a district office right up the road in Greenville."

"Sounds like a plan," I said, relieved he was going to get some help from the state. "And you might want to check his cell phone ping data. Might let us know where he was last before the phone died or was turned off."

"Already on my list," Simpson said.

"Great minds think alike."

14

Carolina and I finished an early dinner at Cut Steakhouse under the heating lamps overlooking the river. I had avoided eating all day so I could tackle the bone-in rib eye that had been on my mind for a couple months. Carolina nibbled at a miso-glazed Chilean sea bass in a Japanese yuzu sauce. I made the strategic decision to skip dessert at the restaurant so we could get back to the apartment and refamiliarize ourselves before she fell asleep. Dr. Ellison called as we were walking back to my apartment building.

"You have an interesting situation," he said.

"Which is a lot better than uninteresting," I said.

"True, if you aren't the decedent or the person who did this to him."

"What did you find?"

"First of all, I don't know this Dr. Melody Farmer, but she conducted a wonderfully meticulous examination. She was not only thoughtful and thorough, but she was patient."

"Patient?"

"You can tell by her examination that she approached the body with an open mind, which is what medical examiners are supposed to do but unfortunately don't always do. Sometimes our conscious and unconscious biases can influence our judgment and get the better of us. Doctors are, after all, human too."

"Don't tell my father that," I said.

"Except Wendell, of course."

We shared a quick laugh.

"Let me start with the blood work and urinalysis," Dr. Ellison said. "There was no alcohol in his system, nor were there any drugs. He was completely clean, and all his chemistries came back normal."

"So much for the theory that he was drunk, got too close to the edge, lost his footing, and fell in."

"Couldn't be further from the truth," Dr. Ellison said. "Let me take you through the four things that stick out to me if you have the time."

We had another seven or eight blocks before we reached my apartment building, and Carolina seemed content snuggling underneath me. The night air was cool but comfortable. The streets were uncharacteristically quiet.

"I'm ready to listen," I said.

"First, your Mr. Escobar was dead long before he hit the water. Farmer was able to rule out drowning pretty quickly. Gross and micro inspection of both lungs show no water had been ingested, and the other deep respiratory airways were also completely clean. If he were alive and breathing when he hit the water—and given that you said he didn't know how to swim—he for certain would have swallowed and inhaled water. Some would've gone into his stomach and some into his airways. The exam does not show that happened."

"What if he was alive but just unconscious?"

"Even if he were unconscious, he would be breathing, and you'd expect to find something in his lungs and airways. I'm very confident he wasn't breathing when he reached the water. That takes me to the heart. I agree with her assessment. But what I find interesting is the mechanism by which the heart was punctured. That's the second item. There's a chest wound no bigger than a sixteenth of an inch in diameter. That's a very small hole, but it was enough for the instrument to penetrate through the chest wall and into the right atrium, which is the upper right chamber of the heart. It was a perfect shot, directly in the middle of the space between the third and fourth ribs."

"What kind of instrument could do that?" I said.

"It had to be long, very sharp, and very strong," Dr. Ellison said. "It entered with great sustained force. Maybe an ice pick in a strong pair of hands or even a drill. Whatever it was, it certainly wasn't something as crude as a knife."

"That sounds painful," Carolina said, grabbing on to my arm tighter.

I nodded.

"The third item I found curious was his bilateral proximal radial fractures," he said.

"Translation," I said.

"The large outside bones of both forearms—the radiuses—were fractured closer to the elbows and not the wrists."

"Why does that matter?"

"A couple of reasons. Let's say someone pushed him off the upper plateau of the embankment above the boulders. Most people who reach out to catch themselves when they're falling forward usually extend their arms outward to break the fall. When that happens, you would typically see one or more fractures in the carpal or wrist bones, and if the height and force were great enough, you would see a fracture of the radial bone close to the wrist. There are other sites where you can sustain fractures, but they're not as common. Escobar's fractures were not at his wrist or near it. They were more midshaft. That makes me think they were not caused by his trying to stop himself from falling."

"So what do you think happened?" I said.

"I really don't know," Dr. Ellison said. "There are several scenarios that run through my mind. First, if he was dead before he was pushed off the embankment, then he wouldn't have been stretching out his hands to break his fall, so I wouldn't expect to see fractures consistent with that mechanism of injury. The other issue is how perfect the fractures are. It's one clean break, and it's in almost the same location on both arms. That never happens in a fall injury."

"What if he was fighting off his attacker, and he put his arms up to defend himself against some object they were about to hit him with?"

"You beat me to it," Dr. Ellison said. "Let me answer that in context of the fourth item I wanted to discuss. Dr. Farmer found debris under the second, third, and fourth fingernails. The second and third nails were partially chipped. She also noted abrasions on both palms. This would be consistent with defensive wounds. He fought back while he was being attacked. He likely scratched the other person in the face, arms, neck—someplace where their flesh was exposed. That could be the debris she's found under the nails. I'm sure she's sending that off for testing. But let's get back to the forearm injuries. Are you with someone right now?"

"Yes, I just finished dinner, and I'm walking home with what I hope will be my dessert."

"Fair enough," he said, laughing. "Can you put me on speakerphone, then hand the phone to her?"

I followed his instructions.

"Now, I want you to pretend I have a baseball bat, and I'm about to swing it at your head, and you are lifting your hands to protect yourself."

I couched a little and raised both of my forearms defensively.

"Hold your position," he said. "Which side of your forearm is facing outward to take the blow from the bat?"

I studied my arms for a moment, then said, "The same side as my pinky finger."

"My point exactly," he said. "There are two bones in your forearm that run from the elbow to your wrist. They're called the radius and the ulna. The radius is the bone on the same side as your thumb. The ulna is the bone on the side of your pinky. If I were to hit you with a bat in the position you're in now, which bone would I fracture?"

"The ulna," I said.

"Precisely. Escobar's injuries are in the radius, and they are almost perfectly symmetrical both in location and size."

"Which means?"

"I don't think Escobar fought back at all, because he was already dead, and those fractures happened after his heart stopped beating."

CAROLINA SPENT THE NIGHT, SOMETHING she didn't often do on a weeknight, but we'd both wanted more than one serving of dessert, and she was too exhausted to get dressed and schlep home. Stryker and I were more than happy to have her spend the night and infuse her vibrant femininity into the apartment. I woke up early while both of them were still sleeping, slid into my running gear, and hit the road.

I had too much on my mind, trying to juggle both cases and, even more challenging, trying to make a determination whether there was any connection between the two. I was bothered by each case for different reasons. Joaquin had been stabbed in his heart, and if that pain hadn't been enough, he'd then bled into a sac that caused his heart to basically suffocate. He had a family down in Colombia that would never again talk to him or hug him, young kids who would spend the rest of their lives wondering who their father really was and what life would be like had he lived to be old and a grandfather to their children.

Holly Blackwell was down in the mountains of North Carolina, medicating herself to fall asleep at night as she waited and prayed and searched for any clues that might tell her whether her father was alive or dead and why he had disappeared. She was dealing with a sheriff's office that seemed reasonably competent but didn't appear to have urgency as one of its great attributes. Kip Crawford's testimony, for all that Simpson had to say about his mental well-being, remained foremost in my mind. When detectives and prosecutors are looking for witnesses, someone like him is the prototype. He had specific recollection, he made keen observations of both the big things as well as those more nuanced, and he was familiar enough with the missing person's habits to discern what was normal and what was not.

I took a left once I reached the lakefront and started running toward Oak Street Beach, where the Drive made a dramatic hairpin turn before straightening out and stretching north along the water to the large prairie-style houses of Evanston. This was one of my favorite times to run, a slight wind coming steadily off the lake with only a few runners and the occasional cyclist and enough room for everyone on the empty paths.

I tried focusing on my stride, but the questions kept scrolling through my head like a ticker tape. I reached the turn at Oak Street Beach and decided to keep going until I reached the North Avenue Beach, where I would turn around and head back. My watch vibrated from an incoming call. It was Burke.

"What are you doing up so early?" I said.

"The superintendent wants all of leadership in for some meeting about a reorganization," he said. "Just moving pieces on a chessboard without a real strategy."

"Gotta make the people feel like you're doing something," I said.

"A bunch of smoke and mirrors," Burke said. "All this is window dressing for a much bigger problem."

"Let me guess: the superintendent himself."

"All those book smarts, I guess you do have some common sense."

"'Common sense is genius dressed in its working clothes.'"

"Jesus Christ! It's not even seven in the morning, and you're already quoting Shakespeare."

"That was Ralph Waldo Emerson. I have to warm up to Shakespeare. He usually surfaces after nine."

"Do you want the information on this Escobar case, or you wanna sit here and debate poetry?"

"I'm not sitting; I'm running. And, yes, I'd like to hear what you have."

"Something came back from the autopsy yesterday that's making O'Halloran broaden the investigation."

I knew what had come up, but I didn't want Burke to know I had already scored the autopsy, which would make him angry. He would accuse me of wasting his time when I had other sources I could use. So I just went along with it.

"It's been moved to homicide. The guy was stabbed to death."

"O'Halloran still leading it?"

"For now. They aren't giving it any priority, for reasons you already know. Since you're working the case from the outside, let me give you some friendly advice: Put some pressure on O'Halloran. I've been told he isn't the most motivated when victims are of certain backgrounds and hues."

"Hues? That's a pretty fancy word before your first coffee."

"Fuck you, Cayne," Burke said. "I've already had two, and I'm working on my third."

I DIDN'T HAVE TO CALL O'Halloran because at nine o'clock on the dot, he called me.

"How's your investigation going?" he said.

"Funny, I was going to ask you the same thing," I said. "But since you asked first, I'll answer: fits and starts."

"Care to expand on that?"

"Irregular bursts of activity."

"Okay, how about you tell me what kind of activity?"

"How about he had been working for a heating and cooling company using a different name and a Social Security number that belonged to that name?"

"Not surprising."

"What the hell is that supposed to mean?" I said.

"Nothing, just thinking out loud. Continue."

"I think he rented this number from a woman named Guadalupe who lives in Pilsen with her three-year-old son, whose name Joaquin was borrowing."

"Have you talked to this woman?"

"Figured I'd leave that to you guys, if you're interested," I said.

"You have her contact info?"

"I have her address."

I gave O'Halloran the address.

"Okay. Tag, you're it," I said.

"The ME performed an autopsy the other day," he said. "He didn't drown, and he wasn't drunk."

"That's a shocker," I said.

"Your sarcasm is unwarranted," he said. "If this is gonna have any chance of working, we need to get along. Shit-talking isn't gonna help."

"Agreed. My bad."

"He was stabbed in the heart," O'Halloran said. "Not sure yet what kind of weapon was used, but for certain, that's how he died. I also think he fought back. There are some markings on his palms, chipped fingernails, debris under his nails—which might be skin and are currently being studied—and fractures in both forearms."

I thought about what Dr. Ellison told me, but sharing it with O'Halloran probably wouldn't be received too well, and we had just signaled a truce, so I held on to it.

"Have you looked at his phone records?" I said.

"We've put in a request for them with the phone company," he said. "I'm expecting them in the next day or so."

"Will you share them with me?"

"Once I've had a chance to look through them, I don't see any problem with you taking a look. Never hurts to have another set of eyes."

"Four eyes see more than two."

15

The next couple days brought a lot more questions than they did answers. Penny picked up the tab not only to have Joaquin's body flown back to Colombia but also for the burial costs. I had told Ivan that he was right all along that his uncle hadn't fallen into the lake drunk—he had been brutally murdered, then thrown into the water. In a few days, Ivan was heading down to be with his family, unfortunately without any real answers about what had happened. Holly Blackwell stayed in North Carolina, hoping her mere presence and daily calls to the sheriff's office would expedite the discovery of her father's whereabouts but having to face the grim reality that the longer he was missing, the less likely they would find him alive.

I finished a session with Mechanic at Hammer's, showered, jumped in the car, and headed over to RPM Italian on West Illinois Street, where my father's girlfriend was having her sixtieth birthday party in a private room. I had purchased her an expensive bottle of wine that had a history I was sure my father, purveyor of all things cultured, would be able to explain when they were alone. I valeted my car, something I despised doing, but I had no choice, since finding a parking spot this time of night was the equivalent of hitting five numbers in the Powerball. I slid the guy an extra twenty to keep me up front.

Once I stepped into the restaurant, I started feeling queasy. I wasn't sure I was ready for such a festive atmosphere when I had so many mixed emotions charging through me. The main dining room was full: young couples mixed in with aging power brokers and suburbanites out for a special night in the city. Tomorrow morning, when they were safely ensconced back in the suburbs, they could boast to their friends about how they had gotten a table at one of the trendiest restaurants in the city, sat across the room from one of the local TV anchors, and made it home without anyone stealing their tires.

An attractive, petite Filipino hostess walked me through the bar area and led me up the back stairwell, which deposited us in a short hallway leading to the private room. As I hit the top step, I could see the assembled party. It was a good-looking group of all ages, dressed nicely, smiling and laughing, carried away in conversation. The table had been decorated with enormous flower arrangements and three large crystal candelabras spaced evenly apart. Soft music piped in from the overhead speakers.

Then I saw my father. He was standing next to a very attractive woman with stylish short hair, fashionable glasses, and a black A-line dress that made it clear she was as familiar with exercise as she was with the law. What stopped me was that he was holding her hand. It wasn't an incidental, casual type of hold. It was the kind of handclasp that only people in love can forge. I had never seen my father hold my mother's hand. Not once. He would occasionally kiss her when either one of them left for a trip, but affection had been virtually nonexistent in our house, at least when it came to Dr. Wendell Cayne. My brain was having a difficult time processing what my eyes were seeing.

"Is everything okay?" the hostess said to me.

I didn't have the words to respond, so I just stood there and stared at their hands, then at the smile on my father's face.

"Is this the party you were looking for?" she said.

"It is," I finally said. I turned and handed her the bag with the wine and bouquet of flowers. "Do me a favor. Please take this in for me. And don't let them know I was here. Just tell them I dropped it off."

Before she could respond, I turned and walked back down the stairs. I didn't realize I was crying until I got into the car.

THE NEXT MORNING, INSTEAD OF heading out for a jog, I ran the shower until it was full of steam. I stepped in and let the hot water fall heavily against my skin and seep into my pores. I inhaled the steam; it felt good going down my airways and up into my sinuses. My mother would have me do that as a child when I had a bad head cold and couldn't fall asleep at night. I just focused on the sound of the water, its constant pitter-patter against the tile floor, and the steady stream from the water jets. I wasn't sure how long I was in the shower or even if I had fallen asleep, but when I finally turned the water off and stepped into my towel, I felt calm and reinvigorated, the drowsiness experienced after a good sleep while getting a deep tissue massage.

I turned the TV to the Golf Channel, fed Stryker, and started making pancakes. My phone rang from the bedroom. By the time I reached it, the caller had already hung up. It was a number I didn't recognize. I brought the phone back into the kitchen with me. As I poured the batter into the pan, my phone rang again. It was the same number.

"This is Sheriff Simpson," the caller said. "This Ashe Cayne?"

"It's me," I said.

"I called a few minutes ago, but no one answered and the voicemail was full," he said. "I was gonna leave you a message but decided just to call back."

"I never empty my voicemail," I said. "Every time I do, it just fills back up. I figure that if someone wants me badly enough and I don't answer their call, they'll just send me a text."

"Fair enough," he said. "I imagine a big-city guy like you stays busy getting calls all day long."

"It can get hectic," I said. "But this is the slow part of the year for me, so it's not too crazy."

"Understood. Well, I know it's been a few days since we last spoke, so I wanted to give you an update on Hank's situation. We got the cell phone ping data yesterday. I've looked through it with one of my deputies. I have to admit, it's a little confusing. Seems to raise more questions than it does answers."

"In what way?"

"Well, his plane landed at 10:24 a.m. He went to pick up his rental car and drove out of the lot at 10:57 a.m. The last ping of his cellular was on a tower near Tar River at 11:23 a.m. After that, his signal goes dead."

"Where is Tar River?"

"Well, that's the confusing part—not where it is, but why he was heading in that direction. The river is about twenty miles in the opposite direction of his cabin. It's directly south of the airport, off Route 13. If Hank was heading to his cabin, he should've left the airport and traveled north on 13."

I thought for a moment, trying to put myself in Hank's mind. "Where is the commercial area of the town?" I said.

"South of the airport. The same direction Hank was heading. Pretty much everything is down there. Hotels, lumberyard, post office, Piggly Wiggly, East Carolina University—it's all down there."

"Piggly Wiggly?"

"Our supermarket in town."

"There a Doggie Woggie too?"

"What's that?"

"Maybe the pet store."

"No, that's called PetSmart."

My attempt at humor fell flat, so I just moved on. "Maybe he needed to stop to pick up some food and supplies from town before he headed up to his cabin."

"That makes sense, seeing as he hadn't been to the cabin for about five months," Simpson said. "But why did his cellular last ping way down south off 13? Why didn't it ping again when he got what he needed in town, then headed back up north? There's a tower about five miles away from his cabin that his cell should've hit."

"Maybe the phone died," I said. "The battery was already low, and he didn't have a car charger with him."

"That's possible, I guess," Simpson said, mulling things over. "Let's say that's what happened. At some point, he would charge the phone and turn it back on, which would mean his signal would hit another tower sooner or later. That didn't happen."

"How good is the service near the cabin?"

"Not good at all. People up there still use landlines because the cellular service is so spotty."

"Well, that could be the reason why he didn't hit any more towers," I said. "He went home and charged the phone, but when he turned it back on, there wasn't any service. Maybe he didn't need to leave the cabin because he had just gotten whatever he needed to fully stock the fridge."

"That's possible too. Once he got to the cabin, he never left."

"How many days after he arrived did you get the call he was missing?"

"Three."

"So he had what he needed for three days. Holly said he liked to go there alone and get away from things. Makes sense he would stay in the cabin and just enjoy the time alone. He had food, a lake full of fish, and a TV. He was all set."

"Well, you seem to have it all figured out," Simpson said.

"Not really," I said. "Just trying to figure out reasons for some of the things that don't make sense. Now, what I can't figure out is the Lawrence Godwin situation. That bothers me. By any chance, were you able to see the surveillance footage from the rental facility?"

"In fact, we did. One of the deputies went down and saw what they had. Hank was on it, clear as day. But he was alone the entire time."

"It's been a while since I rented a car and added a driver, but last time I did that, the other driver had to be there in person to present her driver's license. But now you can add drivers via the rental car app. So that keeps taking us back to the same conundrum about Godwin being there or not."

"Well, that's a bit of a mystery right now for us," Simpson said. "We have someone at the rental agency trying to figure out how that could've happened. As luck would have it, the girl who checked him in is away right now on vacation for a week, visiting family in South Carolina. They haven't been able to reach her."

"Did you get a chance to see the footage yourself?"

"I did. They emailed the clips to me so I could watch it here on my computer. I watched it several times. Hank was definitely alone the minute he got off that plane."

"Was he looking and behaving normally?"

"From what I could tell, he looked fine. Didn't seem anxious. Wasn't in a hurry. We were careful to watch for someone following him. We didn't see that either. He rolls his bag off the plane, walks directly to the rental facility, gets his paperwork, goes to the car, and leaves the airport."

"Maybe he picked up Godwin at the baggage claim, and then they left the airport together," I said.

"Nope," Simpson said. "We checked those cameras too. He didn't drive anywhere near the baggage claim area. We have the car leaving the rental parking lot, going straight out of the airport exit, and jumping on 13."

"Let's go back to Godwin for a moment," I said. "Even if he wasn't with Blackwell, the fact that he was added as an additional driver means the rental agency has a copy of his driver's license somewhere in their system. Unless the rule has changed, which we can verify with a quick call, you would need to show proof of a valid license to be added as a driver, even through the app. So they must have it scanned into their computer system, or his information must've been manually entered."

"Presenting a valid driver's license is still their policy," Simpson said. "But the manager down there checked the system. They have Godwin's name in the computer, but they don't have a copy of his license or the information from it. The manager said this was the first time he'd ever seen anything like this."

"Which brings us back to the missing agent who waited on him at the counter. She's gotta know what happened."

"We're hoping they'll be able to reach her soon, and we'll be able to ask these questions. We can speculate all we want, but she can clear this up pretty quickly."

As we were talking, I was on my computer, looking at a map of Greenville to get a better understanding of the geographical relationship between the airport, Blackwell's cabin, and the cell tower near the river. I did a quick search on Google Maps, then zoomed in on the Street View feature. Route 13 was mostly straight, with not much on either side except for open farmland. Then I noticed a rest stop with a small gas station and a country store with a large, paved parking lot. Had he stopped at the rest stop on his way into town? Had he even made it to town? Maybe he stopped there, got what he needed, then turned around and headed back to the cabin.

"What about bank activity?" I said. "Have you tracked all his credit and debit cards?"

"Sure have," Simpson said. "First thing we did. No activity since he bought something at an airport store in Chicago."

"Nothing at the airport down there?"

"Nothing."

"What about at the rental car counter? Did he use it there for the car?"

"Nothing."

If Blackwell hadn't used his credit card at the counter, that meant he had prebooked the car either online or through an app on his phone. But that didn't make total sense. If he'd booked the car in advance, why had he needed to go to the counter? One of the advantages of prebooking a car was being able to avoid the line of customers who were making same-day reservations or who had other problems with their rental they needed to fix in person. And since he did need to go to the counter, that would mean they needed to do some business with him, see his identification or credit card. Something. But we knew his card hadn't been charged, since Simpson said his last documented activity was at O'Hare. Regardless of which scenario we explored, they all led to the same question: How was Blackwell able to add Lawrence Godwin without his ID being added to the file? It was becoming clearer by the day that this Godwin situation was a problem and that the vacationing reservationist could be the key to figuring out what really happened that morning.

When Simpson and I finished our conversation, I went back to searching the area around the rest stop, still using the Google Street View feature. There really wasn't much else on the road for a couple miles in both directions. I found what looked like a shuttered car dealership. All that was left was an empty, crumbling building and parts of a sign that the sun and wind hadn't yet finished blowing and destroying. I zoomed in closer on the gas station and was able to see the name: Roscoe's Pump & Fill. There were four tanks in total, a small garage attached to the store, and a separate area with a stand-alone air hose. A small grassy area sat next to it with two picnic tables and benches. I assumed this was for people who wanted to take a break from driving, stretch their legs, and have a quiet place other than their car to eat. I googled the name of the gas station, and while it didn't have a website, it had a Facebook page that it looked like someone actually kept current. I searched several links before finally finding a phone number. I figured, what the hell, the likelihood of finding out anything of value was low, but at this point, I didn't have much to lose. "Nothing beats a try but a failure," my grandfather would always say. So I tried.

To my surprise, the number worked, and a man answered the phone.

"I was wondering if I could speak to the owner," I said.

"Mrs. Tutweiler isn't here right now," the man said. "She don't come down too often. Something I can help you with?"

"Well, I'm not sure if you can or not, but I sure hope so," I said. "I was down that way a few weeks ago, and I'll be damned if someone didn't steal my credit card."

"Here at the store?"

"No, must've been somewhere else, but they used it there."

"What a pain in the ass," the man said. "People ain't got no sense of integrity these days. Everybody out for themselves. Dog-eat-dog world."

"Ain't that the truth. What's your name?"

"Clay," he said.

"Like Cassius Clay?" I said, using Muhammad Ali's birth name, which he changed after converting to Islam.

"Well, I'll be damned," he said. "I can count on one hand how many times somebody has asked me that in the last twenty years. Most people just know him as the great Ali. They don't know his history. You must be a boxing fan."

"My whole life. Loved all those old guys. Ali, Hagler, Big George Foreman, Sugar Ray. I watched them all."

"Them was the days when boxing was real boxing," Clay said. "The sport just ain't what it used to be."

"Couldn't agree with you more," I said. "Clay, I talked to the credit card company and reported the card as stolen. They told me someone bought a full tank of gas with it and something inside the store. Set me back over a hundred dollars, then they went into town and spent another couple hundred at the Piggly Wiggly."

"I be damned," he said. "Looks like they was on a spree on your card. I hope they catch 'em and throw the book at 'em. If I caught 'em, I'd take 'em out back for a few. They wouldn't steal nothing for the rest of their lives."

"Well, that's why I'm calling," I said. "I'm trying to catch the sonsabitches so I can turn them in for what they did. I noticed online that you have some cameras out front."

"Sure do," Clay said. "We had new ones installed a few months ago. Had some kids tryna steal gas a few times, and when they couldn't get it, they got pissed and damaged the pumps. Cost Mrs. Tutweiler darn near fifteen hundred to get them fixed. Now we got these high-tech cameras, so anyone try any funny business, we got the video."

"Do you know how to work the cameras?" I said.

"What do you mean?"

"Do you know how to check the recording equipment?"

"I don't personally—above my pay grade—but Tucker knows that stuff inside out. He's one of those tech nerds."

"Is Tucker there?"

"No, he's over at the university right now. He teaches a course or helps with a professor over there. He helps out here when he can. He's Mrs. Tutweiler's grandson. He's gonna inherit it all one day, but between you and me, I don't think he wants it. He likes his computers and electronics."

"Any way you can get him a message to call me as soon as possible? I really need to talk to him and get his help. Sooner I can get this situation squared away with my credit card company, the better."

"You got it, boss," Clay said. "I'll get right on it. Tucker is usually good with text messaging. You know how these kids are. They rather type on a screen instead of picking up the phone and talking like a human being."

"We're in a digital age," I said, "and it doesn't seem like we're going back."

I gave Clay my full name, phone number, the date Blackwell arrived in Greenville, and a reminder of the urgency of my situation, then disconnected the line.

16

Sometimes during an investigation, progress can be painstakingly slow: a trace or two of helpful information, then long, frustrating stretches of sheer nothingness. Sometimes things just happen all at once, and the pace of action kicks off like Usain Bolt exploding from the starting block of a hundred-meter sprint. The call from Tucker Tutweiler rang like the blast from a starter pistol.

"Clay told me you had a problem with your credit card," he said. He sounded young and smart.

"Someone got me," I said. "Spent a few hundred dollars in a matter of minutes."

"Did you lose your wallet?"

"Nope, but that one credit card is missing. Not sure how they could've gotten it. Maybe I used it and left it somewhere."

"But you're sure they used it here at the gas station?"

"Positive. It's on my card statement."

"You have a time of the transaction?"

I thought about what Simpson said. The last ping on the tower had been at 11:23, so I gave it a cushion.

"The charge posted at 12:03 p.m.," I said. I felt like forty minutes would be enough time for Blackwell to have done his business, if in fact he had actually stopped at Roscoe's.

"I have the video for that day already pulled up," Tucker said. "The cameras are motion activated, so I had to make some position changes after we installed them. They were catching the cars driving by on 13. You can imagine that it was almost on continuous record."

"I noticed you had two outside the store," I said. "Any inside?"

"Three," Tucker said. "One facing the door. One behind the counter. And a wide angle in the corner of the store near the soda fountain. Give me a minute while I bring up the exterior recordings first. You know anything about the person or persons who might've stolen your card?"

"I have a good suspicion," I said. "Black guy, about mid-fifties. Short hair. Very fit. Average height."

"You know what kind of car he was driving?"

Holly had texted me the information last week. "Actually, I do. Black Toyota Camry with a North Carolina license plate. DSS-2031."

"If you have all that information, can't you just call the sheriff and have them run the tag on the guy?"

"Well, I'm not a hundred percent sure it's him, so before I make that call, I'm trying to get some verification. If he's on tape making the purchases, then I'll have all the proof I need, and he can't deny it. The video will tell the story."

"Gotcha," he said. "I'm gonna increase the speed of the playback so it won't take all day. Depending on which pump he used, I should be able to see the entire license plate. One of the pumps is slightly out of view, but that depends on how the car is parked."

"Do you save this to the cloud?" I said.

"Everything. That's what I'm in right now."

After several minutes of light banter, he said, "I got something. Give me a sec."

He was silent for a couple more minutes. My heart rate picked up a little. I had come to learn that regardless of how much evidence you collected or how good of an investigation you ran, a bit of luck was always needed and much welcomed.

"There he is," Tucker said.

I breathed a sigh of relief.

"He pulled into the lot at 11:27. Wait, is this the guy?"

"What's wrong?"

"He didn't pull up to the tank."

"Where did he go?"

"Toward the back of the lot on the other side of the store."

"What's back there?"

"A dumpster, and where the clerks park their cars."

"Can you see the license plate?"

"That's what I'm trying to do right now."

He was quiet for a moment. He mumbled something to himself. He didn't seem happy. I felt my good luck slipping away from me.

"I told her we needed that extra camera," he said.

"What camera?" I said.

"My grandmother didn't want to put an additional camera back there. She felt like we had enough, and another would be a waste of money."

"What do you see on the video?"

"He pulled the car toward the back, then disappeared."

"Does he walk into the store?"

"I'm still rolling the tape, but so far, no."

"Are there any other customers there?"

"One lady at the pump. Wait, where did he come from?"

"Who?"

"There's a car that just pulled into view from the back area where the other car went. It's a gray four-door sedan with tinted windows."

"What's it doing?"

"Pulling out of the lot."

"Where's the black Camry?"

"Still in the back."

"Do you recognize that sedan?"

"Nope. Never seen it before. I'm trying to see if one of the front cameras picked up the license plate."

"Can you see into the car?"

"Nope. Windows are too dark."

"Can you see the plate?"

"Not fully," he said. "I'm playing around with the zoom and contrast, but the way the camera hit it, I can only get the last four characters. The first two characters aren't clear enough. But the last four are 3744."

"Is it a North Carolina tag?"

"I can't tell."

"What's the time stamp on the tape right now?"

"11:29."

"Still no sign of the Camry?"

"Nope. I'm at 11:31."

"Is there a bathroom back there?"

"I didn't think of that," he said. "Yes, there's a single bathroom just at the corner of the building, behind the dumpster."

"Do you need a key to use it?"

"No. They stopped that during COVID. No one wanted to touch a key after someone else used it. So we just keep it unlocked during business hours."

"Is there a window where the clerk can see back there?"

"No, the window is closer to the gas pumps. You wouldn't be able to . . . Wait. There it is. The Camry is moving."

"What time?"

"11:33."

"Where is it going?"

"It's leaving out of the north exit, and it's turning back north up 13."

"Can you see into the car?"

"I'm trying. Give me a sec."

I tried to make sense of what Tucker was describing. Blackwell pulled into the gas station. Drove to the back to go to the bathroom. Did his business, then headed back north toward the airport and his cabin. Why had he needed to go to the rest stop to use the bathroom?

"I can't see into the car," Tucker said. "The angles aren't right, and the lighting isn't cooperating."

"Once the car leaves and heads north, does it come back at all?"

"Not for the next hour. I fast-forwarded the playback. It doesn't come back. Are you sure the guy used your card to get gas and something in the store?"

"According to the credit card company. Unless there's some mistake."

"I'm sorry. I wish I could've helped you more."

"Is it possible you can send me the clip of the car coming and going?" I said.

"Sure," Tucker said. "It'll be a big file, so I'll compress it into a zip file and email it to you."

I gave him my email.

"One more thing before you go," I said. "Any way you can take a quick look and see when that gray sedan arrived?"

"Sure." He mumbled something to himself, then said, "10:53 a.m."

"Did the car get gas?"

"Nope, pulled straight to the back."

"Did you see any customers come to the front from the back?"

"Nope. No one walked into frame from back there between the time the sedan arrived and when it left. They probably just used the bathroom."

"But they were there for thirty-six minutes."

"Once they finished in the bathroom, they probably walked around for a bit. A lot of people get out, stretch their legs, and walk around the grass, then they're off."

"Makes sense," I said. "Thanks for all your help."

"Sorry about your card, man. I know it's a real pain in the ass to get a new one and change all your auto payments. If there's anything else we can do to help nail the bastard, lemme know."

I GOT THE EMAIL FROM Tucker within fifteen minutes, then opened it up on my desktop. I downloaded the file, waited for it to decompress, then watched as the recordings populated my screen. I looked at them on a higher speed at first. Everything he had described was exactly as it was. The gray sedan came in and pulled directly into the back. No one came into view from the back area. Blackwell's Camry rolled into the lot and went in the same direction as the sedan. No sign of Blackwell. The gray sedan pulled off a couple minutes after Blackwell arrived. I stopped the tape. The sedan was a new Ford Taurus. I could see the Ford emblem on the trunk and the letters *TAUR* underneath it. Blackwell left a few minutes later. I watched the hour after Blackwell left. He didn't return. Eight customers pulled into the lot and got gas. Some went inside the store, then they left.

I got up to get a glass of lemon water when my phone buzzed. It was O'Halloran.

"We're in the process of picking up your Dario Vazquez," he said. "The team has a visual on him. They plan on taking him in the next few minutes."

I wasn't expecting to hear him say that.

"What happened?"

"We matched his DNA to the sample under Escobar's nails. They must've gotten into a fight. Obviously, Dario got the better of him."

"Where are you taking him?"

"They're bringing him down here to the Second. I'm doing the interview."

"You have anything else other than the DNA?"

"A threat, a dead man, defensive wounds. DNA on the decedent's body. What else do I need?"

"That's a lot," I said. "Any chance I could observe the interview?"

"Unlikely," he said. "Against policy."

"We both know there's flexibility."

"I'll have to check with my sergeant, but I don't think he's gonna go for it. I'll get back to you if he agrees."

As soon as I got off the phone, I called Burke and explained the situation. He then called the commander of that district. Within ten minutes, I got an unhappy call from O'Halloran reporting that his sergeant had approved my request. I was to remain in the observation room and not have contact with the suspect. The interview was starting in an hour, so I needed to get there right away if I wanted to observe.

As I arrived, O'Halloran and Dario were in the room. They were just starting the interview.

"So, Dario, here we are," O'Halloran said.

"It's Rio," Rio said. "Mi abuela is the only person who calls me Dario."

"Okay, Rio it is," O'Halloran said. "So you've been busy."

"I have?" Rio said.

"Haven't you?"

"You're the one who said it. You tell me."

"Well, guy like yourself. Good-looking. Hip. Ladies gotta be digging you."

Rio smiled. "Digging? People still use that word?"

"So Julieta Romero is your girlfriend," O'Halloran said.

"Ex," Rio said.

"Who broke it off?"

"We came to a mutual understanding."

I smiled to myself. The mutual understanding was his friend's smashed nose and my promise to Rio that if he communicated with Julieta or her friends again, I would perform heart surgery on him.

"Were you upset when things ended?"

"Didn't give a shit. I got plenty of bad bitches slidin' in my DMs all the time. Even an all-star is replaceable."

O'Halloran looked down at his notes for a moment, then said, "I hear you have quite a temper."

"No more than anybody else."

"You have five arrests in the last three years for assault and battery."

"I don't let people fuck with me."

"Or your girl. Sorry, your ex-girl."

"What the hell is that supposed to mean?"

"I think you know very well what that means."

Rio leaned back in his chair and smirked. "You brought me down here to give me shit about a dude fuckin' with my ex-girl?"

"No, I brought you down here because I wanna know what you did to the dude who was fuckin' with your ex-girl."

"I already told that investigator or detective that I didn't do anything to that asshole."

"You're a pretty tough guy," O'Halloran said.

"Tough enough," Rio said.

"Where were you on the evening of September 1?"

"I have no idea," Rio said. "If it was night, I was probably fuckin'."

"Of course," O'Halloran said. "I know that's what studs like to do. Can whoever you were fuckin' confirm you were with them that night?"

"I have to figure out who it was I was fuckin'."

"I had a chance to look at your phone records," O'Halloran said, glancing at his notes. "One of your last calls was from a Carmen Delarosa. What was that call about?"

"I don't remember," Rio said unconvincingly.

I immediately texted Carmen and asked her to call me back. "You probably wanna start remembering pretty quickly. Because right now, you're looking at a first-degree murder charge."

Rio popped up in his seat. I thought he was going to come across the table and choke O'Halloran. His eyes were full of blood.

"Murder? Muthafucka, I already told you, I ain't killed nobody. And definitely not some weak ass like that. Stop makin' this shit up."

O'Halloran stayed calm. "Didn't you say you were going to kill him?"

Rio was about to blurt out an answer but stopped himself. "I don't have to answer any of these fuckin' questions without a lawyer."

"That's true," O'Halloran said. "I'm just trying to find out what happened. I can ask you the same questions in front of a lawyer or ten lawyers if you want. But I'm still gonna ask my questions. And if you don't answer me, you'll be answering a prosecutor who's going to try to put you away for the rest of your life. We can play it any way you want, but all I'm trying to do is help you if you really are innocent."

Rio sat back down again and stared at O'Halloran. His shoulders softened. O'Halloran was experienced in reading body language. He knew he had an opening.

"I have to be really honest with you," he said. "You're in a lot of trouble with this one."

"Trouble how?"

"The evidence is not looking good."

"What evidence?"

"Did you get into a fight with Joaquin Escobar on or about September 1?"

"I never met him. I never fought him."

"Did you go looking for him?"

"I did, but I couldn't find him. I can't be guilty for just lookin' for a guy."

"Would you be willing to show me your upper torso?"

"What do you mean?"

"Take your shirt off."

Rio shrugged. "If that fuckin' turns you on, sure." He sat up and pulled his sweatshirt and T-shirt over his head.

"What's that at the base of your neck on the right side?" O'Halloran said.

"What?" Rio said.

"You have linear markings across the base of your neck. Three of them. They look like fresh scars."

I looked closely at the monitor but could barely make them out because of the resolution of the image.

Rio rubbed his neck softly. "Oh, you're talking about this," he said. "My girl got a little excited. You know how it is when you're hittin' that spot and they just go crazy."

"Sure," O'Halloran said. "You know which girl did that?"

"Julieta."

"That would be Julieta Romero?"

"That's her."

"Do you know approximately when that might've happened?"

"Two, three weeks ago, tops."

"You sure?"

"Positive."

I ran through that time frame in my mind. It didn't seem possible. Julieta had left the restaurant and gone into hiding by then. Either he was lying about the date or that it was Julieta he had been with at the time. But why would he lie about it being Julieta? There would be no reason to do that.

"Will she confirm it?" O'Halloran said.

"If you can find her to ask her. I don't know where she is. Carmen will know."

"Who's Carmen?"

"Her girlfriend."

"Girlfriend romantically or a friend who's a girl?"

"They're not lesbos, if that's what you're asking. They're best friends. She called me from Carmen's phone."

O'Halloran closed his pad, then said, "Hold on, I'll be right back."

He walked out of the room. I watched Rio sitting there. He was very confident. He didn't look nervous or as if he were hiding anything. Sometimes when an interviewer leaves the room, watching the suspect's behavior and body language can give you an indication of what they're thinking or feeling. Rio looked like a man who didn't have any worries.

Ten minutes later, O'Halloran returned to the room. He sat down and calmly said, "Now that we got all that other stuff out the way, do you want to start telling me the truth?"

"What in the hell are you talking about?" Rio said. "I've been telling you the truth the whole time."

"Julieta Romero doesn't confirm what you've said."

"Which part?"

"That she scratched you, for one, and for two, that it happened two to three weeks ago. She says she hasn't seen you since the breakup. She left you and then went into hiding because she was afraid that you might do something to her."

"That's a damn lie," Rio said calmly. "She called me from her girl's phone and asked to meet me. We met up. She came back to my place on her own accord, and I smashed it. I don't know what game she's playing, but that's what happened."

"Anyone see the two of you together?"

"No, it was just us."

O'Halloran nodded softly. The interview door suddenly flew open. Three officers entered the small room. Rio looked up, surprised.

"What's going on?" he said.

"You're being arrested for first-degree murder."

The officers made their move toward Rio, and he quickly stood as the chair crashed to the floor. He raised his arms to keep them at bay.

"I want a fuckin' lawyer," Rio said.

"That is your right," O'Halloran said. "Just make sure you tell your lawyer that DNA from your skin cells was found under the fingernails of Joaquin Escobar."

17

I finally got around to looking at Joaquin's call log. I decided to start with the first month. I had a system I liked to employ. It wasn't perfect, but it worked for me. I highlighted with different colored markers the calls according to their frequency. A number called only once had one color, and the numbers called twice a different color, and so on. It took me less than fifteen minutes to get through the entire first month. Over the next hour and a half, I did this until I completed six months of his calls.

The next thing I did was focus on the different groups of calls. I typically started with those numbers called twice, then worked my way up to those numbers called more frequently. Joaquin most frequently called an international number, which I assumed and would later confirm was his wife down in Colombia. The number he had called second most was here in Chicago. I wrote that number on a chart that I had created. I went through this procedure for all six months of calls.

I took a break for a few minutes and stood up to stretch my legs and grab a cold bottle of water. I looked out the window. The dark clouds over the water looked agitated, and the water appeared restless. A lone boat made its way across the water in a rush. The traffic along the running and bike paths was light. My phone rang. It was my father. I thought about sending the call to voicemail but decided to go ahead and pick it up.

"What happened to you at the party?" he said.

"I don't know," I said.

"What do you mean, you don't know? You didn't show up. You dropped off the wine and flowers, but you didn't stay."

"I just wasn't feeling it," I said.

"That's a strange response," he said. "You accepted the invitation, and then last minute, you decided you just weren't 'feeling it.'"

I really didn't want to get into a back-and-forth at that moment. This was a much deeper conversation, and I needed to be completely present to have it.

"How about we talk it over next week?" I said. "Why don't you come to my place, and I will fix you dinner?"

"You haven't invited me to your place in years," he said.

"Well, I just did."

"Fine. Call me next week. But it has to be before that Friday. Connie and I are going to LA for the weekend. Her granddaughter is being baptized."

Hearing him be so integrated in this new woman's life made me nauseated. "I'll call you," I said.

I stood there in the window for a few moments and looked up into the sky. I wondered if the deceased really could see down here to earth and could hear all that was going on. What would my mother be making of all this? Would she feel as betrayed as I was feeling? I needed to distract myself, so I went back to my desk and looked at the phone logs and chart I had established.

I looked at the last number Joaquin called. The call had been placed at 11:27 p.m. on August 31. It lasted for thirty-nine seconds. I picked up my phone and dialed the number. It was a restaurant that sold wings on South Ashland.

"I need a refund for an order I placed a few weeks ago," I said.

"A few weeks?" she said indignantly. "Why are you taking so long to call?"

"Just now getting around to it."

"Was the order placed online or directly with the store? If it was placed online, then you'll need to go onto the website and request the refund."

"It was called in," I said.

"Date?"

"August 31."

"Phone number?"

I told her Joaquin's phone number.

"You can't get a refund," she said.

"Why?"

"Because you placed an order and didn't pick it up."

"What was the order?"

"You don't remember what you ordered?"

"It's been a few weeks."

"Thirty wings. Ten lemon and herb. Ten mild sauce. Ten barbecue."

Sounded like Joaquin was having a party. One person wasn't going to eat all those wings.

"Can I at least get a credit?" I said.

"Next time you come in, speak to the manager on duty. They might do something for you."

I thanked her and hung up.

I went through the other six numbers that he had called on that day. He had made an international call in the morning, which I assumed was to his wife, then to Ivan, Target customer service, AT&T, and a guy named Roberto, which I figured out from his voicemail. The sixth number he called was not what I expected. The call lasted just over nine minutes. When I dialed the number, it went straight to voicemail, but the speaker identified himself. It was Blackwell.

I called Holly and asked her if she knew any way to access her father's online phone account. She said she would call Mrs. McCarley to see if she had the information. I then went back to Joaquin's log. I scanned it for another category I created. Unusual. Numbers that were out of a person's typical geographic range and numbers from calls that came early in the morning or late at night went under this column. There was a Michigan number he'd called six times over the course of six days on the April log. I dialed the number.

"Whistle Stop," a girl who answered the phone said. "How can I help you?"

"Where are you located?" I asked.

"Red Arrow Highway in Union Pier."

"What kind of business is this?"

"Grocery store."

I decided to take a chance. "Do you know a Joaquin Escobar?" I said.

"No, I don't," she said. "No one by that name works here."

"Have you ever heard of his name before?"

"I'm sorry, but I haven't."

"Are you working alone?"

"No, the manager is here."

"Can you ask her if she's ever heard of that name?"

"Hold on," the girl said.

"This is Pam," a woman said, picking up the line. "How can I help you?"

"Hi, Pam," I said. "I was calling to see if you knew someone by the name of Joaquin Escobar."

"Who am I talking to?"

"My name is Ashe Cayne. I'm calling from Chicago."

"No one by that name works here."

"Yes, the girl who answered the phone told me that. I was wondering if you've ever heard this person's name."

"I have not. What is this in reference to?"

"Mr. Escobar, unfortunately, has died under suspicious circumstances, and I'm looking into what happened. He called your store several times back in April."

"Are you a detective?"

"Private."

"I wish I could help you, but we are not familiar with that name."

"Is there any way to look up old orders in your computer system?"

"As long as it's in the same calendar year, we can do a search using the last name and phone number."

"I can give you both."

"What's your name again?" she said.

I repeated my name.

"I shouldn't be doing this over the phone," she said. "I can't really verify who you are, and we protect our customers' private information as much as possible. What's your phone number?"

I gave her my number.

"I'm a little busy right now," she said. "Give me about an hour, and I'll see if there's anything I can find."

"Anything you can tell me would be appreciated," I said. "The family is trying to find answers, so I'm just checking into everything."

I went back to the logs and the chart I had created. I studied the numbers and columns to see if anything else stuck out. I thought about the call he'd made to Blackwell. What had they had to speak about after so much time had elapsed since Joaquin had been let go?

I called Carolina and gave her the last four digits of the tag and the make and model of the sedan at the gas station.

"I need you to run a tag for me."

"What do you have?"

"A Ford Taurus with a DC tag."

"A DC car out here in Chicago?"

"No, a DC car in North Carolina."

I quickly explained to her the surveillance video and how the

Taurus had been at the gas station at the same time as Blackwell. She told me to give her a couple hours and she'd get back to me.

Just as I was disconnecting the line with Carolina, another call came in. I could tell it was a Michigan number from the 269 area code. It was Pam from Whistle Stop.

"This is a little confusing," she said.

"How's that?"

"We have that number, but we don't have that name."

"What name do you have?"

"Diego Santana."

That made complete sense. I should've thought to ask about that name the first time I spoke to her.

"He ordered the same thing every morning. Two coffees, a cinnamon bun, and two breakfast sandwiches. Six mornings in a row. Then he never called again."

"Do you remember him coming into the store?" I said.

"I don't," she said. "But to be honest, we have so many people who come through during the spring and summer who aren't year-rounders that it's difficult to keep track of the names and faces."

Places like Union Pier, Benton Harbor, and Sawyer constituted a stretch of beach towns along the southeast coast of the lake on the Michigan side. This was a playground escape a little over an hour away on the Illinois side for wealthy Chicagoans. I had worked with the wealthy Gerrigan family on a case several years ago that brought me out that way.

"There was something else that was different about his orders," Pam said. "He didn't pay for them."

"Who did?"

"They were paid by a credit card belonging to Patrick Flynn."

"Are you sure?"

"I'm looking at the name right here on my screen."

Patrick Flynn was one of the most powerful aldermen in the city. He was considered to be the dean, having served longer than any other alderman in Chicago's storied political history. He reigned over the Fourteenth Ward, but his power extended over the entire city. He was both an enemy and an ally of Bailey's, depending on when their political interests were shared or when they collided.

I hung up the phone and leaned back in my chair, completely flummoxed, wondering why the hell one of the city's most powerful aldermen purchased coffee and breakfast sandwiches for Joaquin Escobar, an undocumented Colombian immigrant.

18

As Stryker and I were crossing the street coming from our run around the lake the next morning, a gray four-door sedan stopped to let us go by. Its tinted windows reminded me of the sedan that had pulled behind Roscoe's on the surveillance video. The camera hadn't been able to pick up the entire license plate, but it had been able to capture that it was six characters long. Two characters separated from the last four.

When I got back to my apartment, I sat at my computer and looked up North Carolina license plates. They were seven characters long. Three characters separated from the last four. That car wasn't from North Carolina. That wasn't unusual. It could've been a rental car, which meant it could be from anywhere. It also could've just been someone from another state who happened to be traveling through. I went online and found a chart for all the license plates in use across the country.

Starting with Alabama, I went down the list of plate images for each state. I stopped at the District of Columbia. The plate had two characters separated from four characters. I continued down the list to see if there were any others with the same configuration. Idaho, Illinois, and Montana had two-and-five configurations. Rhode Island had two and three. DC was the only tag with the two-and-four configuration.

My phone rang. Carolina's number popped up on my screen.

"You keep it interesting," she said.

"What do you mean?"

"That tag is a ghost tag."

A ghost tag was a tag used by law enforcement to hide the true identity of a vehicle's registrant. This was often done to protect officers from having their personal information compromised. Criminals were able to access databases and discover a car as being registered to police officers or federal agents. Ghost tags were typically used for covert operations by a commissioned law enforcement officer. Carolina's discovery was another unexpected turn of events.

"What kind of covert operation is happening in a town like Greenville, North Carolina?" I said.

"And it's not local," Carolina said. "It's federal."

"What?"

"That car comes back to the feds."

"Which agency?"

"I don't have that."

"Can you get it?"

"It's gonna take me a little more time. Getting behind these tags can be tricky. I need to make a couple calls."

"Okay. As soon as you find something, let me know."

I put a call through to Alicia Gentry, an FBI agent who had helped me with the case of a former school board president whose body had been found half submerged in the Chicago River at a place called Wolf Point. She was a very no-nonsense type of person, direct, and excellent at what she did.

"Ashe Cayne," she said, answering the phone. "I know when you call, there's something going on."

"I could be calling to talk about the great start to the Bears' season," I said.

"Which would be no different from talking about Chicago weather. You don't have to wait too long before it will change."

"Very true," I said, laughing. "Any big cases these days?"

"They never stop."

"Anything you can share?"

"Not right now. What about you?"

"A murdered immigrant and a missing navy vet."

"Two different cases or one?"

"That's what I'm trying to figure out. They have a personal connection, but that's all I have so far. I don't know if the murder is connected with the disappearance."

"Who's working them?"

"A detective in the Second is working the murder. A sheriff down in Greenville, North Carolina, is working the disappearance."

"Why did you take them on?"

"The murder victim's nephew asked me to help find out what happened to his uncle. The man who's missing is a Chicagoan who went to his cabin in Greenville for a little rest and relaxation. His daughter, who lives in Texas, asked if I would help."

"And the sheriff has been willing to work with you?"

"He's not the fastest horse on the track, but he's been communicating and mostly open to my polite suggestions."

She laughed.

"What can you tell me about ghost tags?" I said.

"Which? The ones citizens use illegally on unregistered or stolen cars, or the ones used by law enforcement?"

"The latter."

"What do you want to know?"

"How often do you guys use them?" I said.

"All the time," she said. "We're only supposed to be using them when we're carrying out an operation, but there's been some flexibility."

"What do you mean, flexibility?"

"Well, technically, we are only supposed to use those tags on official business and when the operation is covert. They are not supposed to be used when we're driving around or carrying out non-covert business.

The registration and approval process are really controlled by the state police in your jurisdiction. Recently, there's been a big complaint about how many of these tags are on the road doing non-covert business. A mayor down in Louisiana was driving with ghost tags and got stopped twice for driving and drinking. The cops ran the tags, which came back as 'no record on file,' then let him go without a ticket or even doing a field sobriety. Some sheriffs and police chiefs have been stopped in other counties not on official or covert business but driving with ghost tags. That's not the original intention of the tags. A lot of the staties are now trying to crack down on them. Plenty of people know the usage rules, but most have no problem ignoring them. And no one has really been enforcing it. Until now."

"If you have a tag number, is there any way to determine who's actually driving the car it's on?"

"You mean the agency or the actual driver behind the wheel?"

"Both."

"The agency for sure, but who was driving the car at any particular moment in time would be more difficult."

"If I got you a tag number, could you tell me the agency?"

"Pretty quickly."

Once I got off the phone, I turned and looked at the evidence board I had posted on the wall across from my desk. Detectives in most police departments didn't have these types of evidence boards, but they were popular in TV shows and movies, so I'd decided to give them a try a few years back, and they actually helped me think more clearly about the evidence and the connections to be made between them and the victims and suspects. I always started with a photo of the victim. I added a photo of the suspect or suspects if any emerged. I then drew lines connecting the victim, the suspect, and the evidence. Often it looked like a three-year-old's attempt at drawing a spiderweb, but it worked for me, and I found it to be a useful way to collect my thoughts and sort through them as I tried to piece together a narrative.

I sat, looking at the photos of Joaquin Escobar and Hank Blackwell and the one line I had connecting them. On the connecting line, I had written *TNL Heating & Cooling*. I walked to the board and drew another line between them and wrote *9+ min conversation on August 31; call made from Escobar to Blackwell*. As I stood there studying the board, trying to get it to speak to me, my phone rang. It was Carmen.

"Sorry it took so long to get back to you," she said. "We were really busy all day yesterday."

"No problem," I said. "How's everything going with Julieta?"

"Fine," Carmen said. "I saw her a couple days ago. She looked very happy. She wasn't as worried as she had been before."

"That's good," I said. "Rio must've gotten the message."

"Thank God," Carmen said. "I was really worried he was going to do something."

"Where is Julieta these days?"

"She was staying with one of her cousins, but she left and moved into a new apartment. She's doing well for herself."

"Where is she living?"

"In an apartment on the corner of West Eugenie and North Wells. She's on the third floor. She has a view of Lincoln Park."

"New job?"

"I don't think so. But she's taking good care of herself. She looked different."

"How?"

"She had really nice clothes. Her hair and nails were all done. She kinda looked like a new person."

"Maybe that's the best way to move on," I said. "Speaking of moving on, I have a question about a call you made to Rio."

"What call?"

"Two or three weeks ago."

"I never called him. Julieta used my phone to call him."

"Why did she use your phone?"

"Her battery died."

"You told me she had been in hiding and was avoiding Rio during that time."

"She was. She left the restaurant. Left her apartment. She was at my house one night, and she told me she needed to say something to him about a jacket he left at her place. Her phone died, so she used mine."

"Did you hear the conversation?"

"No, she was in my bedroom. I was in the kitchen with my mother. I wanted to give her some privacy."

"What happened after the call?" I said.

"Nothing. We talked for a while, then she left to go home."

"Back to her apartment?"

"No, she was staying with her cousin over in Pilsen."

"How did she get there?"

"She took a Lyft."

"Do you think she saw Rio?"

"When?"

"That night. After she left your house."

"Why would she go and see him? She was scared he would hurt her. She didn't want to see him ever again. Did he say something?"

"He said they saw each other that night."

"He's a liar," Carmen said. "Like I said, Julieta was afraid of him. Why would she then all of a sudden go and see him? That wouldn't make sense."

"I'm just saying what he was saying," I said.

"And I'm just saying he's a liar."

"And a murderer."

"What do you mean?"

"They arrested him for killing Joaquin."

"Are you serious?"

"Very."

"Where is he now?"

"Looking through a bunch of steel bars, wishing he had never met your friend Julieta."

"Do you think he did it?"

"I don't know, but it doesn't matter what I think. I'm not the one accusing him of first-degree murder, and I'm not the one who put him behind bars."

"I wonder if Julieta knows this."

"My gut tells me she does."

MECHANIC AND I HAD JUST finished a session at Hammer's. We sat on a bench in the corner of the gym, trying to catch our breath.

"You think he really did it?" Mechanic said. I had told him about Rio being arrested.

"I don't think he did it," I said. "But how do I go against the evidence? They found his DNA underneath the guy's fingernails."

"You think the girl was being completely honest with you?"

"I don't think she was being dishonest. I think she conveniently avoided telling me that she called him and they got together for a romp in the hay."

"Did you talk to her friend?"

"I did. She insists Rio is lying."

"But why would he lie about being with Julieta?"

"That's the part I can't figure out. Let's say he wasn't with her. I know he's not MIT material, but he would know that they would follow up and ask Julieta if it was true. So why lie when it would be easy to verify the truth?"

"The way you describe the autopsy results, it sounds like they have a pretty tight case. They must have more on him."

"You would think, but a suspect with a history of violence, a witness confirming a threat, and DNA evidence? Not sure they're gonna need much more to send him downstate."

"So the case is closed."

"I don't think so."

"The kid wanted to know what happened to his uncle, and now you can tell him the murderer is about to rot in prison."

"Maybe."

"What's bothering you?"

"All of it."

"Like?"

"I first talk to O'Halloran about the case, and he insists Escobar died by his own hand—drunk, stupid, and too close to the water. O'Halloran doesn't want to entertain any other possibilities because he has so many cases on his desk. Ivan requests an autopsy, which O'Halloran fought, and it comes back showing a homicide. A little over seventy-two hours later, they have Rio in custody, his DNA, and an ex-girlfriend who denies she had sex with him and scratched him on the neck—critical exculpatory information."

"Exculpatory?"

"Something that clears a person from alleged fault or guilt."

"You could've just said that."

"But then I wouldn't have used my word of the week."

My phone rang. It was Carolina.

"Your tag finally came back," she said. "FBI."

"Any name?"

"No name. Just that it belongs to the FBI. Any other information would have to come from back channels that I don't have access to."

"Can you text me the full plate number?"

"Sure. What are you going to do now?"

"Call a friend at the FBI and see what she can do."

"I'll be at your place a little late tonight," Carolina said. "One of the girls is leaving, so we're taking her out for drinks."

"Perfect," I said. "You'll already be warmed up by the time I see you."

Mechanic looked at me.

"FBI," I said.

"In a small city in North Carolina?" he said.

"Stopping for thirtysomething minutes at Roscoe's Pump & Fill."

"It's a long drive from DC. Could've needed a break."

"At the same time and place where Blackwell stopped to use the bathroom before going to his own cabin, which has a bathroom."

"You're suspicious."

"I'm always suspicious until something convinces me why I shouldn't be."

"What's next?"

"Try to find out who was driving that car."

"And if you find that out?"

"I have no idea."

19

It had been several days since I gave Alicia the tag number, and Rio Vazquez remained jailed without bail. There had been no signs whether Blackwell was alive or dead, and Holly had finally gone back to Texas at the urging of Sheriff Simpson. Ivan was still down in Colombia to properly mourn with his family. Mrs. McCarley wasn't able to access Blackwell's phone records because the phone he mostly used was not on the business account. I reached out to one of my father's friends, who was a lobbyist for AT&T, and asked him to help us cut through the red tape of procuring the information. He agreed to help.

I sat back behind my desk, looking at the wall with a half-finished Italian beef soaking my desk. I kept staring at Joaquin Escobar's photo and the name Patrick Flynn. I didn't know much about Flynn other than he had the most power on the city council, and people both feared and admired him.

I picked up my phone and dialed Delroy Thomas. He had been the longtime alderman of the Twenty-Seventh Ward until he was investigated by the FBI, indicted, and eventually convicted for extortion and kickbacks. He spent three years of a four-year sentence in a federal prison camp in South Dakota, then came back to Chicago, opened a popular soul food restaurant, and got his nephew elected to the seat he had controlled for so long.

"Man, I haven't talked to you in a while," Delroy said. "You still playing golf and taking cases in between rounds?"

"That pretty much describes my life, or what I hope it to be."

"You haven't been by the restaurant."

"Which is why I'm calling," I said. "I wanna come by and pay you a visit."

"To eat or talk?"

"Both."

"What's on your mind?"

"Pat Flynn."

Delroy laughed. "The dean," he said. "He's one of a kind."

"Why?"

"Every second of every day, he thinks about what will benefit him. Don't get me wrong. The rest of us are looking after ourselves too, but no one does it as obsessively as Flynn. You could go to him and complain that your landlord won't keep the heat in your building at the legal temperature, and he'll find a way to squeeze the landlord to not only fix your problem but at some point do him a solid in the future."

"Is he as bad as they say he is?"

"Worse."

"How so?"

"He is drunk on power. He not only wants to control his ward, but he wants to have a say on everyone else's ward, and he usually does."

"How has he lasted this long?"

"His constituents love him. The mayor can't do without him. And he has a lot of minions around him who do his dirt to keep him clean."

"Did you have a good relationship with Flynn?"

"Still do. I respected him and gave him his due, and he stayed out of my lane and let me run my ward the way I wanted to run it."

"Does he have money?"

"By the buckets. He has his own law firm that makes close to twenty million a year. And that's after he pays Uncle Sam."

"Does he have a place in Michigan?"

"A big place from what I've been told. Six or seven bedrooms. Pool. Tennis court. Right on the lake. Either New Buffalo or Union Pier. I forget which one."

"How has he made so much money?" I said.

"How do you think?" Delroy said. "How any alderman makes their real money. Leverage. You think these guys can afford all these fancy apartments and cars you see them driving on $143,000 a year? Shit. You gotta be kidding. The power is in the office, but the money is outside."

"How often do you talk to him?"

"Not much now that I'm out of office. But I see him around from time to time. He comes to the restaurant for meetings every once in a while."

"What do you think is the best way to approach him?"

"Depends on what you want to approach him about."

"I'm trying to help a family whose relative was murdered. I want to know if Flynn knew the guy."

"Something like that, you're better off talking to Smiley."

"Who's that?"

"His right hand."

"Is he on his staff?"

"Not officially. But he handles things for him."

"How can I get ahold of him?"

"I'll text you his number."

"Is Smiley his real name?"

"No. His real name is Liam Harrington."

"Why do they call him Smiley?"

"Because no one has ever seen the man smile. Not once."

GUADALUPE RIVERA LIVED IN A second-floor apartment above a cell phone store in the rough section of Pilsen. Mechanic had nothing better to do, so he decided to keep me company for the visit. I wasn't sure what would come out of our conversation, but I had learned a long time ago that sometimes you just poke around, even if you don't know what you're looking for, and you end up finding something.

Guadalupe answered the door cautiously while her toddler, who I assumed was the real Diego Santana, peeked at us from behind her leg. She was a short, attractive woman with long black hair and delicate features, and she was extremely trim. She couldn't have been more than twenty-five.

"My name is Ashe Cayne," I said. "This guy with me is Mechanic. I just wanted to know if I could ask you a couple questions."

"What's this about?" she said.

"Social Security numbers."

"What about them?"

"The one belonging to your son."

She instinctively reached down and touched her son's head.

"Are you the police?" she said.

"Have you ever met police officers this handsome?" I said, smiling. Mechanic never flinched, but he was still handsome in his fierce way.

She smiled too. "If you're not the police, then who are you?"

"Private investigators."

She scrunched her brow.

"Or private detectives, if you prefer that."

"Do you have identification?" she said.

I reached into my pocket, pulled out a card, and gave it to her with another smile, turning up the wattage a little. She looked at Mechanic. He pushed his shirt back slightly and exposed the grip of his gun. She jumped back.

"He's not the card-carrying type," I said.

"Am I in trouble?" she said.

"Not with us."

"Are you going to do something to my baby?"

"Nothing more than feed him if you need an extra hand."

"Come in," she said.

We followed her into a small, tidy room with gently used furniture and a large print over a small TV of Jesus hanging on a cross. Diego stayed behind his mother, eyes locked on us, then jumped in her lap when she sat down. The sweet smell of something baking in the oven permeated the air.

"What do you want to know?" she said.

"How about we start with your relationship with Joaquin Escobar," I said.

"I don't know who that is."

"Diego Santana?"

The toddler switched his stare from Mechanic to lock onto me. He smiled and had dimples big enough to hold silver dollars.

"How do you know my baby's name?" Guadalupe said, tightening her grip on her son and instinctively turning him away from us.

"Because Joaquin Escobar, who was about thirty years older and almost three feet taller than your son, was using the same name."

"How's that possible?"

"We were hoping you'd be able to provide that answer."

"You said this had something to do with Social Security numbers."

"It does. That and borrowed names."

Guadalupe Rivera brushed her son's hair as he continued to switch stares between Mechanic and me.

"I'm a single mother with two kids," she said. "It's very difficult to raise two boys in this city while making minimum wage."

"No disagreement here," I said.

"I was offered a lot of money last year from someone who wanted to use Diego's name and Social Security number."

"How did they find you?"

"I don't know. I didn't ask."

"How much did they offer?"

"Five thousand down and ten thousand more over the next eighteen months. It takes me a full three months to bring home five thousand dollars at my regular job."

"Which is?"

"Janitorial services. I clean banks at night."

"Any possibility you could leave the back door open for me one night?"

She smiled. It was becoming quite obvious that she probably didn't lack male attention.

"Fifteen thousand dollars is a lot of money for a line of letters and a bunch of numbers," I said.

"Especially for someone in my situation. They told me I would not get caught and they wouldn't do anything with the number that would give Diego problems when he gets older and needs it for himself."

"Sounds like a damn good sales pitch," I said. "Continue."

"So I agreed to the deal. They gave me the money. And they pay the balance to me every month in installments."

"Must make paying the rent and electricity bill a lot easier around here."

"It's the only way I'm able to do it."

"When was the last time you received a payment?"

"I get paid on the first Monday of each month."

"Like clockwork."

She looked at me quizzically.

"Consistently," I said.

"Yes. They have never missed a payment, and they have never been late."

"How do you get the money?"

"Cash. They slide the envelope under my door."

"Who did you sell the name and number to?"

She blinked quickly.

"I can't tell you that," she said.

"Even though I make you smile?"

She nodded and smiled.

"What if you did tell me?" I said.

"They would stop paying the money and report me."

"I could do the same thing. Not the money part, but the reporting."

"I don't think you will."

"Why's that?"

"Because you seem like a good man who understands when a woman is in a tough situation."

"You have me figured out in less than ten minutes. You ever think about reading palms? There's an easy fortune to be made in that."

She smiled again, and I was enjoying seeing her do it.

"Not sure if you ever get information about the customers, but the man who bought that number is now dead."

Her eyes widened, and she seemed even prettier.

"What happened?" she said.

"They found him in Lake Michigan with a hole in his heart that someone put there with an ice pick or something similar."

"An ice pick to his heart?" She said the words slowly. Her nervousness had turned to fear.

"Upper right chamber," I said. "About the size of a pencil eraser. Once he was dead, they threw him in the lake for good measure."

"Why did they kill him?"

"That's why I'm here. His family has hired me to find out."

"Did it have anything to do with the Social Security number?"

"I won't know unless you tell me who you sold it to."

She stared at me for a moment, and I could practically see the gears in her mind grinding through critical calculations.

"Does this mean they're gonna stop paying me the money?"

"I don't know, but it depends on how good of a deal you negotiated."

"There was no negotiation. These are not people you negotiate with. They gave me a price and two hours to think about it."

"That was generous of them."

"Excuse me?"

"Never mind."

"Will you promise you won't tell them that I gave you their information?"

"Scout's honor," I said, crossing my heart.

"I don't think these are the kind of people you want to upset," she said. "They seem really tough."

"Tougher than him?" I said, pointing to Mechanic, who hadn't moved since we sat down and now looked half asleep.

"Well, that is a big gun he has," Guadalupe said.

"You should see it when he pulls it out and shoots it," I said. "Sounds like a cannon from the Mexican-American War."

She laughed softly. "You're kinda funny."

"Kinda?"

"Well, you're not funny enough to make him laugh," she said, pointing to Mechanic, who twitched a little for appeasement.

"Jokes don't make him laugh," I said.

"What does?"

"Violence."

20

As soon as Mechanic and I were back in the car, I dialed the number Guadalupe had given me. A man with a gruff voice and heavy touches of an Eastern Bloc accent answered the phone.

"Who is this?" he said.

"That's quite a greeting," I said.

"What?"

"I'm looking for some help."

"Help with what?"

Guadalupe had given me the code phrase.

"I'm trying to help my kid learn math," I said.

"What's your name?"

"Ossie Davis." I was certain the man wouldn't recognize the deceased movie star's name. My father loved everything the actor had been in.

"How soon does your kid need help?"

"Yesterday."

"Then why didn't you call yesterday instead of today?"

"It's just an expression," I said. "I meant to say tomorrow."

"You don't know the difference between yesterday and tomorrow?" he said incredulously.

"I have a lot on my mind," I said. "Can you help me tomorrow?"

"Sure, but in person only."

"That's fine."

"And you need to bring cash in small bills. Nothing bigger than twenties."

"Grant was a better president than Hamilton."

"What the hell is that supposed to mean?" he growled.

"Forget it," I said. "Inside joke."

"Are you serious about this or not? I don't have time to fuckin' waste."

"Understood."

"Bring five thousand cash. Tomorrow night at seven o'clock. Tryzub Ukrainian Kitchen on West Chicago. When you get there, tell the bartender you want a varenukha special."

"See you tomorrow at seven," I said.

"You will never see me," he said, "but someone will be there to make sure you get what you need."

He disconnected the line before I could say anything else.

ALICIA GENTRY FINALLY CALLED ME back. We agreed to meet at a quiet place for drinks that night. She made it clear that this was not a conversation we should have over the phone. I suggested the Bureau Bar in the South Loop.

Alicia was already seated at a corner table by the time I arrived, which was fifteen minutes earlier than our agreed-upon meeting time. She looked like any North Side single woman who made a decent salary and worked out several times a week but had too important of a job to be overly concerned with the pricey designer brands of the Gold Coast shops. She dressed comfortably and fashionably enough to still draw attention.

"I like this place," she said as I approached the table. "Good vibe. Diverse crowd. Low-key."

"The food is good," I said. "And unlike the bars a few blocks north, the drink prices won't force you to take out a second mortgage on your apartment."

I reached down and gave her a kiss on the cheek before taking my seat. She was wearing perfume, something floral. It was the first time I had ever smelled a fragrance on her. I also noticed she had on lipstick. Nothing screaming, but it was there.

"You look fit as ever," she said.

"How else can I chase down the bad guys?" I said.

"Don't you guys shoot first, then ask questions later?"

"You guys?" I said. "I haven't been with CPD for eight years. And even when I was there, that wasn't how I did my work. I had no problems banging heads if the need arose, but I was never loose with the trigger."

"I ordered you a perfect Manhattan," she said, "and I made sure they knew to add equal amounts of the dry vermouth and the sweet vermouth."

"Nothing sexier than a woman who knows how to order a perfect Manhattan the right way."

"What about a woman who can handle a gun equally well with both hands?"

"That's another level," I said, smiling. "That would make Mechanic lose his mind."

"How is that brute doing?"

"Still bruting."

"Does he do normal things?"

"Like?"

"Ask a girl out for dinner or to go to the movies."

"You should ask him yourself," I said.

She feigned disinterest, but I knew she had an eye for him. She just wasn't the type to make the first move.

The waiter brought my drink over. Alicia gave me the liberty to order appetizers. I chose the broccoli-and-cheese egg rolls, loaded nachos, and buffalo cauliflower.

"Tell me what's your real interest in this car," Alicia said, taking a quick sip of her margarita.

"I'm not interested in the car," I said. "I'm interested in who was in it."

"How does their identity affect your case?"

"Not sure yet," I said. "It might not be anything more than a coincidence, but it seems strange."

"Which part?"

"All of it."

"Mind explaining?"

"Start with it being a fed car with a ghost tag. What covert operation was going on down in Greenville, North Carolina, that required them to be worried about the identity of the agent or agents being compromised?"

"You're assuming the actual operation was taking place in Greenville."

"I am."

"It could've been taking place in South Carolina or Florida, and they were just driving through North Carolina to get there."

"I don't buy that."

"Why?"

"There's a field office in Columbia, South Carolina, and three field offices in the state of Florida. Why would a car from DC need to drive all the way down to South Carolina or Florida when they have field offices there?"

Alicia nodded and studied me.

"Let's say the operation was taking place in North Carolina," I said. "That also doesn't make sense. Why drive down from DC? They could've easily used a pool car from the field office right there in Charlotte."

Alicia shrugged. She wasn't going to give me anything. Yet.

"The other thing is the length of time the car was there at the gas station," I said.

"What bothers you?" she said.

"Thirty-six minutes. What was he or she or they doing for all that time?"

"Didn't you say there was a bathroom back there?"

"Not even the worst case of diarrhea requires that much time."

"You said there was a grassy area for walking and relaxing. That's a long drive from DC. Agents can get tired like anyone else."

I noticed she said *agents*. There had been two of them. That's what I had already figured.

"Nice try," I said. "But it's still not adding up for me."

"Why do you think what they were doing has something to do with your missing navy vet?"

"Because two strange things, neither with an obvious explanation, were happening in the same random place at the same time."

"But you and I both know coincidences happen."

"They do," I said. "But we also know it's a play of the odds. An FBI vehicle from Washington, DC, makes the trip all the way through rural North Carolina and stops at the same rest area as a navy veteran from Chicago who just landed in town and should be heading in the opposite direction toward his cabin. Or maybe his cabin was never his destination in the first place."

"Has there been any progress on the vet investigation?"

"Nothing."

"You trust the people down there working on it?"

"Do I have a choice? It's their jurisdiction. They're slower than I like to work, but they seem capable."

"What if you just work your case and ignore the FBI car?"

Alicia took another sip of her drink. I took a nice long swallow of mine.

"You know something, don't you?" I said.

"I do," she said.

"You know that my suspicions make sense."

"I do."

"You know who was driving that car."

"I don't."

I believed her.

"You're purposely not telling me what's going on."

"Because I don't know everything that's going on."

"Does it have something to do with the navy vet?"

"I think you should leave it alone."

"Leave what alone?"

"All of it."

"You know I can't do that."

"I figured that's what you'd say."

"Do you know the names of the agents who were in the car at the time?"

"I don't," she said. "I couldn't get that far."

"Why?"

"Because I was told to stand down."

"By whom?"

"Someone who has a much bigger title and salary than I do."

"Since when has that ever stopped you before?"

"It hasn't."

"So why is it stopping you now?"

"Because that person is the director himself."

21

At six thirty the following evening, Mechanic and I pulled up outside of Tryzub in a neighborhood aptly called Ukrainian Village. It was a low-key community full of brick row houses and town houses surrounding four cathedrals, the most ornate being the Holy Trinity Orthodox Cathedral, which was visible from both sides of the expressway to the east. We sat there for almost thirty minutes. Quietly. Scoping out the block, watching the cars that parked, paying close attention to the few people who walked into the restaurant. Nothing seemed out of the ordinary or remotely dangerous, so we got out of my truck and headed in ourselves.

It was a festive little place decorated with old-world charm. Two large crystal chandeliers with red shades hung over the main dining hall, which was full of open leather banquets and long rectangular tables arranged in an almost communal way. One entire wall had been fitted with symmetrical bookshelves that had been haphazardly crammed with tchotchkes that someone had either imported from the native land or had manufactured to look like they had been. I couldn't tell the difference. The bar was off the dining room in its own carve-out. Most of the barstools were occupied. I slithered between the two that had the most space between them and nodded at the bartender. He gave me the give-me-a-minute look, then made his way toward me.

"I'll have the varenukha special," I said.

He looked over my shoulder, nodded his head, then walked to the other end of the bar to wait on someone else.

Out of the corner of my eye, I caught Mechanic close in behind me to cut off a tall, thick guy who was approaching from behind. He had Mechanic by a good four inches. They stared at each other for a moment and exchanged a few dramatic sentences in Ukrainian, then Mechanic nodded for me to follow. The guy led us toward the kitchen, where the waitstaff was constantly passing through the swinging doors. We turned into a small cove, down a short hallway, past the bathrooms, and through a door marked *STAFF ONLY*.

The room we entered was nothing like the main dining room. It was bright, modern, and sparsely decorated. An older man with thick black glasses and a bad comb-over sat at a small table in the center of the room, eating from a large bowl. It looked like borscht, but I was too far away to be sure. He didn't look up from his bowl until we stood feet away. The big guy said something to him, then walked away and positioned himself in one of the corners not already occupied by other guys his size or even bigger.

The older man said something to Mechanic in Ukrainian. Mechanic spoke back to him, then motioned for me to take a seat at the table.

"How can I help you?" the old man said. His accent was barely noticeable when he spoke English.

"I want to know about the Social Security numbers you sell," I said.

"I don't sell Social Security numbers," he said. "Who told you that?"

"A little birdie outside my window," I said.

He smiled. Most of his teeth were either crooked or partially gone. I now understood why he was slurping soup instead of biting into a filet.

"Are you in need of a number?" he said.

"No, I'm in need of understanding how one gets a number," I said.

"This is not information that we share. If you need a number, we can help you. If you don't need a number, then you are in the wrong place."

"I need to know who bought one of your numbers."

The man returned to his soup and took another slurp. Once he wiped the corners of his mouth, he said, "That is not how this works. You bring five thousand dollars. You tell me how long you want the number, then I give you the final price. You accept the price or not."

"I'm not buying a number," I said. "Someone who bought one of your numbers was killed, and I'm trying to find out why."

"Are you saying he was killed because he got a number?"

"No. I don't know why he was killed, but I'm trying to find out."

"People trust me to protect them," he said.

"People trust me to find answers," I said.

"We have a conflict."

"Only if we let it be that."

The old man said something in Ukrainian, then one of the men walked over to him and knelt to hear the old man's instructions before walking out of the room.

"I help you if you help me," the old man said.

"What kind of help do you have in mind?" I said.

"In order for my business to continue to be successful, I need to trust the people I do business with."

I nodded.

"I trust that when I help a customer out, they will also protect me from any unwanted attention."

I nodded again.

"Once you find out about what happened to this man, I want you to let me know if it has anything to do with the help he was given and if that will somehow come back to me."

I put out my hand, and he took it. The guy who had left the room returned with a book and handed it to the old man.

"Was it just a number or the name and number?" the old man said.

"Name and number," I said.

"Name?"

"Diego Santana."

He turned the pages of the book, then stopped. He ran his finger down the page, then motioned with his other hand for someone to bring him something to write with. A guy different from the one who had brought him the book brought him a pen and a piece of paper. The old man scribbled something on the paper and slid it to me.

"You need to be careful," he said. "Many of my customers are not the type you want to invite to a tea party."

When Mechanic and I got back to my truck, I turned the engine on, and we sat there for a moment, watching customers file into Tryzub. I pulled the piece of paper from my pocket and opened it. The old man had written down a number.

"Unfuckinbelievable," I said, leaning back against the headrest.

"What's wrong?" Mechanic said.

"I've seen this number before," I said. "I'm sure of it."

"Where?"

"Delroy Thomas gave it to me the other day when I spoke to him. This number belongs to a guy they call Smiley. He's the right-hand man of alderman Pat Flynn."

MY FATHER ARRIVED AT MY apartment five minutes before our scheduled dinner, wearing a two-piece charcoal gray suit and a blue paisley tie. He hadn't been to my apartment in so long, I couldn't remember how many years ago it had been. We always ate at his house, on his turf. I wasn't nervous, but I was definitely uneasy about how the evening would turn out. I had fixed an oven-roasted mushroom, artichoke, and dandelion greens salad to start, and for the main course, we were going to have eggplant parmesan I made from my grandmother's recipe, with long-grain white rice in a tahini sauce.

"This place isn't as small as I remember," my father said, handing me his coat as we entered the living room. Stryker walked up to him, sniffed, then backed up and stared. I hung his coat in the closet, then took a seat on the couch. I had a glass of cognac waiting for him next to a chair by the window. The cognac was Frapin Château Fontpinot XO. I was assured by my man who advised me on liquor that anyone who really knew cognac would be in heaven drinking this.

We got comfortable. My father picked up his drink and took a sip. He worked it around his mouth, then swallowed. He nodded his approval.

"You've been busy," he said.

"I'm working two cases at once," I said.

"Isn't one case enough?"

"It is. But the other one came out of the first one, and I wanted to help this woman whose father suddenly disappeared."

"Why is it that every case you take on is so dramatic?"

"Dramatic is more exciting than boring."

"It's always murder or disappearance or kidnapping. Don't you ever investigate more of the garden-variety?"

"Such as?"

"Stolen artwork."

"No one has ever come to me with that problem. But that's something I might consider. It would be different."

"You have quite the view here," he said, looking out the window. "This is the only thing I like about these new high-rise buildings."

"On a clear day, you can see all the way to Michigan."

"Connie has a place in Michigan," he said. "Sawyer."

We sat there quietly for a moment.

"Are you hungry?" I said.

"Famished," he said. "I haven't eaten all day."

We stood and walked into the dining room. I had two candles already lit at both ends of the table. He had always liked candles. It created the appropriate ambience, he would remind me. He walked around the table and took my seat. I didn't say anything. I put the salad on the table along with a pitcher of ice water. I filled our glasses, then we served ourselves. He blessed the food, and we started eating.

After a couple minutes of silence punctuated by serious chewing, he said, "What really happened?"

"I thought I was ready, but I wasn't," I said.

"She was very excited to meet you. So were many of her friends, who had heard about you independent of Connie or me."

"Sometimes you think you're ready for something, then when the time comes, you realize you aren't ready."

"Did you come to the restaurant?"

"I did."

"Why didn't you come upstairs?"

"I did."

"What stopped you from coming into the room and joining us?"

"I saw you holding her hand."

"That bothered you?"

"Not until I thought about Mom."

"Are you feeling like I'm trying to replace your mother?"

"No. I know that Mom could never be replaced. I'm feeling like you are making amends for things you did wrong with Mom."

"Such as?"

"You were never affectionate with Mom."

"How do you think you came into being?"

"Sex doesn't always mean affection," I said.

"Your mother and I had been together for over forty years. We were very comfortable with each other. We were affectionate."

"I never saw it."

"Maybe you did but didn't recognize it."

"I don't ever remember seeing you hold her hand."

"You say that as if it's the gold standard for displaying affection."

"Most people who are in love hold hands."

"Most, but not all. Your mother and I expressed our affection toward each other differently."

We sat there for a few moments, eating the salad. I wondered what my mother would have said had she been sitting there, listening to the conversation.

"This is very good," he said. "Cooking well is something you definitely got from your mother. I can barely cook rice."

I cleared the table, freshened his cognac, and brought out the eggplant parmesan. Everything had baked just right, and the sauce looked rich and savory. I poured the tahini over the bowl of rice.

"Your grandmother's recipe," he said between bites. "You've definitely mastered it."

"I don't want Constance to feel as though I resent her," I said.

"She doesn't."

"She looks like a really nice woman."

"She's a wonderful person. Smart. Funny. Considerate. Witty. The two of you would really get along."

"How serious is your relationship?"

"As serious as one can be at my advanced age."

"She looks much younger than I had imagined."

"She's fanatical about what she eats and her daily workout routine."

I took a bite of the eggplant parmesan. It really was good.

"I don't want Mom to be forgotten," I said.

"Is that what's bothering you?"

"I think so."

"Ashe, let me assure you that I could never forget your mother. She was and will always be my only true love."

22

The next morning, Stryker and I went out for a run along the lake. We headed south toward Grant Park, first passing the Chicago Yacht Club, then entering the long straightaway that carried us to the Museum Campus, a fifty-seven-acre portion of Grant Park that was anchored by five of the city's most visited attractions. This was my favorite time of the year to run. The paths were largely deserted, the cool air felt good seeping deep into my lungs, and the wind was just enough to inspire me to keep picking up my pace.

I ran all the way down to the monstrosity of dark, old McCormick Place, cruelly left standing under the hulking shadows of the shiny new convention center just a few yards west of it on the other side of Lake Shore Drive. My watch vibrated. I looked down at my wrist. It was a text message from Burke.

Meet me in your office in an hour. I'll bring the doughnuts.

An hour later, as Burke had promised, he walked through my door with a bag full of Stan's Donuts and a large cup with enough coffee to put out a house fire. He took a seat across from me by the window and rested the bag and cup on the small table between us.

"Not sure how many more winters I have left in me," he said.

"You've been saying that for the last five years," I said. "Another winter is threatening, and you're still here."

Burke ripped open the bag and pulled out an old-fashioned. He opened his mouth and took half of it in one bite. I was always in awe watching him eat and drink.

"I've seen enough winters," he said. "The old lady has also. I'm tired of scraping ice off the windshield and blowing snow off the driveway. I want to wake up on a January morning and walk outside in a T-shirt and feel like it's too hot even for that."

I availed myself of a chocolate frosted that had been patiently waiting for me in the bag. I took a bite a fraction of the size of Burke's and immediately felt a rush of sugar. The dough was soft and fresh.

"This city is complicated," Burke said.

"That it is," I said.

"Nothing's ever simple here."

"That's true."

"Your case with this immigrant is a problem."

"For whom?"

"For you."

"Enlighten me."

"I've been trying to access the file since you asked me about it a while ago."

"I've been patient. But it hasn't been lost on me that this is the longest it's ever taken you to do something as simple as this."

"It's not simple."

"Thus your previous statement about the city being so complicated."

"Things are not always as they seem."

"Phaedrus finished that by saying, 'The first appearance deceives many.'"

"There's a lot of deception out there," Burke said, his eyes scanning the lakefront and some of the skyscrapers visible from our vantage point.

"Who's doing the deceiving?" I said.

"I don't know."

"You don't know because you can't figure out the deception, or you don't know because you can't figure out who's behind it?"

"Both."

I took another bite of my doughnut, which put me about halfway through it. Burke was already working on his third.

"Something is going on," he said, delicately wiping the corners of his mouth with a napkin. He was always vigilant about keeping his thick mustache free of residue. For a man so large, he sometimes had a bewildering refinement to his movements.

"What makes you think something is amiss?" I asked.

"Because when I went to access the file, it wasn't there," he said.

"What do you mean, it wasn't there?"

"Not in the system."

"But O'Halloran has been working the case for weeks. They have a suspect behind bars. How is there no file?"

"I didn't say there wasn't a file. I said there wasn't a file in the system. I figured it had to be a mistake, so I called the tech guys. They confirmed there was nothing in the system except the arrest report. No supplementary report. Nothing."

"He's hiding the file," I said.

"For now," Burke said.

"When the DA starts working the case, he's going to have to put the file in the system."

"That's true, but it could be months, even up to a year, the way they've been processing cases these days."

"What else did your sources say?"

"To keep far away from it."

"Was that advice or an order?"

"Advice from someone in the loop who I trust," Burke said.

"Did they give you context for this sagacious advice?" I said.

"Sagacious?"

"Wise."

"Is it ever possible to have a single conversation with you without needing a dictionary at some point?"

"Depends on my mood."

"What about the other person's mood and them not wanting to be bothered?"

"Then I limit my usage to a single occurrence."

"How generous of you."

"Any indication of who the player or players might be in all this?"

"None."

"Any way your person in the loop might know?"

"Definitely."

"Will they tell you?"

"Only if it really means a lot to me."

"Which depends on how much it means to me."

"I don't want to ask if I'm going to potentially jeopardize them. This needs to be really important to you."

I looked out the window. The sky looked angry. The water looked annoyed. Soon the city would be blanketed in snow, and everyone would be bundled up against the chill.

"Tell me what you know about Pat Flynn," I said.

"You asking to be curious or asking because it means something to your case?"

"Both."

"Pat Flynn is the greediest, most power-hungry, most arrogant little man I've ever met," Burke said. "And those are the good things I have to say about him."

"Escobar spent six days in Michigan back in April. Each of those six days, he got breakfast from a little shop, and Pat Flynn picked up the tab."

"Flynn doesn't do anything for free. If he was picking up the tab, there had to be something in it for him."

"He has a right-hand man by the name of Liam Harrington."

"Smiley."

"You know him?"

"Everyone does. The man could hit the Powerball for half a billion dollars, and he wouldn't smile."

"How does he operate?"

"Outside the lines."

"He's the one who purchased the Social Security number and name that Joaquin was using."

"I'm not surprised he'd do something like that, but why?"

"That's what I'm trying to figure out."

"Have you talked to him?"

"Not yet."

"He's not the most agreeable person."

"Maybe I'll win him over with my charm."

Burke rolled his eyes.

"Or a nice, big nine-letter word," I said.

"Smiley never got past seventh grade," Burke said.

"Then maybe he'll be impressed."

"You sure this is the direction you want to go in?"

"It's the only direction in front of me right now."

"You could turn around and just leave that part of it alone."

"What if there's an answer hiding in there somewhere?"

"There are different ways to get answers. You're a creative guy."

"True, but I'm not a magician."

"Can I offer some advice?"

"You'd do it even if I said you couldn't."

"Make sure you've done your homework before you approach these guys. Flynn and Smiley don't play by the same rules as everyone else. There are a lot of people and companies in this city that owe them favors. They can get to anyone at any time."

"I just got chills hearing you say that. Sounds like I better eat my Wheaties."

"You're not taking me seriously."

"I am. Very much so. I just have a problem when people like Flynn abuse their power repeatedly, and no one is willing to do anything about it."

I HAD IT ON GOOD authority that Liam "Smiley" Harrington played hockey every Wednesday night in an adult league at the McFetridge Sports Center on North California Avenue. Said authority also informed me that he drove a black late-model Cadillac Escalade with vanity tags that had his three initials. Mechanic and I sat in my truck with the engine running to beat back the evening chill. Smiley emerged with a large hockey bag, wet hair, and a puffy coat that stretched across his wide shoulders.

Mechanic and I met him as he opened his trunk.

"Smiley," I said.

He turned without any expression and said, "How can I help you?"

"How was the game tonight?"

"We won."

"How did you play?"

"Well enough. Something I can help you with?"

"Thought I would ask you about a mutual acquaintance of ours."

"Who's that?"

"Diego Santana."

"Never heard of him."

His denial was much too fast.

"How about Joaquin Escobar?"

"Him either."

Another no-consideration response.

Smiley then turned and started loading his gear into the very large and very neat trunk of the Escalade. He had splurged on some extras for the SUV. The wood paneling and TV screens gave it the feel of a card room in a country club.

"Neither of those names rings a bell?" I said.

He closed the trunk with the push of a button, then turned and faced me. "Who the hell are you?" he said.

"A concerned citizen."

"Well, maybe you should be concerned about your own goddamn business."

"That's the problem. Now that Joaquin Escobar is dead and his family doesn't understand why someone would kill him, it's become my business."

Smiley looked at Mechanic and said, "You might wanna do your buddy a solid. Tell him to go home quietly, and I'll forget we ever had this conversation."

Mechanic didn't respond. He just stared at Smiley, who then looked at me, confused by Mechanic's silence.

"He's not very verbal," I said. "He's more of the physical type."

Smiley looked at both of us one last time, then walked around and got in the hundred-thousand-dollar truck, backed it up, and drove out of the lot. A message had been sent. Now we would have to wait for a response.

23

I had just sat down to a plate of fettucine with diced chicken, sun-dried tomatoes, and a light cream sauce. My office buzzer sounded, followed by my phone vibrating to let me know someone was at the door. I tapped my screen and saw the image of a well-dressed man in what looked like a long wool coat standing in front of the camera. I pushed another button in the app that allowed me to talk to him.

"How can I help you?" I said.

"My name is Everest Ford," he replied. "I'm looking for Ashe Cayne."

"In reference to?"

"My client Dario Vazquez."

"He told me with much attitude that only his abuela calls him Dario."

"Yes, he's told me that too. Rio. I am representing him."

"You are dressed too nattily to be a public defender."

"I'm not. I am a private defense attorney."

"You charge by the hour?"

"That's customary for the work I do."

"Same for me," I said. "And if this conversation continues, the billable hours, as I'm sure you're familiar with, will start adding up."

Undeterred, Ford said, "I would like to speak to you about his case."

"And I'd like to meet the Dalai Lama. But right now, I'm about to knock back a plate of pasta and an ice-cold root beer."

"I'm sorry to barge in on you like this, but if there's a better time, I can come back when it's more convenient."

I tapped another button in the app. The door buzzed, and the lock released. All this activity and I was still seated comfortably behind my desk. This new system was fun.

Everest Ford walked in, all five feet of him and a pile of wavy dark hair that stood as tall as he did. His coat looked expensive, but his suit did not. I wasn't sure what to make of that. His skin was the color of an envelope that had been left in the sun too long. He had a slight but sturdy build. His mustache was thin and razor-sharp. I wasn't able to see his shoes.

"I hope you don't mind if I eat while we talk," I said.

"Go right ahead," he said.

"Make yourself comfortable," I said, pointing to the new leather tufted armchair I had recently installed on the other side of my desk.

He almost disappeared when he sat down.

"So how can I help you?" I said before taking my first forkful of pasta. I got a tomato and a piece of chicken all in one stab. It was a good start.

"Rio wanted me to talk to you," Ford said. "He insisted you could help him."

"Why would I want to do that?" I said.

"Maybe because you have a conscience."

"Something your client has repeatedly failed to show he possesses," I said.

"Listen, man, just being honest with you, I know Rio hasn't been the most upstanding citizen."

"Ding, ding. You just qualified for the understatement-of-the-decade award."

"He said you had a sense of humor."

"It tends to be taste-specific."

"I know who you are," Ford said. "I've read all about you. You're a good guy. Very accomplished."

"Mind telling my old man that?"

"You also don't seem to be the kind of man who lets his personal feelings get in the way of doing what's right."

"Just so we understand each other, I'm not sure what you've read or what image you might've formed of me, but I'm far from being an angel."

"Understood. But you have delivered and facilitated a lot of justice in this city."

"Now, that would be a good slogan to put on my business card."

He smiled. His teeth were shiny. "Rio told me about the conversation you had."

"He also tell you that his cretin of a friend tried to make a run at me?"

"He did."

"And did he tell you that after said friend's nose was rearranged at no cost, I then informed him that I would perform a surgical maneuver on his heart if he ever tried to contact his ex-girlfriend again?"

"He did."

"So what more is there for me to say?"

I loaded up my fork again and took a healthy bite. The flavors melded perfectly in my mouth. I had always been willing to tell anyone who would listen that leftovers were often better than the original meal.

"You could tell me if you think he did it," Ford said.

"In my professional opinion, he did not."

"Well, if you think he didn't do it, then that's all the more reason to help clear him of this illegal prosecution."

"May I be very blunt?"

"I respect bluntness."

"I don't like your client, and I think he's a complete waste of sperm."

"I represent clients all the time who I don't like personally. But everyone has a right to counsel."

"The Sixth Amendment applies to you lawyers with your fancy degrees, but not to a little worker bee like me trying to scratch out a living."

"You're very modest," Ford said.

"Not on the golf course when my driver is working and I'm smashing bombs off the tee."

"You play golf?"

"Not as much as I'd like to."

"Is there anything I can do to convince you to help my client?"

"Probably not."

"Can I appeal to your sense of morality?"

"Sure, whatever's left of it."

"Then I'm doing that right now."

I loaded my fork for the third time, trying not to splash any of the sauce on my shirt. Cream stains were the hardest to get out.

"And if I were to help," I said, "who exactly would be paying for my services?"

He paused briefly and considered my words. Obviously, this was something he hadn't thought about. I wouldn't have thought about it either, but because I really didn't like him, I was going to make him pay.

"Wait," I said. "He thought I would do this pro bono?"

"I'm sure a payment arrangement can be made," Ford said. "What is your fee for this type of work?"

I told him, and he popped back a little. "Expensive."

"'We must be prepared to pay a price for freedom, for no price that is ever asked for it is half the cost of doing without it.'"

"So you agree to help him?"

"Sure."

I stuck my hand out across my desk. He accepted it and grasped it a lot more firmly than I had expected.

"Do we need to give you a down payment for your retainer?"

"Nope."

"Do we need to sign a contract?"

"We just did."

MY FATHER'S FRIEND AT AT&T, Mickey Lester, got back to me with Blackwell's call logs. I sat down at my desk and went through my typical process of organizing and analyzing the numbers. I zeroed in on the day before he went to North Carolina and the day he arrived. After two exhausting hours, I had five numbers of most interest. The first number I called was a North Carolina number. It belonged to his second cousin, who lived just outside of Greenville. He informed me that Blackwell had called him when he'd arrived, and they had agreed to have a barbecue in a couple days. That was the last he had heard from Blackwell, which was very unlike him. He always saw him when he came to town, and often the cousin would go up to the cabin and go fishing.

The next number Blackwell had either dialed or received a call from twenty times over the last three weeks before he went missing. The incoming and outgoing calls associated with that number occurred at all hours of the day. Blackwell called the number just before midnight prior to his departure from Chicago the next day. I dialed the number. It went to voicemail. I recognized the name in the recording. Deanna Turner. She was the alderman for one of Chicago's toughest, most hardscrabble wards, the Sixteenth, also known as Englewood.

Deanna Turner was a single mother of two who had been a neighborhood activist and gained popularity when she successfully demanded the firing of two sergeants from her local district who had shot an unarmed teen at a traffic stop. The teen had survived but was paralyzed from the waist down. The superintendent had defended the officers at first, but after Turner's grassroots activism gained momentum, he had no choice but to force their resignations.

The third number made the list for three reasons. First, Blackwell had been in contact with the number for the last five months. Second, it was the number he'd called after he'd spoken to his cousin once he had landed in North Carolina. Third, it was the only number in the log with a South Dakota area code.

I dialed it. It rang several times before the voicemail recording kicked in. It was an automated recording, the type that lets you know the number you've reached, then gives you instructions to leave a message.

I was just about to dial Burke's number when he called in.

"Your ears must be burning," I said.

"Not as much as your ass will be if some people have their way," he said.

"If I didn't know you better, I'd say that sounded a bit racially insensitive."

"Well, you do know me better, so you know I don't do that bullshit. You ruffled some feathers the other night."

"Harrington?" I asked.

"Yes," he said.

"Smiley wasn't smiling."

"And neither is his boss."

"So they got the message," I said.

"What message was that?"

"I'm out here, and I'm searching, and I won't stop until I get some answers."

"And they're gonna send a message back," he said.

"What's that?"

"I don't know, but it's coming."

"Who did they call?"

"Bailey."

"Who did Bailey call?"

"The first deputy superintendent, who called my area deputy chief, who called me."

"That sounds like a lot of time on the phone instead of being out there catching the bad guys."

"My DC wanted to know what you were up to."

"What did you tell him?"

"You're working the case of the Colombian they found in the lake several weeks ago. I shared with him some of what you shared with me just to make him feel like I was on the same level and also like I was mostly removed from the situation."

"Did he believe you?" I asked.

"He did."

"What did he tell you?"

"To call and warn you that there are some rumblings at HQ. Rumblings that no one really likes."

"I haven't even had a chance to chat with Flynn yet."

"And you're probably not going to. But you will talk to Bailey."

"Why?"

"He personally wants to know what you're up to."

"What's his angle?"

"What it always is. Leverage."

"When will he be calling me?"

"I'm told very soon."

"Now for the reason why I was going to call you," I said. "I need you to run a phone number down for me."

"What's in it for me?"

"You sound like Flynn."

"You ever take a minute and think about how one-sided our relationship is?"

"Not really."

"That's what I figured."

"Wasn't exactly one-sided when you called and asked me to take the Kantor case."

"I was relaying a message from upstairs."

"And at the end of the day, you looked good in front of the brass."

"Whose number is it?"

"That's what I need you to help me figure out. Blackwell called it several times over the last five months, and it was the last call he made after he landed in North Carolina."

"Did you call it?"

"I did, and it went to voicemail."

"Maybe they don't want to talk to you."

"Or maybe they don't want to explain why they were one of the last calls Blackwell made before he disappeared."

24

Delroy's Catfish Corner occupied a small, weathered brick storefront deep in the far West Side of the city. Once the powerful alderman of the Twenty-Seventh Ward, Delroy Thomas now held court in his bustling soul food restaurant, where the most important political and civic leaders, as well as beat reporters, gathered daily to swap stories and trade information. It was just after seven o'clock on a Friday night, and the place was jumping. The Isley Brothers crooned "For the Love of You" over the din of clanking silverware, lively conversations, and sporadic bursts of laughter. The cramped, hot dining room was decorated with a few banquettes along the perimeter, and scarred wood tables filled out the rest of the floor. The wobbly ceiling fans carried the smell of frying fish from the kitchen. Delroy and I were sitting over large plates of ribs, mac and cheese, and collard greens cooked with ham hock. A gallon of sweet iced tea sat between us. I poured myself a glass, took a sip, and almost went into a diabetic coma.

"They all gettin' paid," Delroy said. "That's how the system works. Always been that way, and it don't matter how many get put away—it's always gonna be that way."

Chicago had routinely been named the most corrupt city in the country, largely because of the aldermen and their penchant for cheating, grifting, lying, and abusing their power. Over thirty had been convicted since 1973, and many more had been indicted but had escaped the claws of justice. The aldermen ran their wards like mini fiefdoms. There were fifty of them in total, spread across fifty wards throughout the city. The aldermen made up the city council, thus setting the agenda and making laws for the city. In fact, they had been described as mini mayors because their rule was so great and dominating within the geographical confines of their wards. Mayor Bailey might've had the title and office, but the aldermen held the real power of the city. Without them, he wouldn't be able to get anything done.

"What about Deanna Turner from the Sixteenth?" I said.

"She's new to the game," Delroy said. "She has a lot of ideals and aspirations. Calls herself an activist. It won't last. It never lasts. The temptation is too great."

"Romantic interests?"

"She has two kids from a deadbeat who they say is strung out somewhere in a crack house in Englewood. She's a damn-good-looking woman. No one knows who she's going home to at night."

"Maybe Blackwell."

"Maybe. He's older, but when you have the kind of money he has, it doesn't make a difference. Women can get past the age difference and other differences too."

"He has that kind of money?"

"He ain't got Kantor or Packer money, but for a brutha living on the South Side, you damn right he's got some money. The man was a genius. Once he left the navy, he chose a business that he could learn on the job. He also knew there weren't a lot of us doing that kind of work and definitely not many of us owning our own businesses in that field. Washington became mayor, and all of a sudden, city hall started paying attention to Black-owned businesses and their struggles to get city and county contracts. Blackwell opened his own shop. No other Blacks were doing that work, so he started collecting all these subcontracting gigs. And we're not talking hundreds or thousands of dollars. Some of these jobs pay well into the seven figures."

"I saw lots of photos of him at construction sites," I said. "Groundbreakings, ribbon cuttings. He's even in a photo with Penny Packer at the University of Chicago."

"Blackwell has played the game like it's supposed to be played," Delroy said, licking the extra sauce from his fingers. "He's not flashy, doesn't need to show you how much money he has in the bank. He just goes on about his business quietly."

"He's missing," I said.

"Who's missing?"

"Hank Blackwell."

"What the hell are you talking about?"

I explained all that had happened up to that point without going into the messy details of the investigation.

"Don't sound right," Delroy said. "The Blackwell I know ain't the kind of man who just up and disappears."

"Sometimes we don't know people as well as we think we do."

"And there ain't been a peep from him in weeks?"

"Thereabouts."

"People mostly know him for his business, but they forget he's ex-military. He knows how to take care of himself."

"I've been thinking the same thing."

"I don't know what else he might've been up to, but I'd bet good money no one could take Blackwell easily."

"Which means he could've had a plan all along to disappear."

"And leave everything that he has?"

"If what he has somewhere else is more than he has here."

"You think Turner knows something?"

"I think she's had a lot of conversations with a missing man who suddenly dropped off the face of the earth."

"Sounds like you need to talk to her."

"That's my plan."

"Is this why you were asking about Flynn?" Delroy said.

"That was for something else I've been working on," I said.

"A different case?"

"Appears to be for now."

"How many cases you working at one time?"

"Usually just one. But I have a soft heart and agreed to take on Blackwell's case too."

"Does Flynn have anything to do with Blackwell?"

"Not that I can see. But Flynn has something to do with a guy from Colombia who was found in the lake with a hole in his heart."

"You talk to Smiley?"

"I did."

"Let me guess: He had nothing to say."

"Other than he knew nothing and it was in my best interest to forget the conversation ever happened."

"He's a bad dude," Delroy said.

"How bad?"

"He has a body count."

"Flynn is aware of that?"

"Flynn is the reason why he has that count."

"How does Flynn get away with this shit?"

"Two words: Fear. Leverage."

CAROLINA WAS WAITING FOR ME at my apartment with the promise that I'd deliver two servings of mac and cheese, spicy cabbage, fried chicken, and some molasses corn bread, of which she would likely take nothing more than a nibble. Burke called in as I made my way from the shadowy outskirts of the West Side back to the luxury high-rises of Streeterville.

"You're really swinging for the fences with this case, I tell ya," Burke said.

"Why play the game if you're not gonna go for it all?"

"Your South Dakota number comes back to an E. Cummings."

"Like the poet E. E.?"

"Who's E. E.?"

"The name of the poet. The guy who wrote everything in small letters. No capitalization and strange punctuation."

"Can we stick to the topic?" Burke groaned. "The number you gave me belongs to E. Cummings. The 'E' stands for Edward."

"If you tell me his middle name is Estlin, I'm gonna hang up this phone."

"I don't know his middle name or even if he has one. Does this have something to do with that damn poet?"

"His name was Edward Estlin Cummings."

"I have no fuckin' clue the guy's middle name, nor do I care. What I do know is, he's an FBI agent based in Virginia with an address in DC."

"Blackwell lands in Nowhere, North Carolina, and calls an FBI agent with a famous name—or at least partially famous—then goes off the grid within the hour? How strong are your contacts at the FBI?"

"I've been doing this for over thirty-five years."

"How about making a call?"

"I already did."

"Proactive."

"I don't normally say this, but you sure you wanna keep going down this path?"

"What's my alternative?"

"You keep stirring up shit, and it keeps stinking. Leave it alone, and the smell eventually goes away."

"Thanks for the advice. I'll invest in a good pair of nose plugs."

BAILEY WANTED TO MEET ME away from all the eyes and ears of city hall. So we agreed to meet at a tiny barbershop in the neighborhood of Bridgeport. This was where he'd gotten his hair cut as a little boy and where he still got it cut, now by the son of the man who used to own the shop. When I entered the empty shop, the man sitting in the middle of three chairs looked up casually and nodded for me to go to the back. I walked the short length of the room and opened a small plywood door that looked like it had been recently stained. Badly. There were dried splotches all over the brass doorknob.

Bailey sat at a small card table. Alone. A pile of poker chips and two decks of cards sat in front of him.

"Thanks for coming," he said. "I know you have a lot going on."

I took a seat across from him. The room had four drab, undecorated pale walls; a small makeshift bar; a refrigerator; and a farmer's sink. I imagined on Friday and Saturday nights, men assembled back here once the shop was closed, pulled out cigars and wads of cash, then got down to business.

"Golf and the occasional murder," I said.

"I heard you joined Olympic. Nice track."

"It would be a lot nicer if I could get out there and play it more."

"I hope you don't feel like I summoned you here," he said. "I just wanted to check in. I do my best to keep tabs on what's going on."

"We both love this city," I said. "We both will never leave this city. We need to be able to coexist. And we can do that even without liking each other."

"I don't dislike you," Bailey said.

"Then I guess I'm speaking for myself," I said. "You're not my favorite person in the world."

Bailey nodded softly. "So what are you working on these days?"

"Stuff."

"What kind of stuff?"

"Murder. Mysterious disappearance. Garden-variety stuff."

"Thank you for your work on the Kantor case last year," he said. "The family is very appreciative of your efforts. As am I. Elliott was a pillar in our city. He didn't deserve what happened to him."

"None of them deserved it," I said. "But money doesn't make us impervious to some of life's cruelties."

"I hear you're all charged up about this immigrant who was found in the lake last month."

"Not sure I would use the words 'charged up.' I just want to do my job and make sure whoever is responsible has to answer for what they did."

"I've been told he was here illegally."

"So that means it's okay for someone to shove an ice pick into his heart?"

"I'm not saying that at all. I'm just repeating what I heard."

"What else have you heard?"

"That you talked to Smiley the other day outside of McFetridge."

"We had a quick chat."

"Was it any help to your investigation?"

"He didn't have anything to say but a couple denials and a thinly veiled threat. But denials sometimes speak louder than admissions."

"Do you think this has something to do with Smiley?"

"I think Smiley is familiar with the deceased."

"Do you know in what capacity?"

"I'm not comfortable saying right now until I get more information."

"Do you think Flynn is involved?"

"I've heard you and Flynn aren't exactly bosom buddies."

"We've found a way to, as you say, *coexist*."

"But your existence would be a lot happier if he failed to exist."

"Literally?"

"Figuratively."

"That would be an accurate assessment that anyone who knows an ounce of our city politics could make."

"Thus you would be interested to know if I had any knowledge regarding him that would figuratively make him no longer exist."

"Very."

"I don't like when I get the feeling I'm being used," I said.

"I'm sorry you feel that way," he said. "That's not my intention."

"What is your intention?"

"To help you."

"Help me how?"

"Any way I can."

I considered his offer for a moment. There was nothing he could really do right now to help me, and if there was, I wouldn't accept it anyway. He'd be helping me only to help himself. What he really wanted was what Delroy had said all aldermen hoped to obtain: leverage. If I got something on Flynn and gave it to Bailey, that would put Bailey at a distinct advantage.

"I'm good right now," I said.

"Smiley and Flynn can be very tricky," he said.

"So I've heard."

"They also don't tend to play by the same rules as everyone else."

"Who really does these days?"

Bailey nodded and said, "Fair enough."

I stood to leave.

"You never answered my question about Flynn," Bailey said.

"Which one?"

"Do you think he's involved with this man who was found in the lake?"

"I'm sure he was. I just don't know in what capacity."

A glint of excitement livened Bailey's weary eyes.

25

Deanna Turner's aldermanic office was located on the corner of Sixty-Third Street and South May, in a squat L-shaped row of small storefronts. A ramshackle gas station barely remained standing at the other end of the parking lot, and a discount liquor store sat across the street. The other buildings were either boarded up entirely or in various stages of delayed refurbishment.

After a brief wait in a barren lobby of vinyl chairs and plastic potted plants, I was buzzed through an inner door, led down a short hallway, and deposited in an office with a stunning view of a vacant lot decorated with several old vehicles in all phases of disrepair.

Turner stood from her large desk and walked around to greet me. She was tall, attractive, and very fashionable. We shook hands, and she offered me a chair at a small oval conference table that sat adjacent to a wall full of plaques and framed certificates.

"Thanks for taking the time to meet with me," I said.

"Your message was a bit vague, but you mentioned Hank Blackwell," she said.

"I take it you know him."

"The fact that you're here indicates you already know that I do."

She was soft-spoken but very direct. I found the contrast to be quite appealing.

"Did you know that he was missing?" I said.

"Missing how?"

"Missing as in he can't be found."

"Who is looking for him?"

"I am."

"Why are you looking for him?"

I smiled. "Because he can't be found."

She smiled. "I heard you could be clever," she said.

"Only when I'm trying to impress."

"And charming."

"Only when my cleverness doesn't seem to be getting the results I'm hoping to achieve."

"I know of your work," she said.

"Can't hide anything with Google at everyone's fingertips."

"What you did with the Marquan Payton case was one of those watershed moments for the city."

"It wasn't about me. It was about doing what's right. Plenty of people could've taken a stand and done the same thing I did."

"But they didn't," she said.

"Not for lack of opportunity," I said.

"When you say Hank is missing, are you saying he's in danger?"

"Unfortunately, that's usually what 'missing' ends up being."

"Why are you the one searching for him?"

"Because his daughter is in Texas suffocating in fear, and the sheriff down in North Carolina where he went missing isn't exactly lighting the investigative world on fire."

"Hank is a bright light in our community," she said.

"He's a fascinating man," I said.

"You've met him?"

"No, but I've read about him and talked to others who know him."

"He knows a lot of people," she said.

"And some of them are very fancy," I replied.

"Any in particular?"

"Pat Flynn, for starters."

"I don't know if I'd consider Pat as fancy."

"He has a lot of power."

"More than he should have," she said.

"He makes a lot of money with that law firm of his," I said.

"He does."

"And he owns one of those extravagant manses on the other side of the lake."

"I've heard that also, but I've never been there."

"How's it been, working with him?"

Turner smiled. "In one word? Challenging."

"How about two words?"

"Often frustrating," she said.

"That description is becoming a motif," I said.

"You've talked to others?"

"Yup. And so far, no one has used the word 'delightful.'"

"Pat sees the world differently than most of us," Turner said.

"How's that?"

"The rules that apply to us don't apply to him."

"Sounds pretty arrogant."

"That's a fair description."

"I've also heard he likes to get his way."

"Don't most men with some power?"

We sat there for a moment. I enjoyed talking to her. Sometimes a person could be even more attractive when they were a good conversationalist. She knew how to talk.

"What was your relationship with Blackwell?" I asked.

"He's my constituent," she replied. "I'd like to think he is also my friend."

"Nothing more than that?"

She smiled. "Why would there be?"

"You're an attractive woman with considerable power. At least here in your ward."

"Here's the charm you mentioned earlier," she said, smiling.

"Wrapped around the truth," I said.

"Hank and I have nothing more than a professional relationship."

"You speak often," I said.

"We do. He does a lot of work in our community. I rely on him to get some things done and vice versa."

"Is it normal for the two of you to speak late into the evening?"

"Not particularly."

"You were one of the last persons he spoke to before he went missing. And that call was late into the evening before he left for North Carolina."

She nodded.

"Might I ask what you spoke about?"

"You can ask, but I won't answer that," she said.

I lifted my eyebrows.

"The content of that call was off the record. I'm going to keep it that way."

"If you tell me, I'll also keep it off the record, so there will still be no record."

"Clever," she said. "But I'll pass."

"Did you know he was going to North Carolina?"

"I did."

"Did he mention plans on meeting anyone there?"

"He didn't."

"Did he seem his usual self?"

"He did."

"Do you know any reason why he'd be missing?"

"None."

THE FOLLOWING AFTERNOON, I SAT across from Rio Vazquez and Attorney Everest Ford in the large visiting room at the Cook County Jail, one of the largest single-site jails in the country. Rio was one of nine thousand inmates being housed in the massive complex. He sat there, looking small and helpless in the drab brown uniform with a large black *M* on the left breast pocket of his shirt.

Rio looked thin and badly in need of a good night's sleep. His hair had been finger-combed, and his face had been colored by dark stubble that was heavy in some areas and lighter in others.

"Thanks for coming, Mr. Cayne," Ford said. "We look forward to working with you." He nudged Rio softly.

"Thanks," Rio said sheepishly, his eyes staring at the table. Gone was all the inflated bravado he bared on the streets of Pilsen.

"You getting along alright in here?" I said.

"I'm making it," Rio said. "But it's a fuckin' dump, and I don't belong in there. This is all bullshit."

"It's the DNA, gentlemen," I said. "The threat to kill Escobar doesn't prove anything, and millions of people say that kind of thing every day and don't mean it. But DNA underneath the fingernails? That's tough to argue away."

"I never saw the man in my life," Rio said. "No clue what he looks like. Offer me ten million dollars, and I still couldn't pick him out of a lineup."

"Well, how would you explain your skin cells being found underneath his fingernails?" I said.

Rio shook his head. "I can't explain it," he said. "All I can think is, they made some kind of mistake in the lab where they did the test. They can't be perfect, right? They have to make mistakes sometimes like anybody else."

"We could challenge the chain of custody of the evidence," Ford said.

"What the fuck does that mean?" Rio said.

"We could make an argument about how the evidence was handled," Ford said. "There are certain protocols and standards for collecting and handling evidence like this. That's one of the ways O.J. got off."

"Everyone knows that muthafucka was guilty," Rio said. "I'm no murderer like he was. I ain't do shit."

"Sometimes getting acquitted of a charge has nothing to do with guilt or innocence," Ford said in his lawyerly fashion. "An acquittal can rest on technicalities that have nothing to do with whether a crime was committed or not."

"You sounding like you don't believe I'm innocent," Rio said, raising his voice. "Whose side are you on?"

"I told you when you first hired me that I believe you're innocent," Ford said. "Otherwise, I wouldn't be sitting here."

I knew that to be untrue, but there was no need for me to throw more gas on a fire that was growing pretty well on its own. I continued to spectate.

"The DNA is the weakness in our case," Ford said. "I need to figure out a strategy to deal with that. Just standing up in front of the judge and saying we don't know how it got there, but you didn't put it there, is not going to work."

"Then think of something," Rio said. "That's why I'm paying you all this fuckin' money. You're already ten thousand into my pocket, and I don't feel like I'm any closer to getting outta this shithole."

I decided to jump in, since I was into his pocket for half that amount.

"Let's talk about the scratches on your neck," I said. "Do you remember the exact night that happened?"

"Yup. When I was with Julieta."

"Where did the two of you have your dalliance?"

"Dalliance?"

"Sexual involvement," Ford said.

"Why the fuck couldn't you just say that?" Rio said.

"One word versus two," I said. "Less is more."

Rio shook his head. "She came to my place," he said.

"How did she get there?"

"She caught an Uber."

"According to her testimony, she's saying she talked to you that night, but she never saw you."

"That bitch is lyin' her ass off," Rio said. "We talked. She told me how much she missed me, then she asked me if I wanted her to come over. I was surprised she called. But I wasn't gonna turn down the pussy."

"Did anyone see her come to your apartment?"

"I don't know. Maybe if somebody was outside on the stoop."

"The first thing we need to do is prove she was at your apartment that night," I said.

"Why can't you go and talk to her?" Rio said.

"Because now that I'm helping you, it would look like I'm trying to coerce or intimidate her on your behalf. Did anyone else see those scratch marks?"

Rio looked down momentarily. He nodded.

"Who?" I said.

"Another girl I was messin' with."

"Explain."

"She came over after Julieta left."

"Lothario," I said.

"What does that mean?" he said.

Ford gave me a look to leave it alone.

"Never mind," I said. "What happened with this other girl?"

"She came over about an hour after Julieta left. We was doing our thing too, then she saw the scratches on my neck when I took my shirt off. She got upset, cussed me out, got dressed, and left."

"Have you seen her since then?"

"She came to visit me yesterday."

"What's her name?"

"Carmen Delarosa. Julieta's girlfriend."

26

That night, Carolina and I sat at a small table in a hole-in-the-wall on Taylor Street called Chilango. There were plenty of high-priced Mexican restaurants with faux-leather-clad menus and linen tablecloths, but for my money, no one made a better empanada than Chilango. I had a plate half full of barbecue chicken empanadas, the other half full of beef-and-rice empanadas. Carolina had two lonely spinach-and-ricotta empanadas on her plate, and I was certain she wouldn't make it halfway through the second one. We sat squeezed between a table of college students and an old couple that hadn't said anything to each other since they'd sat down.

"Promise me that will never happen to us," I said.

"What?" Carolina said.

I wiggled my eyebrows in the old couple's direction.

"Impossible for us," she said.

"Why?"

"Because you could never sit through an entire meal without talking golf or a case or quoting an obscure poet."

"I didn't know Heraclitus was obscure."

She smiled. "Does that mean what I think it means?"

"You should avoid allowing your beautiful mind to travel to the gutter, especially when eating the city's best empanadas."

"Where I come from, that's not the gutter. That's proper female anatomy, and there's nothing wrong with appreciating it."

"Where I come from, that is the name of a pre-Socratic Greek philosopher known for the doctrines he wrote: that things are constantly in a state of change, opposites coincide, and fire is the basic material of the world."

"Sounds like your two cases," she said.

"That would be the proper inference," I said.

"They sound like a real mess."

"They are definitely in the entropy period," I said.

"Don't try to get all scientific with me," she said. "I took a year of chemistry in college. I know what 'entropy' means."

I took half an empanada in one bite, then followed it with a long pull of guava juice that was almost as sweet as the iced tea at Delroy's. If I kept going like this, I was going to find myself on a daily regimen of diabetes medications.

"Most cases tend to get confusing before they clear up," I said. "It's just an unwritten rule of investigations."

"But there are some things you're clear about now?"

"Definitely."

"Such as?"

"Are you gonna take a bite of one of those empanadas or just sit there and stare at them affectionately?"

"I was waiting for you to get through some of yours so we could finish at the same time."

"Hank Blackwell is not dead," I said. "He is a military man. A planner. A strategist. He went to North Carolina for a reason."

"Which is?"

"That answer is in the 'Confusing' column."

I dipped my empanada in pink sauce and took a bite. The crust flaked in my mouth and on my lips like a well-made empanada should.

"Joaquin Escobar got himself too deep in something that had to do with Pat Flynn and whatever scheme he was working on at the time."

"What scheme was that?"

"Another answer that goes into the 'Confusing' column."

Carolina took her first bite of an empanada. She nibbled at the corner and didn't even make it to the cheese and spinach.

"Alderman Deanna Turner knows more about Blackwell's disappearance than she's letting on."

"Are you sure?"

"A hundred percent. She tried to sell me on the important role he played in her ward and what he did for the community. But there was more there."

"How many aldermen talk to their constituents just before midnight?"

"And what was so pressing that she couldn't wait until the morning to discuss?"

"Didn't he catch a flight in the morning? What did she need to say to him before he caught that flight?"

"Hey, I'm supposed to be the crack detective."

"Behind every man is a good woman."

"Behind every woman... Forget it. I digress."

Two guys came into the restaurant looking like two beached orcas lying in the middle of a golf course fairway. They wore long navy blue coats, loose-fitting black pants, and the type of black shoes that could also pass for sneakers if more casual dress were required. They awkwardly joined the queue at the register but hadn't stopped looking around since they'd walked into the joint. I kept one eye on them and the other on my plate of empanadas.

"Julieta Romero is not playing on the level," I said. "She's lying, either by her own decision or because someone is forcing her."

"What is she lying about?"

"She was with Rio that night that she said she wasn't. She also wasn't as afraid of him as she led others to believe."

"Why would she make all this up?"

"Add that answer along with the others on the 'Confusing' side."

The two men placed their order, took a number, then squeezed into adjacent seats at the counter by the window.

"Carmen also isn't playing on the level," I said.

"It's not the first time a girl has nibbled on the crumbs of her girlfriend's crumbled relationship," Carolina said. "Not that it's admirable or anything, but it's not uncommon."

"The question is whether Carmen was hiding the relationship because she felt guilty and embarrassed or if she was hiding it because there was something more sinister at work."

"What's more sinister than sleeping with your girlfriend's ex who you pretend to be protecting her from?"

"Assuming they really were in the so-called ex phase of the relationship when the sloppy seconds started."

"Which complicates it even further."

"Which is why most of everything with Carmen needs to be pushed into the 'Confusing' column."

The cashier walked from behind her counter and carried three large bags of food and two enormous drinks to the men still anchored by the window. They took the bags and drinks, swayed their bodies left and right until they could get off the stools, looked at me longer than I would've liked, then walked through the door.

"So what's next?" Carolina said, completely unaware that seven hundred pounds of flesh had just been menacing us.

"Put the one and a half empanadas still on your plate in a doggy bag, take you to my apartment, and study another Greek philosopher not as obscure as the one previously mentioned."

"Who might that be?"

"Uraclitus."

THE NEXT MORNING, I SAT in my office, working only by the light coming through the window. I had drawn a *Clear* column and a *Confusing* column on the evidence board and filled it with all the thoughts I could drain from my mind. I picked up the phone and called Alicia Gentry.

"You're still at it," she said.

"A man is still missing, and a daughter is still crying," I said.

"If nothing, you're persistent."

"'Neither snow nor rain nor heat nor gloom of night stays these couriers from the swift completion of their appointed rounds.'"

"Honorable."

"The 'swift' might be a stretch."

"Are you still chasing ghosts?"

"The ghost now has a name."

"Which is?"

"Edward Cummings."

"And I'm assuming you want me to do something with this name?"

"After you don't confuse it with E. E. Cummings."

"Who the hell is that? I thought you were a Shakespeare guy."

"Only when I'm feeling less adventurous."

"What do you want me to do with this name?"

"Check it out and tell me whatever you feel comfortable sharing."

"I won't ask how you figured out it was him."

"I adore you," I said. "But even the best of lovers have their secrets."

I DROVE OVER TO TNL Heating & Cooling. Mrs. McCarley was in her chair, combing through papers, as I entered the office. She looked up and smiled when she recognized it was me.

"A sight for sore eyes," she said.

"A ray of sunshine on a cloudy day," I said.

I walked over and took my usual seat in front of her desk.

"How are things going around here?" I said.

"Hectic," she said. "We have too many jobs and not enough men to cover them."

"Don't you have a number two here?"

"You're looking at her."

"You know how to install and fix HVAC systems?"

"Better than half the men we got on the payroll. I only stopped because my knees couldn't take all those stairs and the constant bending and standing. That's a young person's work."

"Still nothing from Blackwell?"

"That's what I wanted to ask you."

"Not a peep."

She lowered her reading glasses and let them fall onto her ample chest. "You think he's dead?"

"I do not."

"You think he's in trouble somewhere?"

"I do not."

"You think he's caught up in something bad?"

"I don't know."

"Dear Lord, this is one big mess," she said.

"What do you know about Deanna Turner?" I said.

"The alderman?"

"Is there another?"

"Not that I'm aware of."

"Have you dealt with her before?"

"Not really. I mostly work with the people who report to her."

"Did Blackwell deal with her?"

"Of course. Bosses talk to bosses."

"Peons talk to peons."

"That's the way of the world."

"Is it possible the bosses had eyes for each other?"

"Eyes as in . . . ?" She rubbed her hands together.

"Yes, those kind of eyes."

"I don't think so. Blackwell is a very straight shooter, and he likes his money too much. He wouldn't mix business with the type of pleasure he could get somewhere else."

"She's an attractive woman."

"If you're into the tall, skinny type."

"And she's single."

"Single and married seem to be the same these days."

"Any reason why Blackwell would have business to talk to her about at midnight?"

"No idea."

I looked at her desk and noticed one of those large old-fashioned cardboard check binders.

"How are things financially?" I said.

"Better than ever."

"Do you have access to the account?"

"Of course I do. I wear five hats. Chief accountant is one of them."

"Did Blackwell access the account also?"

"Sure. It's his business."

"Is it possible for me to take a look at the account?"

"I don't see why not," she said. "If you think it might give you a clue about what's going on, then I don't have a problem with that. C'mon and pull that chair around here."

I did as she instructed and sat beside her. She smelled of the kind of fragrance that grandmothers always wore to church on Sundays. She tapped the keyboard, clicked several windows, entered a password that seemed like it was one letter short of the entire alphabet, then leaned back so I could get an unobstructed view.

"Can I use the mouse?" I said.

"Be my guest."

I looked through the last three months of statements, starting with September and working my way back. I first noticed the balance. Just over five million dollars. I wasn't sure what the cash flow requirements were for a business like this, but five million sitting in a bank account seemed like a lot of money. There were many more debits than there were credits, which is the goal of any business owner. Make more than you spend. As I got toward the beginning of September, I noticed a check for twenty thousand dollars written to Blackwell

Industries. I made a mental note of that and looked at August. There was no unusual activity for that month, except another check written to Blackwell Industries. This was also at the beginning of the month and for the same twenty thousand dollars. I looked at July. Same amount. Same time of the month. Same recipient.

"Can you print these statements out for me?" I said.

"Sure," Mrs. McCarley said. She pushed a few buttons, and the printer behind us came to life.

"What is Blackwell Industries?" I said.

"His personal account."

"Do you have access to it?"

"No, only he does."

"Every month, he wrote a check to that account for twenty thousand dollars. Do you know what that was for?"

"No idea."

"Did you ever think to ask?"

"I did. But I didn't. I need to pay my rent more than I need to dig into someone else's affairs."

"What do you think the money was for?"

"I have no idea."

"Was Blackwell paid a regular salary like everyone else?"

"You mean, was he part of the weekly payroll?"

"Yes."

"Never."

"So how did he get paid?"

"He wrote one check to himself at the end of each year."

"Was it always the same amount?"

"Always."

"How much?"

"One million dollars even."

27

I walked into Atotonilco Taqueria just before three o'clock, figuring it would be the sweet spot right between the end of lunch and the beginning of the after-work rush hour. I had figured correctly. A few couples sat at the small tables, but no one was standing in line to order. Carmen was in the prep area behind the counter, pouring sauce into small containers. She smiled and walked in my direction.

"How are you?" she said.

"Living the dream," I said.

"Did you want to order something?"

"Actually, I was hoping I could talk to you for a few minutes."

She looked up at the clock behind the shelves of pots and pans.

"My next break is in fifteen minutes," she said. "It's better if we talk outside. I'll meet you there."

"Sounds like a plan," I said.

I walked outside and stood next to my truck.

Carmen walked out of the restaurant and came bounding toward my car.

"How's everything going?" I said.

"We had a busy day," Carmen said. "It's slow now, but it'll pick back up after five. One of the girls called out sick, so there's just three of us today."

"How's Julieta?"

"She's good. I think. I haven't talked to her lately."

"You guys too busy for each other?"

"You know how it is. Everyone's got so much going on. Work. I'm trying to get back to finish school at Columbia. Family stuff."

"Talk to Rio lately?"

"Ewwww," she said. "Disgusting. No way."

"He's an asshole, but he's a handsome guy," I said.

"Plenty of handsome guys out there who aren't assholes."

"Does Julieta know you and Rio were having your private moments?" I said.

"What are you talking about?" she said, not too convincingly.

"You and Rio were fucking," I said. "Does your girlfriend know that?"

"Who told you that?"

"Mr. Debonair himself."

"What an asshole," she said.

"So I can take that as a yes?"

"It was only after they broke up," she said, as if that made it more acceptable.

"I'm the last one to pass judgment," I said. "Do I think that's a shitty way to treat a friend? You betcha. Do I care? Not for a second. Who you lie down with is your business. I just want to know about the last time you were together."

"What about it?"

"It was the night Julieta called him from your phone, right?"

"Yes."

"Did you know she went to his apartment after she left your house?"

"That's what he told me."

"Did you know he had been with her an hour before you arrived?"

"I didn't know that when I was going there. He told me after I saw the scratches on his neck. He's such a dog. He says they aren't seeing each other anymore, then he goes and sleeps with her again."

"Which means he cheated on you with the girl he was cheating on."

Carmen's eyes glazed over. "Something like that, I guess," she said. "What are you going to do now?"

"Find Julieta and talk to her."

"Are you gonna tell her about Rio and me?"

"And make a situation that's already messy even messier?"

"Yes."

"None of my business," I said. "I just needed you to confirm that you had been with Rio and that you saw those marks on his neck and that he told you they were from Julieta."

"Will that help him?"

"A little, but not enough to get out of County."

"Will you see him again?"

"If I don't get hit by a bus first."

"Will you tell him I'm sorry?"

Silly youth, I thought to myself, then got into my truck and went searching for the other third of the love triangle.

I DROVE OVER TO JULIETA'S apartment building and parked across the street. I figured the element of surprise might work better than calling and setting up a meeting with her, so I sat there and waited. As I watched a nanny brigade of strollers and lapdogs walk by, my phone rang. The number had a North Carolina area code, but I didn't recognize it.

"This Ashe Cayne?" a caller said in a Southern twang.

"The one and only," I said.

"This is Kip Crawford down here in Greenville. Remember me?"

"A voice I could never forget," I said.

He chuckled. "You got anything on Black?"

"Nothing since we last spoke," I said.

"Simpson and his boys got anything?"

"Nothing. I don't even know if they're still looking."

"Doesn't surprise me one bit. That's exactly why I called you. I didn't even bother with those knuckleheads. I haven't met you in person, but even on the phone, you come across as a man who knows how to handle business."

"Only took one conversation for you to figure that out. Took my girl almost three years. Better late than never, I guess."

Crawford laughed. "And you got a damn good sense of humor. That goes a long way in life."

"I heard a guy once say, 'When you have a sense of humor, you have a better sense of life.'"

"Whoever that was, he was a wise man."

"Have you heard anything about Blackwell on your end?" I said.

"No, but I saw something that I think you should know about," he said. "You got the time?"

"I'm all ears, except where I'm all muscle."

Crawford chuckled, then said, "I got some hunting cameras out on the back of my property and different places in the woods. I can keep track of the animals that come and go, especially this time of year, when they're looking to eat. Well, I went earlier today to take a look at the cameras. I saw something on one of them that's bothering me."

"What's that?"

"A man walking through the woods who shouldn't have been walking through the woods."

"Why shouldn't he have been walking through the woods?"

"Because it's private property. We got big signs all over the perimeter and interior letting people know the land is private. People like to come up here and hunt, but Black and I don't want nobody up here."

"Is your land adjacent to Blackwell's?"

"Our joint line runs from the street all the way down to the water. When Black isn't here, I walk his property and look after it, make sure nobody is putting up hunting stands and setting traps."

"What was the man doing?"

"From the camera that caught him and the way he was walking, he was coming back from the lake."

"You have a date and time?"

"It's stamped on the video," Crawford said. "He walked by the camera at 8:54 p.m. on September 15."

"Do people normally walk through there at that time of night?"

"Only if they're up to no good."

"What do you think he was doing?"

"I don't know, but I don't think he was hunting."

"Why do you say that?"

"He wasn't dressed like he was hunting. He didn't have a long gun or anything. He looked like a guy walking through the woods."

"Is there a clear shot of his face?"

"It's pretty clear," Crawford said. "Not like you can see the color of his eyes or anything, because it's black-and-white. But put it like this: If you knew him, you would know it's him in the video."

"Is he carrying anything?"

"Nope. He's just walking."

"Is he alone?"

"Just him."

"Is it possible he was out on another property and got lost?"

"It's possible, but he doesn't own any properties up here. I know everyone for miles around. I've never seen him before."

"Is there any way you can send me that video?"

"I'm sure there is, but I'm not the best at this technology stuff. I'd have to call my son who lives in Charlotte and ask him how to do that."

"I just need the footage with the man in it."

I gave Crawford my email address.

"I'll talk to my son after he gets home from work. Expect an email within the next forty-eight hours, after he gets everything sorted out. His name is Luke."

I disconnected the line and continued watching Julieta's apartment building. No one had entered or exited since I had been sitting there, and it was going on an hour. I got out of the truck, walked over to her building, found her name on the intercom panel, and pushed the buzzer next to her name. There was no response. I waited a few minutes just in case she was in the bathroom, then pushed it again. Still no response. I went back and got into my truck.

As I continued to watch the front of her apartment building with my attention occasionally drifting to the goings-on in the park and the birds chasing each other among the trees, I thought about Blackwell. What was he up to? He'd never made it to his cabin that day he landed. Had he ever intended on going there? I also thought about E. Cummings. An FBI agent had been talking to a navy vet. FBI agents didn't call to talk weather and sports. They only called when there was business at hand. A ghost-tagged FBI vehicle had happened to be at the same rest stop as the one Blackwell had visited at the same time on a deserted country road. No way was it coincidence.

A white Lexus SUV with shiny chrome rims pulled up to Julieta's building. The passenger door opened, and Julieta stepped out, carrying a couple shopping bags with designer names I was too far away to read. She was dressed in a light suede jacket and tight black jeans tucked into a pair of knee-high boots. She bent down and said something to the driver, then turned with a big smile on her face and walked up the short flight of steps to the front door. She struggled with the key and the handle for a moment but eventually made it inside. The Lexus did a U-turn and drove past me. A young guy with a baseball cap, shades, and a gold chain draped across the front of his sweatshirt sat in the driver's seat. I took out my phone and typed his license plate into my Notes app.

The sun had made a quick descent, and shadows now crept along the sidewalks and in between the buildings. I was about to get out of the truck when I had a different idea. I picked up my phone and called Mechanic.

"You busy?" I said.

"Cleaning my guns."

"How would you like to do a little reconnaissance?"

"Who's the target?"

"An extremely attractive girl with emerald eyes."

"That sounds like fun."

I brought him up to speed on Julieta and the love triangle and her difficulty telling the truth. We had agreed that I would spend a couple more hours sitting there, then he would relieve me and cover her until midnight. He would stick with her tomorrow, and maybe we would get a chance to see what Julieta Romero was really doing with all her spare time.

28

Despite his wealth and power, Pat Flynn's aldermanic office was not much different from any other alderman's. He occupied a suite of rooms on a generic block containing a row of two-floor storefronts. I parked my truck and walked across the street to the front door. Several of the windows had been blocked by those old-fashioned aluminum window blinds that always seemed to be coated in a half inch of dust. As I approached the door, I noticed that not only was this the site of his aldermanic office, but it also housed his law firm. This arrangement seemed too cozy, if not unethical.

I opened the door and was met by a middle-aged woman who likely visited the next-door bakery too often. She sat behind a white laminated counter. Her mess of red hair had been clipped and twisted in some arrangement that could best be described as confusing. She was furiously typing as I approached.

"One second," she said, not looking up and continuing to work the keyboard. I noticed her fingernails were painted the same shade of red as her hair. She finished with the flourish of a concert pianist concluding a Beethoven symphony.

"All set," she said, looking up with a smile.

"How many keyboards you go through over the course of a year?" I said.

She kept smiling. "If I had a nickel for how many times people have walked through that door and asked me that very question, I'd be sipping piña coladas on a beach in San Juan."

"Well, to those of us who make our way jabbing and cursing at keyboards, it's a wonderful performance to witness."

"Why, thank you, young man," she said. "How can I help you?"

I noticed the nameplate on the counter said BRIDGET MURPHY.

"I was wondering if I could have a moment with Mr. Flynn," I said.

"Do you have an appointment?" she asked.

"I apologize. I didn't know I needed one."

"Are you wanting to see him for legal work or as the alderman?"

"Alderman."

"Okay," she said. "That means you would go down the hall on the left. He does take walk-ins, but those slots fill up really fast, and they get squeezed in between the appointments. My advice would be to make an appointment; that way, you're guaranteed a time and don't have to sit around for too long."

"Well, since I'm here, would it be possible to sneak a few minutes of his time between appointments?"

She turned toward the computer monitor, raced her hands across the keyboard in a nanosecond, and said, "Unfortunately, Alderman Flynn isn't in right now. He won't be back in the office until tomorrow. And tomorrow, he's booked solid."

"Does that mean he's in his lawyer office?"

"I don't think he's there either," Bridget said. "Give me a moment."

She picked up the phone, and as fast as she typed on her keyboard, she punched in a number. She asked if Flynn was in his office, listened for a moment to the response, which seemed to be extensive, then hung up the phone.

"No, he's not there either," she said. "He's out on business. What's your name, young man? I'm happy to set up an appointment for you."

"Ashe Cayne," I said. "Is Smiley around?"

"You know Smiley?"

"We ran into each other a week or so ago."

"He doesn't work out of the office."

"Where's his office?"

"He doesn't really have one. He comes by now and again, but he keeps his own schedule. Hard to pin him down sometimes. I can get a message to him if you'd like."

"I really wanted to speak to the alderman."

She leaned forward and lowered her voice as if others might hear us. There were only the two of us in the lobby. Maybe she was worried the potted plants might be eavesdropping.

"I'm not supposed to tell you this," she said, "but the alderman is on his way to a meeting with the mayor at city hall. We have an office there also. All aldermen have an office in their ward and an office in city hall. No guarantees, but if you're lucky and fast, you might catch him down there." She winked.

I winked back, gave her a high-kilowatt smile, then turned around and walked through the door.

CITY HALL WAS A MASSIVE eleven-story Classical Revival–style limestone rectangle that sat on an entire city block downtown. I visited the building as infrequently as possible. There's an old saying: *Nothing good happens in city hall.* I agreed with that assessment. The aldermen's offices were scattered on different floors of the building and were noted simply by their room numbers. They were small, cramped, and really only in use when the city council was in session or the aldermen had business to conduct downtown. Most preferred their offices in their wards, which were much more spacious and far away from the never-ending political theater on North La Salle, the building's most popular entrance.

I made my way to room 300, office 1. The glass double doors were marked with a city logo and Pat Flynn's name stenciled in gold letters with his title: *CHAIRMAN, FINANCE COMMITTEE*. I opened the door and was met by a young woman with long blond hair, bright blue eyes, and a slender neck.

"Can I help you?" she said. She wore an expensive V-neck white cashmere sweater that people at country clubs liked to tie around their necks and flap about their backs. I looked down at her very neat desk. *EMMA RATNER*. A copy of *Netter Atlas of Human Anatomy* sat bookmarked next to her very white and very clean keyboard.

"Med student?" I said, pointing to the book.

She looked down, then back at me with a smile that probably had many boys and professors lying awake late at night.

"Oh God, no," she said. "I couldn't deal with all the blood. But I do enjoy studying and looking at the human body. Kind of my nerd fetish."

"Erudite," I said.

She smiled again. I was enjoying looking at her.

"Are you here to see the alderman?" she said.

"If he's available to be seen."

"Unfortunately, he's not here right now."

"Any chance you might know where he is?"

"In with the mayor."

"Important meeting."

She gave a slight roll of those beautiful big blue eyes.

"When will the meeting with His Honor be over?"

"Who knows?" Emma said. "Sometimes it's a few minutes. Sometimes it's an hour. I can't say for sure. Was the alderman expecting you?"

"Maybe."

"I don't understand."

"I didn't tell him I'd be coming, but he knew I'd be coming."

She narrowed her eyes.

"Inside baseball."

"The two of you are supposed to go to a Sox game?"

"No, just an expression."

"I'm confused," she said.

"I tend to have that effect on people."

"You like talking in circles."

"Only when I get tired of talking in squares."

She laughed. "You have a good sense of humor," she said.

"And you have a good everything," I said.

Her cheeks flushed a little.

"I'd have you speak to Garrett, but he's in with the alderman," she said.

"Who's Garrett?"

"Chief of staff."

"So they left you here alone to answer phones and talk to randoms like me."

"You're not random," she said. "What's your name?"

"Ashe."

"Nice name," she said. She opened her top desk drawer, pulled out a small pad and pen, and wrote my name on it. She cocked her head and examined what she had written.

"Everything okay?" I said.

"Yeah, just thinking," she said. "I've never seen this name before. It looks good on paper."

"And underneath the clothes."

"You're a bit of a flirt," she said.

"Keep that a secret between you and me. But I also have a nerd fetish I will share with you."

"What's that?"

Before I could answer, she suddenly stiffened, and that radiant smile I had been enjoying so much quickly disappeared from her face. She sat up in her chair and swept her hair behind her ears, then looked out the door. I turned to see what had gotten her attention. A small man with circular glasses; thin, white hair; and a ruddy complexion walked toward us, surrounded by several people who seemed busy just trying to keep up with him. He was talking and gesturing. They were nodding and scrambling. A young guy opened the door once they arrived and let Flynn enter first.

Flynn looked at me with a scowl, then at Emma and said, "What's he here for?" His three minions reflexively gathered around him to create a buffer.

"To clean your floors," I said before Emma could get a chance to answer. I heard her snicker softly.

"He wants to talk to you," Emma said.

Flynn sized me up, then turned and began walking away. "Write his name down and give him an appointment next week," he said, still on the move.

"The name is Ashe Cayne," I said.

He immediately stopped and turned back around. Some of the color drained from his face. "Follow me," he said.

I walked in his direction, and the others tagged along behind me.

"Alone," Flynn said firmly.

We walked into a small office at the end of the hall. It barely had enough room for the desk and two chairs that had been stuffed in there. Flynn took off the jacket of his double-breasted blue pin-striped suit and carefully hung it on a hanger and stand in a corner. He walked behind his enormous desk full of paper stacked neatly at various heights. He wore an old-school blue shirt with an English cutaway collar. He leaned forward and crossed his arms on his desk. The face of his gold Rolex watch matched the tiny green shamrocks embedded in his blue tie. His nails were professionally manicured, and his fingers had that waxy appearance that older people tend to get as they age.

"Let's cut through the bullshit," he said. "I know exactly who you are."

"Then you know why I'm here," I said.

"Haven't a single clue," he said. "Why don't you tell me?"

"I'm here about a man named Joaquin Escobar," I said.

Flynn shook his head and raised his hands. "Never heard of him," he said. "Why do you assume I know this person?"

"I'm not assuming anything," I said. "That's why I'm asking."

"Well, this will be a short meeting, because I don't know him. So there's nothing more I can say."

"He's an immigrant from Colombia," I said. "A wife and three kids back home. He came here looking for work and a better life for his family. Once he got himself established, they were going to join him. Now he's six feet underneath the ground in a small plot of land on a mountainside in Colombia that faces the sun most of the day. He was found in Lake Michigan last month."

"That's unfortunate," Flynn said. "These types of accidents happen far too often on the lakefront."

"It wasn't an accident. Someone stabbed him through the chest and into his heart. They used something like an ice pick. His death was slow and painful. Then they tossed his body in the lake to make it look like it was an accident."

"I assume CPD is looking into the matter."

"They are. They arrested a guy named Dario Vazquez. But he likes to be called Rio. He only lets his abuela call him Dario."

"Well, that's good. Despite all the negative attention our men and women in the department get, they do a lot of good work for the people in this city."

"Rio didn't kill Escobar," I said.

"I'm confused," Flynn said. "You just said the cops arrested him."

"You're an attorney who passed the bar," I said. "You're fully aware that just because someone is arrested, it doesn't mean they're actually guilty or the state attorney will be able to make the charge stick."

Flynn nodded. "You say this Rio is not the one who did it."

"That's what I said."

"What do you know that the cops don't know?"

"I'm not sure. The cops might know what I know but are still keeping the guy locked up in County."

"Are you implying the cops are purposely incarcerating a man they know to be innocent?"

"That's one way to put it."

"Does this man have representation?"

"He does. A guy named Everest Ford."

"Never heard of him. But I don't know every defense lawyer in this city. Where does Rio live?"

"In your ward."

"Then let me get my chief of staff in here to take down the information and see if there's something we can do about it."

"Do something about the victim or the accused?"

"I'm not sure what we can do for the victim. You said he's already dead and buried in Colombia."

"But his wife and three sons are still alive and hurting and looking for answers. Something needs to be done about that."

"I can have Garrett look into that also."

Flynn pushed back from his desk, preparing to stand. He was not so subtly indicating our meeting had come to an end.

"I asked you earlier if you knew Joaquin Escobar," I said.

"As I said before, I don't know him," Flynn said.

"What about Diego Santana?"

"Excuse me?"

"Maybe you know Diego Santana."

"Who is that?"

"Joaquin Escobar."

Flynn wrinkled his brow.

"Escobar used the alias 'Diego Santana.'"

"Why would he do that?"

"Because he needed to work and make money, and he needed a Social Security number to do that if he wanted to be paid on the books. The place where he was working didn't want to pay him off the books."

"So he procured a Social Security number under someone else's name."

"Under the name of Diego Santana, who's a cute three-year-old boy who lives with his single mother and eight-year-old brother in Pilsen."

"Unfortunately, that's all too common. These people are trying to find a way into the system, but the system has requirements and standards, and for many of them, they're too difficult to meet. So they try another method, even if it's illegal."

"Maybe the system needs to be modified."

"I've been championing that for years."

Which made sense given the ethnic makeup of his ward.

"You still haven't answered my question," I said. "Do you know a Diego Santana?"

"I meet so many people in the ward. I can't say for sure. I don't recall the name right off."

"Maybe you can get Smiley on the phone."

"What would Smiley have to do with this man?"

"He's the one who bought and sold the name and Social Security number to Joaquin Escobar."

"I know nothing about this," Flynn said. "But I will look into it."

"How's your place in Michigan?"

"I beg your pardon?"

"Don't you have a summer home in Michigan?"

"I do."

"I heard it's quite a house. Six or seven bedrooms. Equal number of bathrooms. That's a lot of house to sit empty nine months of the year."

"That's the definition of a summer home," Flynn said. "You use it in the summer, and summer is only three months long."

"You like going to the Whistle Stop?" I said.

"The one on Red Arrow Highway?"

"Unless there's another one I don't know of."

"It's a nice little place. The owners used to live in my ward. They live out there full-time now."

"I had a chance to talk to them."

"You did?"

"Not the owners, but someone who works there."

"They're nice people."

"Kinda strange, though," I said. "Diego Santana went there several times back in April. He liked their cinnamon buns and breakfast sandwiches."

"Both are very good there."

"That isn't the strange thing. The fact that you paid for his order six days in a row, and yet you claim you have no recollection of who he is? Well, that's the strange thing."

Flynn stood. "Thanks for stopping by, Mr. Cayne," he said. "I'll talk to my staff, and we'll see about our constituent who you say is locked up for a crime the police are aware he didn't commit."

He opened the door, and I nodded as I passed by him. The three minions flew into his office as if a big vacuum cleaner had sucked them in. Emma Ratner remained anchored to her desk.

"Chaucer and W. E. B. Du Bois," I said.

She looked at me quizzically.

"My nerd fetish."

She smiled. I smiled. Then I calmly walked out of the office of Alderman Pat Flynn.

29

One of my favorite places to think was in the North Rose Garden overlooking Buckingham Fountain. Thousands of roses had been planted in long rectangular plots, bordered by meticulously trimmed hedges and vine-entangled trellises. I typically took a seat on a bench away from all the commotion near one of the world's largest fountains that was days away from being turned off for the season.

Tourists gathered in front of the fountain, snapping photos to send to their loved ones back at home or to post on Instagram. Mothers and nannies watched as their toddlers ran circles around the fountain, then waited for them to collapse back in their strollers from exhaustion. The wind blew lightly, but not enough for a serious jacket.

My phone buzzed. It was a number I didn't recognize. I answered it.

"Alicia Gentry," she said.

"I didn't recognize the number," I said.

"I'm calling you from a different number that won't be in existence once we finish this call."

"Understood."

"Ed Cummings is a mid-career agent," she said. "He works out of DC and does a lot of special work with Justice. He has a clean reputation. Very cautious. Very by the book."

"Any connections to Chicago?"

"None that I was able to find."

"North Carolina is a long way from DC. Is that travel distance customary for agents when there are field offices already in the area?"

"Hard to answer that," Alicia said. "I don't know what he's working on or if he was working at all, but every case is different. Depending on the circumstances and who's involved, we pack our bags and travel."

"Does he work only with Justice?"

"Full-time."

"Partner?"

"Yes, but I can't give you that."

"Do you know what he was doing down there?"

"I didn't ask because I don't want to know. Asking too many questions can cause red flags."

"I owe you a drink."

"For all that work?"

"You drive a hard bargain. Drink, then a nice dinner at a place with linen tablecloths."

"That's a deal," she said. "And be careful out there. I don't know all the players and what they're playing at."

THAT NIGHT, STRYKER AND I were feeling restless. He kept going to the door, walking in small circles, then lying down and moaning. He wanted to go outside and play. The day had been unseasonably warm for mid-October, and the night, for reasons I didn't understand, was forecast to be even warmer. Everyone in the city couldn't stop talking about how lucky we had been so far this fall. The naysayers, purveyors, and those who luxuriate in endless negativity couldn't stop talking about how severe a winter we were going to have because fall had been so mild. I texted Karla Coe to see if she and Rex were up for a playdate in Grant Park. We agreed to meet in thirty minutes in the northern section just opposite the playground in Maggie Daley.

Stryker and Rex saw each other from a distance, then raced forward, head-on like two trains speeding on the same track. They collided in midair, rolled on the ground, barked and squealed, got up, and then chased each other in wide circles.

"If only I could have so much energy at this time of day," Karla said. "I barely have enough energy to heat up a frozen dinner."

"If you're exhausted fighting for the little guy," I said, "imagine how they must feel living that life every day."

She shook her head. "Feels like I haven't had eight hours of sleep in eight years. How's your case going?"

"Which one?"

"You have another one other than the murdered immigrant who purchased the Social Security number?"

"I have a missing South Side businessman who flew down to his cabin in North Carolina and hasn't been seen since."

"Do you know what happened to him?"

I filled her in on the details of the Blackwell case. She was a good listener, and maybe because she spent most of her days analyzing and strategizing, she also asked excellent, insightful questions. I found that talking to her made me think more clearly about the information I shared.

"Experience has taught me that when something seems too coincidental, more often than not, it's not coincidental," I said.

"I feel the same way," she said.

Rex and Stryker ran all the way to the middle of the park, several hundred yards away, chasing birds, then each other, then the occasional dog that happened to cross their paths.

"That FBI agent sounds interesting," Karla said.

"And mysterious," I said.

"I once dated an agent," she said. "Many years ago."

"How was that?"

"Didn't last very long. I had my first job working at a big firm. He had been a full agent for four or five years. He was so cute. I melted every time I saw him."

"What happened?"

"I never saw him."

"How could any guy with testosterone and a pair of working eyes not want to see you every second of every day?"

"I said the same thing," she said, laughing. "But it was the job. He was never around, and when he was, he was always preoccupied with work. It didn't matter where we were—out to dinner, in a movie theater, at the symphony—he was always on call. He'd answer his phone, step outside to have his conversation, and sometimes wouldn't return."

"What kind of work did he do?"

"I'm not exactly sure because he would never tell me anything he was doing, but I think he had something to do with WITSEC."

WITSEC was the federal witness protection program, which provided witnesses and their families with protection to ensure their health, safety, and security. It was run by the US Marshals Service and worked with witnesses involved in cases handled in federal courts or by federal investigative agencies. One of the ways WITSEC did this was by creating entirely new identities for people and providing them with documentation, housing, and assistance with basic living expenses.

"Why do you think he worked with WITSEC?" I said.

"One time I was at his apartment," she said, "and he got a call in the middle of the night. We'd been sleeping. He took his phone and stepped out of the bedroom, but he didn't close the door all the way. He said something about moving someone to a safe house. He also said he had their new passports. I put it together that it had something to do with witnesses in a case and he was protecting them."

"Did you ever ask him?"

"No, because it would've been a waste of time. He never would've told me what it was about. Everything was always a big secret."

"You ever run into him after you broke up?"

"Never. I moved here to Chicago after a couple years. He stayed in DC, so we lost touch."

When she mentioned DC, that got me thinking about Edward Cummings and Blackwell.

"Did he work only in DC?" I said.

"What do you mean? That's where his office was."

"Yes, but did he travel?"

"All the time. He was never home."

"Where did he go?"

"All over."

"Do you remember how he traveled?"

"You mean mode of transportation? He would fly if he was going out to California or somewhere far away. But if it was on the coast, he usually drove."

"Would he ever drive as far as North Carolina?"

"All the time. That was nothing for him. Six or seven hours depending on traffic."

"Did he drive alone?"

"Never. Always had a partner."

"When he went on these trips, how long would he be away?"

"Days, sometimes a couple weeks. It depended."

"Would he ever call you?"

"Occasionally. But I could never call him. He said because of where he was, he needed to call me."

That stop at Roscoe's was making a lot more sense. *When something seems too coincidental, more often than not, it's not coincidental.*

30

Mechanic called me as I was about to turn in for the night. Stryker had worn himself out with Rex. I had heated up some leftover chicken cacciatore. Stryker and I were both lying on the couch as the TV stared at us. I kept reminding myself every fifteen minutes to get up and get into bed, but I wouldn't move and then I would doze off, and the cycle would start all over.

"Update on Green Eyes," Mechanic said. "She's a busy girl."

"How busy?" I said.

"She spent half of her day shopping on Oak Street, the other half in a beauty salon, and now she's having a visit from the guy who never smiles."

"Flynn's guy Smiley?"

"Yup. Same guy we saw at McFetridge."

"Where are they?"

"He just went up to her apartment. With his own key."

"What do you mean, 'with his own key'?"

"He didn't ring the buzzer. He walked up the steps, took out a key, opened the door, and went inside."

"How long has he been there?"

"About twenty minutes, give or take."

"What the hell is going on?" I said.

"I have no idea, but it's a lot more than what meets the eye."

"Text me when Smiley leaves."

"Will do."

I stayed on the couch and drifted off, wondering how Smiley and Julieta knew each other and why he had a key to her new apartment. I also couldn't figure out how a girl with no job was doing things a girl who had a very good job or a very rich boyfriend would do.

Twenty minutes later, my phone buzzed me awake. Mechanic had sent a text.

Smiley just left. Still no smile.

It was almost midnight. I got up, brushed my teeth, and climbed into bed. Stryker was still asleep on the couch.

THE NEXT MORNING WHEN I walked into the living room, Stryker was in the same position I had left him in before going to bed. I finally got him up on his feet, and we headed out for a short run to Oak Street Beach and back. Yesterday's warmth had vanished, and the temperature was barely peeking above freezing. I planned on visiting Julieta early before she set about her day of spending and pampering. I walked into my building's garage, which was mostly enclosed, but part of it remained open to the outside, and the heat blowers had not been turned on yet. I opened up my phone and hit the app that started the car remotely. By the time I reached it, the steering wheel and seats would be warm and the engine would be ready. I tapped the button and within two seconds heard an explosion, as if ten sticks of dynamite had just been ignited. The garage shook, and car alarms on all levels started screeching and honking. A woman who was getting into her tiny sports car stumbled and fell to the ground. Harold, my doorman, came running into the garage, out of breath.

"What the hell happened?" he said.

"My car app just saved my life," I said. I lifted my phone to show him and noticed my hand trembling.

We ran over and helped the woman off the ground. She had hit her head on an adjacent car, and a small stream of blood slid down the side of her face. She had a dazed look in her eyes. I took off my jacket and pressed the lining softly against her head.

Within minutes, we heard the wail of sirens. I left the woman with Harold and walked up the ramp to the second floor, where I'd parked my car. The Defender, or what was left of it, was on fire. The windows had all been blown out, the hood was resting on top of another car thirty feet away, and the doors were hanging by their hinges. I stared at the charred driver's seat, which only had the frame and springs remaining, and shook my head. I'd been shot at before and almost stabbed several times, but this was the closest I had ever come to dying. I dialed Burke and told him what happened. He said he was on his way. I walked back to a distance I thought was safe and waited for the first responders to arrive.

"Today was your lucky day," Burke said.

We were standing along the perimeter as the firemen and bomb squad went about putting out the fire and collecting whatever forensic evidence they could find on the type of bomb that had been planted to kill me. Several other cars had been badly damaged: windows smashed, mirrors hanging by wires. Some vehicles were leaning on their sides yards away from where their owners had parked them last night.

"That's one way of describing it," I said.

"Makes me think all of your investigating has hit a nerve."

"Good investigations into bad acts tend to do that sooner or later."

"Who do you think did it?"

"Flynn and Smiley would be at the top of my list."

"But there could be others."

"Rio is in County. I'm trying to help him out. Wouldn't help his chances of rejoining society if I were lying over there in a million tiny pieces."

"What about that missing HVAC guy?"

"Possible. But I don't know where he is or who might be responsible for him being where he is, so I have no idea whose nerve I might've struck."

Several of the other building residents had come into the garage—some because they needed their cars to drive to work, others because word of the explosion had already spread. Seeing their lives inconvenienced and their property damaged angered me.

"Any cameras in this garage?" Burke said, scanning the perimeter.

"We had some, but they kept malfunctioning. They took them down to replace them with a new system, but the contractor realized he didn't have all the equipment ready for installation, so they've been waiting."

"Murphy's Law."

I thought about Carolina. She could've been part of the debris they were currently sweeping up had she spent the night and had we decided to go grab breakfast before she headed off to work. Stryker also could've been in smithereens if he'd had an appointment with the vet that morning. My mind kept running through all the potential for collateral damage because some asshole didn't want me to uncover something they did that was wrong.

"I heard you talked to Flynn yesterday," Burke said. "Was Smiley there?"

"Nope. Just the two principals behind a closed door," I said.

"Did he have anything useful to say?"

"You know how it goes. It's what they don't say that's usually the most useful."

"Maybe you should keep low for a while."

"Which is exactly what they want me to do."

"Go to Packer's place in Arizona and play some golf."

"I'm not going," I said. "I'm gonna finish my job."

"If it doesn't finish you first."

After talking to a couple detectives about the little I knew of the bomb and who rigged it to my engine, Burke drove me to my office, where suddenly I felt safe and hidden in the three small rooms that I occupied alone. Against my wishes, he insisted on parking an unmarked car across the street. I kept the lights off, took a seat by the window, and looked out across the park and into the lake. The gray water looked cold and cranky. The clouds had the foreboding appearance of a punishing rain. I turned, faced the board, and studied the photos of Escobar, Blackwell, and Flynn. Next to them, I had written the names of the second triangle—Rio, Julieta, and Carmen. How were these triangles connected? What had Escobar done that was so bad that someone had wanted to kill him?

My phone buzzed from an email notification. I opened it and saw the name Luke Crawford. I walked over to my desk, sat down behind my computer, and brought up the email. He said he had done the best he could with the footage, but it was taken at night, so there was only so much he could do. I clicked the video, waited for it to process, then sat back and watched the fifteen-second clip.

A white male who looked to be somewhere in his late twenties, early thirties, came into frame from a position lower than the camera. He was walking uphill. He was wearing gloves and a baseball cap. His clothes, a long-sleeve pullover and pants, were nondescript. He walked fully into frame, then turned to his left and walked out of frame. The clip ended. I played it several more times, this time in slow motion. First, I watched it while studying the environment, looking at the peripheral portions of the frame. I looked at the trees and brush to see if I noticed anything else—maybe another person or any kind of reflective surface that would indicate some type of object nearby. The next pass, I focused on him exclusively. There was one frame where I could get a decent look at his face. I couldn't see the level of detail I wanted, but someone with better software would be able to clean it up and enhance it. I marked the time stamp. The next frame that caught my attention was when he began to make the turn that took him out of frame. There was something about the way his shirt gapped and bulged on the right side of his body. Was it a gun, fat, or just an artifact? I marked down the time stamp.

I attached the video to an email, noted the time stamps, and sent it off to Rayshawn Jackson, a digital-and-video whiz who had helped me a couple years ago with the case of a prima donna local news anchor who'd been stalked. I then sent him a text and asked him to do his best to get back to me as soon as he had something.

My door opened, and I instinctively pulled back the top drawer that held my Walther PPQ 9mm caliber. Mechanic walked into the office carrying a brown bag with grease stains at the bottom.

He walked over to the window, set the bag on the table between the two chairs, took off his coat, and sat down. I joined him. He pulled out a large ham-and-cheese croissant and handed the bag to me. I dug my sandwich out. It was still warm.

"At least we now know how serious they are," he said. "A single gunshot in most places, chances of survival are damn good. A bomb, almost no chances."

"It's a big mess over there," I said. "My brain would've been a mural on one of those concrete walls."

"You think it was Smiley?"

"I do."

"We should hit him back fast."

"I had a feeling you'd say that."

"How you answer this kind of shit is important."

I took a bite of the croissant. The cheese was warm and soft, the bread flaky. It was the perfect breakfast sandwich. We sat there for several minutes, chewing, looking out the window, not saying anything.

"I think it's time I have a chat with Julieta," I said.

"Let's roll," Mechanic said.

We took finishing bites of our sandwiches, threw away the bag, then left the office. Mechanic had parked his Viper in the alley behind the building, which gave us less area to clear if the bombers were aware I was still upright. Everything looked fine, so we jumped in the car and headed over to Old Town. We were parked across the street from Julieta's building in less than fifteen minutes. Mechanic turned the car off so the exhaust coming from the rear pipes wouldn't be seen.

I didn't want to talk to Carolina right now because she would get upset and have a thousand questions about what happened. If I talked to her and didn't come clean about the bomb, she would be even more irate when I told her later, which was what I was planning to do in person this evening. So I texted her instead. I asked her to find the owner of Julieta's apartment. She wished me a good morning and sent a heart emoji and a lips emoji.

Mechanic and I sat there in the cold for about two hours before Julieta finally emerged. She wore a short-body leather jacket and matching boots that rose to the middle of her toned thighs. If nothing else, she was a gorgeous woman. She got into the back of a Prius, which we followed east through downtown, turning on Pearson and then heading toward Water Tower. The car stopped in front a restaurant called Wildberry Pancakes and Cafe, adjacent to the Ritz-Carlton. We pulled up across the street next to a small playground and park. We lost her after she entered the restaurant.

My phone vibrated with a text message. It was from Rayshawn.

I got the video. Finishing up something that's on deadline. Will get this for you in a couple hours if that's okay.

            No problem. I appreciate it.

We continued watching the restaurant. A steady flow of traffic moved between it and the Ritz. We also kept an eye out to see if anyone else might be watching her. We didn't see anything. Mechanic looked up the menu and commented on how many varieties of pancakes they had. He was mortified that someone would make a key lime pie pancake. He was a plain, no-frills eater. The less, the better.

Carolina texted me.

> 6 apartments total. All owned by LuckyShamrock Enterprises. Which is owned by Green Dragon Real Estate Holdings. Which is owned by Patrick Flynn.

> Good work. As always. Dinner on me tonight.

> I'm in the mood for sushi.

> I have the perfect spot. I'll bring the credit card; you bring your appetite and beautiful face.

Twenty minutes later, Julieta emerged from the restaurant alone. Instead of getting into a car, she walked toward Water Tower.

"Let's go," I said.

We got out of the Viper and casually walked across the street, scoping out all directions to make sure no one was about to do to us what we were doing to Julieta. We followed her into the lobby, but instead of taking the escalators that went up to the shops, she hung a right and walked to the bank of elevators that led to the suite of professional offices.

"You stay with her," I said to Mechanic. "She doesn't know what you look like. Text me when you get upstairs."

I hung back in the lobby as Mechanic walked over and waited with her, then got on the same elevator. I picked up my phone and called my father.

"This is a pleasant surprise," he said.

"Good morning to you too, Dad," I said. "Everything good?"

"Of course it is. Why wouldn't it be?"

I was not going to tell him about the bomb. There had been a time when my father hadn't perceived how serious a threat my work was, but last year, his town house was broken into because of a case I was working. My work made my seemingly invincible father very vulnerable to a criminal element that was no longer willing to keep it a fair fight. Not only had violent crime skyrocketed in the city, but the boundaries of what and who these lowlifes would hurt had been obliterated. Everything and everyone was fair game.

"Just checking to make sure you're okay," I said.

"I already had breakfast, and I'm about to leave the house to go play tennis. I have a doubles match this morning up north."

"How are you getting there?" I said.

"What do you mean? I'm driving there, of course."

"Where was your car last night?"

"My car?"

"Where did you park it last night?"

"Boy, is something wrong with you? Why are you asking me all these silly questions? What's going on?"

"Can't a son check in on his father to make sure everything is alright?"

"Any other son, yes, but you doing it is different. When was the last time you called to check in on me like this?"

"I don't know, and it doesn't matter. What matters is that I love you and I'm doing it now."

"Everything is fine. My car is fine. My health, fine. Hopefully my game will be fine, because this is a grudge match and I don't want to lose."

I didn't want to say or do anything else that would raise his suspicions, but after last year's close call, I didn't want to take any chances.

"Is your remote start working?" I said.

"I assume so," he said. "I haven't used it in a while. Why do you ask?"

"What year is your Mercedes?"

"It's only a year old, if that."

"I think I read somewhere about some type of electrical issues with the remote start. If your year and model are having problems with that, they're suggesting you bring the car in for service immediately."

"That's the problem with all this new technology," he said. "When it works, it's great; when it doesn't work, it's a big headache."

"Where are you now?"

"Upstairs in the second kitchen. I just finished eating."

His garage was built underneath his town house in what used to be a bomb shelter. It was encased by enough concrete that, should there be an explosion, you would barely hear a thump upstairs.

"Do you have your keys with you?"

"They're in my gym bag."

"Try the remote start."

"Why? I'm about to go downstairs. I can just turn on the car once I'm inside."

"I want to see if it works."

"You really are acting strange," he said.

"Don't always be so obstinate. I'm trying to help you troubleshoot. Start the car and let me know it works, and I'll leave you to your match."

"Give me a minute." He mumbled something. I could hear his steps on the hardwood floor. "Okay," he said. "To appease you and so I can get on with my day, I'm pushing the button." He paused. "There, it's pushed."

"Go down and see if it worked."

"You're really getting on my last nerve," he said.

"Indulge me."

I heard him going down the steps and opening the internal door to the garage. I didn't realize I was holding my breath until he came back on the phone and calmly said, "My car has started. Purring like a kitten. Now I'm getting on with my day."

He disconnected the line, and I exhaled slowly.

31

Mechanic called me almost as soon as my father hung up.

"I texted you, but you didn't respond," he said.

"I was on the phone with my father," I said.

"Is he okay?"

"He's fine. He thinks I'm crazy for making him start his car remotely while it was sitting downstairs in the garage. But he did, and there's wasn't an explosion, so all is good."

"Green Eyes is in with the dentist right now," he said.

"Where are you?"

"Walking around a small pharmacy down the hall."

"Is it quiet up there?"

"I've only seen two other people on the entire floor since I've been here. I don't know how these people are staying in business."

"Maybe they charge a lot of money. Margin game."

"What do you want me to do?"

"What floor are you on?"

"Nine."

"Keep browsing pharmaceuticals. I'm on my way up."

By the time I found the pharmacy and Mechanic, he was trying to appear seriously interested in foot orthotics. He was the only one in the store, and the young girl behind the counter was busy on her phone and not paying us any attention. He pointed to the office door Julieta had gone in.

"What's the plan?" he said.

"Ambush her when she starts walking to the elevators."

Mechanic nodded his approval.

Ten minutes later, the office door opened. We were in the digestive aid aisle, looking at various remedies for constipation. Julieta stepped out and headed in our direction. We quickly exited the store, and the store clerk never looked up from her phone. Gen Zers. We met Julieta halfway between the office and the elevator bank. She stopped when she recognized me, and smiled.

"Ashe," she said. "What are you doing here?"

"I was gonna ask you the same thing," I said.

"Routine teeth cleaning," she said. She smiled to offer proof. Her teeth were so white they looked fake.

"I'm overdue for a cleaning myself," I said. I turned to Mechanic and said, "What about you?"

He shrugged.

"You're not at the restaurant anymore," I said.

"No, I decided to try something different."

"A new job?"

"Not yet. Still looking. Trying to find the right fit."

"That's important," I said. "Being happy at work means you won't feel like you're working at all."

"I'll have to remember that," she said.

"Talk to Rio lately?"

"God, no," she said. "I don't want to see or talk to him again. Ever." She scrunched up her beautiful face for emphasis.

"I talked to him a few days ago," I said.

"You did?"

"I did."

"What did he say?"

"That the two of you had been in very close contact during the time you said there was no contact."

"When was that?"

"The night you called him from Carmen's phone, left her house, then went to see him."

"I don't remember that."

"That's strange. He remembers."

"You talked to Carmen?"

"I did. She remembers that night very clearly."

"I had so much going on back then, I wasn't even thinking clearly."

"That's not what you told the cops when they called you."

"How do you know what I told the cops?"

"Because I used to be one of them, and I still talk to them when necessary. Considering Rio is sitting in County for allegedly committing a murder I don't think he committed, I decided to talk to the cops."

"Are you on his side?"

"I didn't know there were sides in all this."

"Well, I told you what he did to me. I told you what he wanted to do to Joaquin. We are not on the same side."

"Then why did you go see him that night?"

"I was afraid of what he would do if I didn't go."

"Then why didn't you tell that to the cop when he asked you?"

"I need to go now," she said. "I'm late for an appointment."

She started walking away.

"How are you affording that nice, new apartment and all that shopping you've been doing?" I said. "That's a lot for someone who's still looking for that perfect job."

She stopped and turned around. "Have you been following me?" she said.

"Why does Liam Harrington have a key to your new apartment?"

"I'm not answering any more of your questions," she said. "And you should mind your own business if you know what's good for you."

One of the elevator doors opened as soon as she was about to press the button. She stepped in and turned around to face us. She had that blinding smile on her face as the doors closed. Conniving and deceitful for sure, but man, was she a heart crusher.

BY THE TIME I GOT back to my office, Rayshawn had sent me an email. I opened it up and downloaded the photos. Every time I went to him for help, it amazed me how incredibly talented he was at producing digital magic. He had isolated two photos and drastically improved the contrast, resolution, and sharpness to a point where they were much clearer than they had been on the video. The man's face was now identifiable, and the bulge on his right hip was definitely a gun.

I opened them up on my phone, then attached them to a text I sent Alicia Gentry with the message **Who is this man?**

I called Mrs. McCarley to find out more about the company's contracts and their business flow.

"Do you have a list of the projects you all have worked on in the past couple years?" I said.

"All the jobs?" she said.

"Just the big commercial jobs."

"General contracting and subcontracting work?"

"Both. Have you had a lot of big-city projects?"

"Yes, thank God," she said "Those big-ticket contracts stop us from losing our shirts on the small residential jobs. Can't make a lot of money servicing air-conditioning units and replacing furnace capacitors and igniters."

"How is the list organized?"

"Date, location, scope of work, and the fee."

"Can you email the list to me?"

"Sure. Give me about an hour to get everything together."

"Who goes out and gets these big jobs for the company?"

"Blackwell used to do it," she said.

"Why did he stop?"

"Because he didn't need to do it anymore. The jobs started coming to us."

"Are most of those jobsites in your ward?"

"Hardly any."

"Where are they?"

"Almost all of them are in the Fourteenth."

The ward of Alderman Pat Flynn.

I went back to the board. What was Julieta Romero up to? The more I talked to and about her, the more I began to realize that she was a more central figure to all this than I'd first thought. My mind shifted to our first meeting and how she had orchestrated everything so flawlessly, agreeing to meet only in the safety of Carmen's house. Was Carmen in on all of it, or was she just an opportunist who saw her chance and did the American thing and went for it, consequences be damned? I looked at Blackwell's side of the board. I had never thought of there being a connection between Julieta and his disappearance. That might've been my mistake from the beginning, treating the players and their actions and their narratives in different silos. Was there a way to make all of it fit together? Could Julieta be the glue that brought everything together? I didn't have enough right now to make that idea work, but I stared at her name and was confident she definitely wasn't the sweet, innocent victim of a love triangle that had soured. She knew things. She did things.

I called Burke.

"You still in one piece?" he said.

"Last time I checked," I said.

"I've been told the explosion was so bad, it's unlikely they will get much from it," he said.

"I'm not surprised."

"But they'll keep working on it, and they won't give up until they've exhausted all avenues. They work very similarly to the way you do."

"I know no other way. Which is why I'm calling about the girl Julieta Romero. The one who's afraid of Rio. So she claims."

"So you doubt."

I filled him in on her new apartment and fabulous lifestyle and Smiley letting himself into the building that Flynn owned. I also explained the love triangle between her, Rio, and Carmen. I then told Burke about my conversation with her at Water Tower and her warning to me about minding my own business.

"You think there's something sexual going on there?" Burke asked.

"Between her and Smiley or Flynn?"

"Yes."

"Jesus Christ, I hope not."

"You said she was beautiful."

"More than beautiful."

"Beautiful women like rich older men."

"That's true, but Flynn is more than older. He barely has a damn pulse. Money and power attract, but there's gotta be a line drawn somewhere."

"You think Flynn is bankrolling her?"

"That part seems fairly obvious, even to the untrained eye. The question is, What has she done to deserve it?"

"Other than be beautiful and all the things men like to physically do with beautiful?"

"Exactly."

"Sounds like she got a little tough during your conversation today."

"More than tough. She was cocky. People tend to get cocky for two main reasons: Either they're really confident, or they're pretending to be."

"Which do you think it is with her?"

"The former."

"Why?"

"I don't know, which is the reason for my call. I think knowing who she's been talking to and when she's been talking to them might help me figure out that answer."

"You want the phone logs ASAP."

"See, there's a reason they promoted you to commander."

"It might behoove you not to be a smart-ass when you're asking me for a favor, which I'm under no obligation to deliver."

"You never used words like 'behoove' before you started wearing that white commander shirt."

"I'll get the call logs," he said. "Expeditiously."

"It's nice having friends in high places."

"I wish I could say the same."

32

"I think you need to find a new apartment," Carolina said.

We were sitting in her town house in the West Loop, something we rarely did for reasons I didn't understand, because I liked her town house, and being in her space always made what we had feel more real and more meaningful.

"Who's to say they wouldn't find the address of this new place?" I said.

"There's no guarantee they wouldn't. But there's a guarantee that they know where you live now and where you park your car, and they'll likely come for you again since the bomb didn't do the job they were expecting it to do."

"I've been thinking about that too."

"Are you scared?"

"Angry."

"What if they come again?"

"Well, as of now, I don't have a car for them to blow up. I already put the Porsche away for the winter. I'll have to go rent something until my insurance sorts things out and tells me what they plan on doing."

"A real pain in the ass."

"Lucky that I still have an ass that can be pained."

"That's a positive attitude."

"'Attitude is a little thing that makes a big difference,'" I said in my best imitation of a British accent.

"It's been a while since you quoted Churchill."

"I need to channel his fighting spirit right now. I shall never surrender."

She leaned over and kissed me softly.

"I'm worried about you," she said.

"You shouldn't be," I said. "You should be worried about whoever did this. They crossed the line."

"But they have the advantage."

"How's that?"

"They know who you are and where you live and work."

"But I have Mechanic, and they don't."

"What's Mechanic saying about everything?"

"Very little. Per usual."

"How do you interpret that?"

"He's going to kill them."

"You think so?"

"If I don't get to them first."

"You really think the girl with the green eyes is behind all this?"

"I think she has a big part in what is going on. I don't know how big, but she touches everyone except Blackwell."

"I like it when you spend the night," Carolina said.

"More than you like it when I leave?"

She smiled and looked me directly in the eyes. "I can't believe I'm saying this, but I could get used to this."

"How about we study some more Greek philosophers, then?" I said before ducking under the covers.

THE NEXT MORNING, I MADE it to my office safely. No bombs. No guys with dark clothes and scowls. Burke still had an unmarked car parked outside my office. I waved to the cops as I entered my building. They didn't seem too excited. They barely gave me head nods in return. I caught the elevator up to my floor, organizing the day in my head. When I reached my office door, I noticed a small package in a gold envelope sitting outside it. I stopped and backed up down the hall, got back into the elevator, rode it down to the lobby, zipped up my coat, and walked out the front door.

I called Burke.

"There's a package in front of my door," I said.

"What kind of package?" he said.

"Unmarked gold bubble mailer, about eight by twelve."

"Where are you right now?"

"Outside the lobby."

"Is the unmarked car there?"

"Sitting across the street, soaking up the sun and taxpayers' money."

"Anybody else on your floor?"

"Only three other tenants. One guy is a travel agent. He's usually out of the country. The woman across from me doesn't get in until eleven. And there's a guy at the far end of the hall who I've only seen once and have no idea what business he's in. I never know if he's in there or not."

"Walk out of the building and go wait by the car across the street. I'm sending a squad over right away."

I did as he had instructed. Within ten minutes, an impressive assemblage of blue-and-whites, unmarkeds, and a bomb squad wagon came racing down Michigan. They jumped the divider to make a U-turn and pulled in front of my building. I waited outside while they carried in the robot, two dogs, and other heavy equipment to do their work. Burke showed up a few minutes later. He was still wearing short sleeves. Everyone else had on coats. His face was a seasonal red.

"Let's wait in the car," he said.

We got into his car, which thankfully had the heat on instead of the air that he normally ran. The warmth felt good on my ears and fingers.

"This is a problem," he said. "You're too unprotected."

"I have you," I said. "You're a commander."

"I can't run a detail around the clock."

"I wouldn't expect you to."

"How the hell are you gonna stay alive if you stay out in the open?"

"How am I going to do my work if I stay inside?"

"How are you going to do your work if you're dead?"

"That won't happen anytime soon."

"Don't be so cocky," he said. "The cemetery is full of tough guys who thought the same thing."

"I'm not tough," I said. "I'm an inveterate investigator."

He gave me a look, then turned his attention back toward the building.

"That kid Rio," he said. "I accessed his file."

"I thought you were worried about fingerprints."

"I was able to get around it."

"And?"

"The file is nearly empty."

"How's that possible? It's a homicide."

"I know. There was only one supplementary I could find, and that was the autopsy report from the ME's office."

"Either O'Halloran isn't working the case, or he's working it but keeping everything out of the system."

"Shadow file," Burke said.

"What the hell do they not want us to know?" I said.

"I don't know, but I think it goes all the way upstairs."

"To the superintendent's office?"

"Possibly. And take a wild guess about who's in tight with the supe."

"Flynn."

"As I told you before, don't underestimate him. He's a very powerful and dangerous little man."

Burke's radio crackled. "All clear," someone said.

We climbed out of the warm car and into the strong wind. Burke kept his coat in the back seat. The bomb squad was filing out with all their equipment as we entered the building. One of the guys was standing in the lobby with the opened envelope and balled-up paper in one hand and a small flash drive in the other.

"It's clean," he said before handing it to me and joining the others leaving the lobby.

Burke and I took the elevator up to my office. I got behind my desk and stuck the flash drive into the computer. I opened the drive on my desktop, and several images popped up on my screen. Blackwell stood with Deanna Turner outside a building at night. He was holding a Subway bag in his hand. The next image must've been taken just a couple seconds later, because now she held the same bag. Burke and I looked at each other but didn't say anything. The next image was the two of them at night again, but this time, I could see the reflection of water in the background. Their hands were outstretched toward each other, both grasping another Subway bag in a handoff. The last image was a large construction site. I couldn't tell where it was. There weren't any people in the photo, just heavy machinery and lots of cement and rebar. A few letters on the mixing truck were just visible: *G, L, H*. The last photo was of Turner, Blackwell, and Flynn dressed in formal attire. It looked like they were at a gala. The three of them were holding drinks and talking to each other. They looked happy.

The next image was a list. It had been titled "Fourteenth Ward Contractors." I counted eighty-six businesses. There was no other information about the companies other than their names. The only one I recognized was Blackwell's TNL Heating & Cooling. I clicked on the last image. It was a spreadsheet. PAT FLYNN, ATTORNEY-AT-LAW had been typed on the top line, and a column of business names had been arranged underneath it. There were twenty-two names. TNL Heating & Cooling was the only name I recognized on this list also.

"Who are the man and woman with Flynn?" Burke said.

"Deanna Turner, alderman of the Sixteenth Ward, and Hank Blackwell, the missing businessman," I said.

"Someone was watching them."

"That's the thing about this city. There's always someone watching."

"Potbelly makes a much better sandwich than Subway," Burke said.

"But nobody can digest grease better than a Chicago alderman."

"Did you know about their relationship?"

"I knew they had some kind of relationship, but I just didn't know the nature of it. I talked to her. She didn't want to talk. But I knew she called Blackwell just before midnight the night before he left for North Carolina."

"Flynn is really powerful."

"You keep saying that."

"That's because he has a body count. He's been around since the old Bailey was in office. This city runs through his veins."

"But just like the male lion who's been leader of the pride, all kings eventually die. Whether of natural causes or at the mercy of rivals and a waiting pack of hyenas, their reigns come to an end. Pat Flynn can fight to the end or lie down, but either way, he will be devoured just as he has devoured so many over the years."

"Many have tried and failed."

"I wasn't part of that many."

Burke stood and walked to the door. He turned and looked at me for a moment. The sun coming through the window caught his eye a certain way.

"Be smart," he said. "I like having you around."

He walked through the door, and never looked back.

I had a lot of thoughts racing through my mind. Who'd given

me this information? It had to be someone who knew I was hunting Flynn and working on Blackwell's missing case. They wanted me to see the connections between the three of them, something I hadn't thought of before until now. The businesses and the lists meant something. I needed to print them out and study them. I converted the lists from images to PDFs so I could read them easier. Just as I pushed the print button, my phone rang. It was Mrs. McCarley.

"I ran into a little problem," she said.

"What kind of problem?" I said.

"I have a master list that I keep of our projects. I update it every month, print it out, and keep it in my top desk drawer. Well, it's not there anymore."

"You lost it?"

"I couldn't have lost it. I never take it away from this desk. No reason to. It's either on the desk or in the drawer. That's it."

"What do you think happened to it?"

"I think Blackwell must've taken it."

"Why do you think that?"

"Because not only is the list gone, but his passport is also."

"His passport?"

"He went to renew his passport just as spring started. He said it was about to expire. Instead of having the new one mailed to his house, he had it mailed here to the office. I got it and kept it here in the drawer for him. It was sitting here since June. I also kept that list of our big commercial projects in here. Both of them are now gone."

"Can't you just print the list again from your computer?" I said.

"That's a problem too," she said. "That file is gone."

"What do you mean, it's gone?" I said. "Files don't just disappear on their own. Did you forget what name you saved it under?"

"I remember the name. But the file is just gone. It's not here."

"Does anyone else use your computer?"

"No. Nobody else but me would need to use it."

"When was the last time you saw the passport and that printout?"

"I really don't remember."

"Did you see it in September?"

"Yes. I print the list out on the first Monday of every month. I saw it the first week of September but maybe not this month..."

"Can you re-create the list?"

"I can, but my Lord, that's gonna take a long time. I'm at my wit's end keeping everything going without Blackwell. I've already told his daughter we're gonna have to do something soon. I can't do all this by myself."

"Do the best you can," I said. "Whenever you get a chance to work on it, just let me know."

33

My phone's buzzing and dancing across my desk was what woke me up. I was uncertain how long I had been asleep, but it was definitely the better part of an hour. I got up and answered the caller, whose number I didn't recognize.

"Are you alone?" Alicia Gentry said.

"If you don't count the four walls of my office," I said. "Really only three. The fourth is all windows."

"Where did you get those photos from?" she asked.

"Hunting camera in the woods of Greenville, North Carolina."

"The guy's name is Tanner Osborne."

"Anything else you're willing to share?"

"He works out of DC. Very well-respected. Keeps a low profile. Does a lot of covert missions. Works a lot with Justice."

That made me think about my last conversation with Karla Coe. She'd mentioned that her ex-boyfriend had been an agent working out of DC. She suspected he'd been dealing with witness protection. At that moment, several of the pieces of the puzzle started falling in place for me.

"Osborne have a partner?" I said.

"Not like how detectives or patrolmen have consistent partners day in, day out. We work together and sometimes often with another agent, but it all depends on the situation. What's the operation? Are there going to be interviews? Is it just stationary surveillance? Are the conditions potentially dangerous?"

"Does Osborne work a lot with E. Cummings?"

"He does."

"Is there any way to know where Osborne is right now?"

"Yes."

"Do you know?"

"I do."

"Will you tell me?"

"I won't."

"Let me ask you a yes-or-no question."

"I can't stop you from asking."

"Is Osborne currently in the country?"

"No."

I called Burke.

"Any way you can go back to your FBI connection?" I said.

"Depends on what I need," he said.

"Information."

"What kind of information?"

"Safe houses."

"You want to know about FBI safe houses?"

"Specifically, where they're located in the Southeast."

"What are you up to?"

"Trying to piece all of this together."

"Care to share what these pieces are?"

"When I know about those safe houses, I think I'll have my answer."

"This is a really big ask," he said.

"I wouldn't put you in this position if it wasn't important."

"I'll make the call."

I started to feel like a plan was taking shape, thanks to the assist from whoever had dropped off that flash drive. I dialed Flynn's office in city hall. Emma picked up.

"How's that anatomy-nerd-fetish thing going?" I said.

"Already knocked out ten pages today," she said. "How's Chaucer?"

"About halfway through 'The Miller's Tale.' I like 'The Knight's Tale' better. Lots of love and ethical dilemmas."

"Sounds interesting," she said. "I'll read it and let you know what I think."

"Then we can compare notes," I said. "Speaking of notes, I have a note I need to get to the alderman. Is that possible?"

"Actually, I was told that if you called, you were to speak to Garrett, his chief of staff."

"Is he there?"

"One moment."

The line went silent. About half a minute later, a deep voice vibrated through the phone.

"Garrett Peterson," he said. "How can I help you?"

"I have a question about some companies," I said.

"What kind of companies?"

"I don't know. I was hoping you could help me figure that out."

"You want me to help you figure out what some companies do? Why can't you just google them and look at their websites?"

"Since the alderman knows them, I figured it might be faster just to ask you."

"I'll take the names down and see what information we have that I can share with you."

I gave him all twenty-two names, which he took down diligently. When I was done, he said, "Is there anything else I can help you with?"

"Yes, tell your boss that if his memory has gotten any better, I'm still interested in Diego Santana."

"I'll be sure to let him know," Garrett said.

THAT NIGHT, MECHANIC AND I had a ferocious workout at Hammer's. We took a long steam, then a cool shower and got dressed.

"How about we grab a bite?" I said.

"And maybe catch the football game," Mechanic said.

"I have the perfect spot in the South Loop. Two cars or one?"

"Let's take two. I've gotta do something a little later."

I parked in the back alley. He parked on Madison, so he walked toward the front door.

I pushed open the back door while at the same time searching my bag for the keys to the rental. As soon as I stepped foot outside, I heard the loud pop of a gunshot, then the sound of metal crunching behind me. I instinctively fell to the ground and rolled behind Hammer's old Cadillac. Another shot rang out. It split the brick behind me. I couldn't tell which directions the fire was coming from, but I knew there had to be at least two shooters based on where the bullets hit. I had dropped my bag when I'd hit the ground. My phone and gun were in it. I looked above me to see if I could spot anyone. I didn't see anything, but with the way I was crouched, my vantage point was limited. I lifted my head to get a look through the windows. As soon as I did, several shots rang out, and both rear passenger windows exploded. I heard footsteps echoing down the alley. Someone was coming for me. I was stuck. I needed to get to my bag, and in a hurry.

I saw an old broom handle lying on the ground against the building. I army crawled toward it and pulled it in. I took off my coat, wrapped it around the end of the handle, then crawled back to my position against the car. My bag was about six feet away between the car and the back door, but it was out in the open. I crawled toward the bag, still holding on to the broom handle with my coat hooked to the end of it.

There were more footsteps in the alley. They were getting closer. Hammer was going to lose it when he came out and saw the condition of his car. I had one chance to get this right. I closed my eyes, slowed my breathing, and then, all in one motion, lifted the broom handle so my coat was visible through the openings of the shattered windows. The gunfire was immediate. I threw the broom handle up in the air as a decoy, then at the same time, lunged for the bag. I grabbed it just before they spotted me and sent several rounds in my direction. The bullets ricocheted off the ground and struck the front tires of the Cadillac, causing it to collapse to the ground.

My phone had been shattered, but I had my gun.

The footsteps started again. I could tell they were coming from the east end of the alley. I got on my stomach and looked under the rear of the car. I didn't see anything. There were two lights in the alley, one adjacent to the back door, the other about ten yards down, above the dumpster. I aimed for the closest light and took it out with one shot. The area around the Cadillac was now in total darkness. I crawled closer to the rear of the car, aimed at the light above the dumpster, and took that out with one shot also. The alley was now enveloped in complete blackness.

I knew one shooter was somewhere on the other side of the Cadillac, but I didn't know how far away. I got on my knees, aimed my gun through the busted-out windows, and fired two shots. Several shots came back in return; one round pierced the roof of the car. He was above me. I got to my feet, still in a squatting position, and fired at the top of the building across the alley. I waited to see the return muzzle flash, which came quickly, then fired several times in that direction. I heard a groan and, a couple seconds later, a loud thud against the ground. I looked under the Cadillac. He was lying there, motionless.

I had to figure out the location of the other shooter. I reached into the busted window of the car and opened the door. The interior light came on, followed by a stream of gunshots that smashed the front windshield. One of the shooters was to the west, opposite from where the footsteps had approached. More gunshots rang out as I ducked back under the car. There was a small area on the other side of the door where the building jutted out slightly into the alley. If I could make it over there, I would have enough cover to find the other shooter. I crawled to the front of the car, then bolted. More gunshots exploded but I made it to the other side without getting hit. I heard footsteps coming from the west. I slowed my breathing, waited a few seconds, then crouched down, pivoted into the open alley, and fired west, hoping to draw return gunfire so I could expose the shooter's position. I received fire from both directions. I went back to fire again, but after one shot, the gun clicked empty. The sound echoed down the alley. They knew they had me. I backed up against the wall and calculated my chances of running at one of them and hoping they'd miss in the darkness. My chances were extremely low with two shooters. I had to do something, because just standing there was a guarantee things would end badly. I made up my mind to try to run across the alley to a spot that would give me greater cover. Just as I jumped into the open, the sound of a cannon exploded. I knew it well. Mechanic and his .500 Magnum. A body hit the ground, and a gun clanged onto the asphalt. Mechanic stepped out from the eastern part of the alley. The faint interior light of the Cadillac illuminated his silhouette. He lifted his finger to his mouth, then pointed above me. I nodded. There was just the slightest amount of movement on the roof. Mechanic waited for it to stop, then took one more shot. Everything fell silent.

34

"Three bodies and a shot-up Cadillac," Burke said. "Might've been more helpful if you'd kept one of them alive."

We stood just outside the police tape. The alley was awash with flashing lights and an army of officers working the scene. The wagon had come to collect the bodies. Mechanic was being interviewed by detectives, which meant it wouldn't be a long interview. And Hammer was leaning against the building, staring at his bullet-riddled car.

"It was either them or us," I said. "We wanted to leave this alley on our own feet more than they did."

"Any idea who they are?"

"I think I saw two of them over at Chilango on Taylor Street last week when Carolina and I were there getting empanadas. Something didn't look right about them. But they didn't do anything."

"We'll ID them and go from there."

"Probably won't do much good. Low-level thugs for hire. You won't be able to trace back who sent them. I'm sure they erased the trail."

"You check in on your father and Carolina?"

"I did. They are both upset but fine."

We watched as they bagged the biggest of the three, loaded him onto a stretcher, and pushed him into the back of the wagon. That was the one I had hit on the roof.

"I talked to my guy about those safe houses," Burke said. "The locations don't stay the same, but the number of houses in a region does. They maintain two in North Carolina, two in South Carolina, three in Georgia, five in Florida, and one in Puerto Rico."

"Makes sense," I said.

"What does?"

"Blackwell didn't disappear. He's alive and well. The FBI had it planned the entire time. They used him flying to his cabin in North Carolina as a cover. The exchange had been set up at Roscoe's. They arrived before he got there and waited. They pulled into the back because they knew there weren't any cameras there. Blackwell got out of his car and into the back of their vehicle. Osborne got out of their sedan and got into Blackwell's car. Osborne drove to Blackwell's cabin with gloves on. Went and made it look like Blackwell had arrived. But Osborne made two critical mistakes."

"Which were?" Burke said.

"First, he chose the wrong room. He loaded Blackwell's personal items into the biggest of the three rooms. Makes sense. You expect someone to sleep in the biggest room of their own place. But Blackwell never slept in that room. His daughter said he always used the back room because it had the best view of the lake. Second, Osborne didn't hang the flags. Blackwell's neighbor, a guy named Crawford, insisted that Blackwell never came to the cabin without flying the Chicago flag and the navy veteran flag at the end of the driveway. He said it was the first thing Blackwell did when he got to his property. Sort of like the monarchy in Great Britain. They fly the sovereign flag over the royal palace where the monarch is currently in residence. There were no flags. Osborne didn't know to fly them."

"You think they took him to a safe house?" Burke said.

"Yup, and I think that safe house is in Puerto Rico or a foreign destination."

"Why?"

"Because just before he left Chicago, he swiped his passport from his office manager's desk drawer. That passport had been sitting in there for months, and he hadn't bothered it. Inside that drawer was a printout of a list of his company's big contracts. The passport and that list were in the same drawer. Both went missing at the same time, as did the file on the computer that created the list. The feds could've done a better job."

"Pretty sloppy work for professionals," Burke said.

"Just because they work for a three-letter agency doesn't necessarily mean they do it any better than we do."

"Don't tell them that. A bunch of pompous assholes. Not all, but enough of 'em are. Makes my blood boil."

"That's not the hardest thing in the world to do."

"Be pompous?"

"Make your blood boil."

"You do a damn good job of it too."

"But at least I give you an excuse to get out from behind that big, fancy desk and do some real police work again."

"Nothing is ever simple with you," he said.

"Not true," I said. "Upper seventies, blue skies, negligible wind, and an open golf course. Not very complicated at all."

"You know this is the second time these guys have tried to kill you?"

"And it's the second time they've failed."

"They might've failed, but whoever is behind them is still out there. And they want you covered up in the back of that wagon just like these assholes."

"I want to own a private island with eighteen holes in my backyard. You can want anything; doesn't mean it's gonna happen."

"Maybe you should sit down with the suits and let them know what you've got," Burke said. "Especially since you think they have Blackwell. And you think there's something on that list that's important."

"I'm not ready yet," I said. "You know how they work. They'll try to bigfoot me and shut everything down. I can't let that happen yet."

"Why not? You probably have enough to get this closed."

"Probably. But I still don't have all the answers Escobar's family deserves."

IVAN RAMIREZ WAS BACK IN Chicago after his trip down to Colombia to bury his uncle. He had another two weeks before he went down to Florida to begin the winter golf season. Caddies up north were just like the millions of birds who migrated south when harsh weather made nesting difficult and food availability scarce. Before Ivan left for the winter, I took him out to my course so I could get in one more lesson. We were sitting at the halfway house, eating lunch after finishing the ninth hole, when my phone rang. I reluctantly answered it.

"Ashe, this is Carmen," she said. "I need to speak with you."

"Can it wait?" I said. "I'm about to take a big bite into my hot dog, then finish the last nine holes of my round."

"This is very important," she said. "I'm scared."

"You're kinda early," I said. "Halloween is still days away."

"You think it's funny when people are seriously scared to death and need help?"

I was about to say something about how funny I thought it was that she was playing protector to a girlfriend whose boyfriend she had been cheating with. This wasn't the time. The foursome playing behind us had just reached the ninth green.

"What has you so scared?"

"A man came by my house today and threatened my father."

"Threatened him how?"

"To have him reported to ICE and kicked out of the country because he doesn't have his papers."

"How long has your father lived here?"

"Since he was sixteen."

"What about your mother?"

"She came a year after he did."

"Is she a US citizen?"

"Yes, she took her test last year."

"Then your father should be fine. He's married to a US citizen."

"The man said that it didn't matter. They were married before my mother became a citizen, and my father has to be married to her for three years after she became a citizen in order for him to apply to become a permanent resident."

I was the furthest thing from an immigration expert, and after just the few minutes we had been talking, my head was already spinning, my hot dog was getting cold, and the first guy of the foursome had sunk a twelve-foot putt, which meant they would be getting off the green and pushing us faster than I had expected.

"I'm lost," I said. "I don't know much about immigration rules or law. They're ridiculously complicated, always changing, and always politically motivated. You need to talk to an immigration attorney."

"We can't afford someone like that," she said. "They cost thousands of dollars. Up-front. We don't have that kind of money."

"They have organizations that do this work pro bono. You can find hotline numbers on the internet."

"I understand. I've tried. But we don't have time. The man said he had the connections to get my father picked up tomorrow."

"Do your parents know this man?"

"They've never seen him before."

"Why do you think he's picking on them?"

"Because they want me to keep my mouth shut."

"About what?"

"Rio. They told my parents if I keep my mouth shut about being with Rio that night, they will leave us alone."

It all made sense now. They were cleaning up the trail.

"Did the guy tell your parents his name?"

"No."

Ivan nudged me. The foursome was finishing up on the ninth

green and walking over to the halfway house. We needed to tee off on the tenth hole.

"Where are you now?" I said.

"I just got home."

"I'm going to send you a photo right now. Show it to your parents and ask them if this was the guy who came to the house."

"Okay. Will you help us?"

"I'm a private detective, not an immigration specialist. There's only so much I can do, but let me know if this is the guy, and we'll take it from there."

I texted her a photo of Smiley and threw my hot dog in the trash, because eating a cold hot dog was as gratifying as eating an old leather shoe. I walked up to the tenth tee. Ivan reminded me of my stance and swing path, then I unleashed a low stinger down the middle of the fairway that landed and rolled a good fifty yards more before coming to a stop. There was a lot of frustration that came with the game of golf, but one beautiful shot like this made the memory of all the previous mistakes just disappear.

Carmen sent a return text. **That's the man. Please help us.**

35

I typically liked to go home and take a nap after a good round of golf, but there was something about the cases that kept bothering me, and I couldn't put my finger on it. I felt like I needed to see everything again and follow the timeline. I wanted to organize my thoughts better and create more of a narrative from the information I currently had. I entered the lobby cautiously and had my hand on my hip as I waited for the elevator door to open. How much longer was I going to be looking around corners? I pulled the blinds up completely so the sun lit up the office. I took my shoes off, pulled my chair out, and faced the board. I looked at the images I had printed from the flash drive and posted next to Escobar and Blackwell. I had also printed out the lists. I pulled them from my desk and began studying them.

My intercom buzzed. I opened my phone to see who was at my door. Everest Ford stood there in a leather trench coat, a felt fedora tipped to the side, and a tie knotted big enough to choke an elephant. I unlocked the door from my phone to let him in.

He entered my office in a huff.

"They killed him!" he shouted.

"Killed who?" I said.

"Dario! I mean Rio."

"Calm down," I said. "Join me over here and take a seat."

I got up and walked to the window. He took off his coat, folded it over his right arm, then took off his hat before sitting down. It was a very nice hat.

"Okay, tell me what happened," I said.

"I got a call from County. The woman asked me if I was Rio's attorney on record. I told her that I was. She then said she regretted to inform me that he had died. I asked her what did she mean, he had died? She said that's all the information she had, and her job was just to make notifications. She wouldn't answer any of my questions."

"When was the last time you spoke to him?" I said.

"Yesterday."

"In person or on the phone?"

"In person."

"Did he seem alright?"

"Alright? He was perfect. He wanted to know what was taking us so long to get him out. I told him we were working as fast as we could. I had already put in for another bond hearing with the court. That was scheduled for early November. I figured you might find some exculpatory evidence by then that could earn his release."

"He didn't say he was having any problems back in lockup?"

"He didn't complain about anything other than how bad the food was and how he wanted to go home."

"You didn't notice anything physically wrong with him?"

"Nothing."

"Has his family been notified?"

"I assume so. I've never met his family."

Cook County Jail had thousands of prisoners, but the number of deaths attributed to homicides was surprisingly low given how many gang members and violent criminals were housed in the pre-trial facility.

"Have you gone to County to see what you could find out?"

"I was on my way."

"I'll go with you," I said. "I know a guy who's a divisional supervisor. I'll see what he can find out for us."

COOK COUNTY JAIL WAS A formidable maze of grim brick buildings surrounded by barbed wire fences in the South Lawndale neighborhood. It was comprised of ten divisions that were run like their own prisons. Flip Gatson had been in the class ahead of me at the police academy. He was six foot five and at least two hundred fifty pounds and not an ounce of fat to be squeezed. He looked like it had taken three people to stuff him into his uniform. He met us in the parking lot, then walked us into one of the buildings, down several corridors, and into a small, unmarked office that had no windows. Four chairs sat around a small aluminum table.

"Luxurious," I said, trying to find a more comfortable position in the metal chair but failing to do so.

"Everything here is on a shoestring," Flip said.

"Taxpayers' dollars hard at work in County."

"Or hard*ly* at work," he said.

I properly introduced Flip and Ford. They shook hands.

"Anything you can tell us?" I said. "He called and couldn't get any more information other than Rio had died."

"Twenty-four-year-old healthy men don't simply die," Ford said. "And concealing what really happened won't do any good, because the autopsy will reveal the truth."

Flip raised his hands to profess his innocence. Even his hands looked like they had muscles.

"He wasn't in my division," Flip said. "I run D-10. For some reason he was put in minimum security over in D-2."

"Why can't I find out what happened?" Ford said.

"I don't think it's a matter of you finding out what happened. It's a matter of how long it will take for someone to tell you."

"I've called almost every number I could find and haven't been able to get anyone on the phone who will tell me anything."

"Chain of communication is really big around here, especially when it's about something like this."

"But I'm not just someone off the street," Ford said. "I was the kid's attorney."

I looked at Flip, who looked at Ford, then shot his eyes quickly in my direction.

"Ford, I have an idea," I said. "How about Flip and I have a private talk for a few minutes?"

Ford was readying his protest when Flip said, "I think that's a good idea. Let Ashe and me catch up for a few minutes."

Ford finally got the message, stood, and said, "I'll wait outside."

Once he was outside, I said to Flip, "How bad is it?"

"Real bad. They snapped the kid's neck while he was sleeping. He never really had a chance."

"They know who did it?"

"They always know who does shit like this."

"But no one's talking."

"Not to anyone in uniform."

"When did it happen?"

"Early in the morning."

"Cellmate?"

"He didn't have one."

"How did someone get inside his cell?"

Flip shook his head. "All kinds of ways these guys get into places they're not supposed to be."

"Cameras?"

"Man, this is inside. Cameras all over the fuckin' place. That doesn't mean a damn thing here. They might as well be decorations."

"Who did it?"

"I don't know exactly. But what I do know is that this kind of thing almost never happens in D-2. Those guys are in for small stuff and usually don't stay in too long. They aren't the real bad guys. Those guys are in my division and D-9."

"Was it a hit?"

"Had to be."

"Will they investigate it?"

"I know the supervisor over there. He's a hard-ass. He's also real political. The official statement to the family and that little man standing outside is that there will be a full investigation."

I understood.

"Where's the body?" I said.

"Being processed, then sent over to the morgue. Cases like this automatically go to the ME."

"The kid was a knucklehead," I said, "but he definitely didn't deserve this."

"Unfortunately, those who don't deserve it are usually the ones who end up getting it."

After we left County, I shook hands with Ford and assured him that even though Rio was gone, I still wouldn't stop until his name was cleared and those who had put him away unjustly answered for it. Ford got into the back of a rideshare, and I walked down the block to the Cook County public defender's office, which occupied its own floor in a tall concrete-and-glass building sandwiched between the jail and the criminal court building.

Karla Coe met me in the lobby and whisked me through security and then upstairs into their newly redesigned suite of offices. We walked into a small, bright conference room with new, inexpensive office furniture. The paint still smelled fresh.

"What are you doing in my neck of the woods?" she said as we sat down. The chairs were a lot more comfortable than the one I had sat in a few minutes ago in the jail.

"Still trying to put these pieces together in my cases," I said.

"Have you made any progress since we last spoke?"

"With these investigations, sometimes it's one step forward, two steps back."

"But why are you way over here at County?"

"One of my clients is—or was—here."

"Was?"

"He was killed last night."

"Are you serious?"

"I joke about a lot of things. Death is not one of them."

"Was he one of ours?"

"No, he had a private defense attorney. Guy named Everest Ford."

"Never heard of him."

"Seems capable enough, but wasn't having any luck getting the kid bail."

"What was the charge?"

"First-degree murder."

"Would've come to us if he hadn't been able to pay for an attorney."

"You ever have one of your clients killed while inside?"

"Beat up real badly, but never killed. There are too many bodies in that jail. Longer you're in there, the more likely something bad is going to happen."

"Kid was only twenty-four. And he didn't kill anybody. He was set up."

"Why did he hire you?"

"To find who it was who set him up."

"Do you know who it was?"

"I think I have a good idea."

"But it's too late to save the boy's life."

"Very true. I feel like I let him down. But it's not too late to make them pay for what they did."

"These are the kinds of stories that make me come to work every day," she said. "I know everyone over there isn't an angel, but they are not as bad as the system would have you believe."

"Speaking of the system, I want to ask your opinion about lawyer incomes."

"That's a pretty big topic."

"Specifically, Alderman Pat Flynn's income."

She smiled. "I don't know him personally, but I know of him."

"He runs a law office out of a two-floor storefront on the West

Side. He has a multimillion-dollar house in Southwest Michigan and supposedly makes millions of dollars as an attorney. He's not a partner in some big firm downtown. How is he making that kind of money in an office that's next to a Mexican bakery and looks like it could be selling used tires out the back door?"

"Flynn is very powerful," Karla said.

"Everyone keeps telling me that."

"Because it's true."

"But he's that damn good of a lawyer to make the kind of money he's bringing in every year?"

She laughed. "Flynn isn't making all that money from his legal skills. He makes it from being an alderman with a lot of power. He's been the chairman of the city council's finance committee for years. It's the most powerful committee in city hall."

"I get all that. But it's the *how* I'm wondering about. He can't just cook the books and steal city money without people seeing and knowing what he's doing."

"You're wrong, actually. He can do both. People know what he's doing, but no one steps in to stop him."

"Not even Bailey?"

"Not even Bailey."

"Do you know how he does it?"

"Does what?"

"Pads his pockets."

"I've heard rumors like everybody else, but I can't confirm anything."

"What have you heard?"

"If you want to do business in Pat Flynn's ward, then you need to take some of your business to Pat Flynn."

36

I didn't want Delroy Thomas to see the evidence board in my office, so I met him at the front door and sat down with him in the waiting area that I never used. It had two comfortable chairs, a potted plant my former-boxer-turned-florist friend had given me, and a recently purchased print of Basquiat's *Boy and Dog in a Johnnypump*.

Delroy took off his fur-lined trench coat, carefully folded it over the back of his chair, and sat down. His burgundy alligator shoes matched the Windsor-knotted tie and tufted pocket square sprouting from the left breast pocket of his wide-pin-striped suit. He wore several gold rings, and his French cuffs were secured by a pair of bejeweled links that sparkled when he moved his hands.

"I wanted to ask you about Pat Flynn's work a little more," I said.

"You still digging around?"

"I am, and I'm finding a little bit here and there, but I need to understand what it all means."

"Flynn ain't too hard to understand. Money, greed, and power. Everything that man does involves at least one of those things."

"How has he stayed in power for so long?"

"Half the people fear him; the other half owe him."

"How is he making all this money?"

"All kinds of ways."

"Explain."

"Let's start with the finance committee," Delroy said. "Most people don't understand how important and lucrative it is to be the chair of an aldermanic committee. Any committee. It could be the transportation committee, special events, aviation, contracting oversight and equity—it doesn't matter. If you're a committee chair, then you have special powers and allowances that other aldermen and regular committee members don't have."

"Can you be more specific?" I said.

"I can, but you got any water in this place?" Delroy said. "My throat is dry as church dust."

I went to the office, fetched him a bottle of water, then returned to the waiting area. He took a long swallow, cleared his throat, then began.

"Each committee has a chair and a budget set aside for the committee to do its work. Over six million dollars gets divided up every year among the committees, but it's not divided equally. The amount each committee gets depends on tradition and how much clout the chair has. Take Flynn, for example. He's been there for over thirty years. His committee's budget is bigger than everyone else's, even though they do a lot less work than some of the other committees and they meet less often. No one's watching, and no one's telling."

"How much does each alderman get annually?" I said.

"You mean their salary?" he said, taking another swallow of water.

"I know the aldermen get just over a hundred and forty thousand in salary, but what about to run their office?"

"It's probably gone up since I left, but when I was there, we got a hundred and ninety thousand to pay our staff and a hundred and twenty thousand to pay for other office expenses. But see, this is why being a committee chair is important. When you become a chair, depending on which committee you sit on, you now get a lot more money to spend. You're supposed to spend that money on staffing the committee, but what the aldermen do is take the committee staff and have them do work that's not committee-related but for the alderman's main office. So in effect, they can increase their staff at no cost to them because they're using the committee money allocation to hire more people who will also do their work."

"How much does Flynn get?" I said.

Delroy chuckled. "Let me ask you something. The average committee chair gets a budget of anywhere between a hundred and fifty thousand to two hundred and fifty thousand. So given that context, what do you think Flynn gets?"

"I have no idea. Double? Triple?"

Delroy sat back and laughed. "Man, forget about not being in the ballpark," he said. "You ain't even in the right state. That man oversees a budget of 2.3 million dollars."

"Jesus Christ! Over two million dollars."

"That's what they could count on the books. The real number is closer to 3.4 million. Check this out. Most committees might have a staff of three or five at the most working for them. Flynn, over the course of the year, has—catch this—between sixty and seventy-five."

"Unfuckinbelievable."

"Believe it. And that's how he gets paid. He hires friends, children of friends, friends of political allies, relatives of business owners who bring business to his firm. One hand washes the other. Old-school. Everybody on the council finds a way to create an angle. If you're an alderman and ain't doing that, you're a damn fool."

"Hold on for a sec," I said.

I went to my office, picked up the lists I had printed out from the flash drive, and brought them back to Delroy.

"What's this?" he said.

"Someone gave them to me," I said.

He studied them carefully, then smiled.

"What's so amusing?" I said.

"This is what I just told you."

"You understand what they mean?"

"Damn right," he said. "Someone is trying to show you all the businesses that got city contracts in Flynn's ward and how many of those businesses hired his law office to do their legal work."

That was just the way Chicago worked and why it topped almost every list that talked about city corruption. It wasn't just that the people who worked in the system were corrupt; the system itself was built in a way that begged for corrupt shenanigans, then turned a blind eye when it happened. Nothing was simple or easy in Chicago's political jungle, where life was a daily war for survival, demanding that parents eat their young and that the weakest be sacrificed to the predators to protect the rest of the pride.

"Getting business from people you give city contracts to at the very least sounds unethical," I said. "Is it legal?"

"I'm not a lawyer or nothing, but it doesn't sound legal to me. Right or wrong, he's been pulling that shit for years and getting away with it."

"Maybe not much longer," I said, smiling.

"Be careful, brutha. That little Irishman is a vindictive muthafucka."

DELROY LEFT, AND I WALKED into my office and took a seat in front of my board. I ran my eyes over everything I had posted. There was a lot of work to do within a relatively short period of time. I understood more of the connections among the players, how things had gone down, and the timeline. But despite all that I had learned over the last weeks, I was still left with the two questions I had when Ivan had walked into my office: Who killed Joaquin Escobar and why?

My phone rang as I was pondering those two questions. It was a North Carolina number. I answered and was greeted by Sheriff Simpson's singsong voice.

"It's been a little while," he said. "Thought I would check in with you to see how things are going."

"Good to know you guys are still kicking down there," I said.

"And punching," he said, laughing softly. "I got something that might be of interest to you."

"You and Hank Blackwell are sitting in your office, having a cold one and talking about old times."

"I wish. That would be one helluva ending. No, what I have is information."

"I'm listening."

"There's a small airfield strip about an hour and a half south of us in Duplin County. It's called Eagles Nest. It's privately owned, but it's for public use. Fella by the name of Bo Daniels owns it, and his daddy owned it before him. Well, we were sitting here, bouncing off ideas of where Hank might've gone if he were still alive and able to move on his own power. We checked buses, trains, and the airport. But what we didn't check was the private airfield in Duplin. One of my deputies went down there a couple days ago just to see if they might've seen something, and they did."

"They saw Blackwell?" I said.

"Well, making a positive identification is still a problem," Simpson said. "Right now, we have a confirmed sighting of three individuals leaving on a private plane on September 15 at 1:33 p.m. Two of them were Caucasian males, and one was African American. The man who was working the airstrip at the time didn't get a good enough look at them to confirm that Blackwell was one of the three men. But my deputy showed him Hank's photograph, and he said it was possible Blackwell might've been in the group. He said the man was very fit and wore sunglasses and a baseball cap. They were only on the ground for about fifteen minutes. They got on the plane, locked up, and went on their way."

"Did he notice anything else that was different or caught his attention?"

"He said that when they got out of the car, both Caucasian males had suitcases, but the African American did not."

"What happened to the car they were driving?"

"Someone came later that day and picked it up."

"Did he get a make and model?"

"Gray Ford sedan with DC tags."

"Did he get their names on the manifest?"

"That's the tricky part of the story," Simpson said. "When he went to collect the paperwork, no names or destination were disclosed."

"How's that possible?" I said. "Even private planes have to enter the names of the pilots and passengers and intended destinations."

"Yes, private planes do, but not if they belong to the United States government."

"Which branch?"

"FBI."

"Did you call them to confirm?"

Simpson laughed softly. "This ain't the first investigation I've worked, Ashe," he said. "I called them myself. No response."

"Meaning no one would answer the phone?"

"Oh, no, they answered the phone alright, but they wouldn't give me any information about that plane or the people on it. Every conversation my deputies and I had led to a dead end. No one knew anything. They took my name and number and promised to get back to me. It's been three days, and nobody's called. And I don't think they're gonna call. Whatever the three of them were up to, the FBI's holding that information real tight."

"How about the FAA?" I said. "They had to file a flight plan."

"We checked them also. We gave them the time and location. They don't have any record of a flight plan being filed."

I wasn't surprised. There were ways around filing a plan, especially if the flight was part of an operation that needed to be kept confidential. Government agencies did confidential pretty well.

37

It had been a while since Holly Blackwell and I had spoken. I sent her a text message asking that she call me when she was home alone and didn't have any distractions. The call came in just after seven o'clock, when Stryker and I were walking into the apartment.

"My husband is out at a business dinner," she said. "He won't be home for a couple hours."

"How have you been doing?" I said.

"Tired," she said. "Unless you're in this situation, the average person doesn't understand how exhausting not knowing and hoping can be. It just wears you down. I have tiny moments when I get distracted by things like doing something at work or buying groceries or listening to a song, but those moments don't last long. Once they end, the thoughts and feelings always come rushing back."

"It's important not to give up," I said. "I couldn't keep doing my job if I gave up because the odds weren't looking good."

"I haven't given up. But I just want the waiting to end one way or another."

"That's why I'm calling you," I said. "I wanted to wait for the right time to tell you something, but in cases like this, I don't know if there's any such thing as the right time."

I spoke for another few seconds before I realized the line had disconnected. I called her back.

"One of us dropped out," I said when she answered.

"I hung up," she said. I could tell she was crying.

"I think your father is alive," I said.

"What?"

"I don't have the proof I'd like to have, but I have enough evidence that indicates your father is still alive."

Her sobs transitioned into a happy cry. I gave her space. I heard soft whispers thanking God.

"I can't believe I'm hearing these words," she finally said. "Ashe, are you certain about this?"

"That's why I was saying I didn't know if there's a right time to tell you," I said. "I am as certain as I can be without having laid eyes on him myself."

"But you're confident he's not dead?"

"Very. I have a general idea of where he probably is, but I haven't been able to figure out why exactly he's there."

"Where is he?"

"Puerto Rico."

"Puerto Rico? You think my father is vacationing in Puerto Rico?"

"I don't think he's vacationing," I said. "I think your father had been transported to a safe house under the supervision of the FBI."

"What? Safe house? FBI?"

I explained to her all the information I had, specifically the footage from the gas station and the footage Crawford had sent me. I told her about the phone call from Cummings when Blackwell arrived in North Carolina and the government charter that left that same afternoon from the airstrip south of Greenville. She was skeptical at first, but then she understood my reasoning for believing her father's disappearance had been staged and the FBI had taken him.

"I hear all that you're saying," she said, "but I know my father better than anyone. If he were alive and okay, he would've called me. He would never leave me guessing and hurting like this."

"I don't think it's your father's choice."

"Why? What do you think's going on?"

"I don't know if they've taken him into custody or they're protecting him. In either situation, they probably don't want him communicating with anyone until whatever it is they're doing with him has been worked out."

"But what could my father have done to be targeted by the FBI? They only come after you if you've done something really bad."

"I don't know what he did," I said, "but my gut is that he knows things that some powerful people don't want him to know, and the FBI is afraid something might happen to him because he knows this information."

"What information do you think he knows?"

"That's what I'm still trying to figure out."

"It sounds like you know who these people are who don't want him to know this information," she said.

"I do, but I won't tell you."

"Why?"

"Because the less you know, the safer you'll be. Maybe I shouldn't have even told you all this, but I know you're down there, worried and not getting any answers. I wanted you to have some comfort knowing that he's alive."

"Well, I'm glad you told me," she said. "This is the news I've been praying to hear. I felt it in my heart all along that he wasn't dead."

"I also wanted to tell you this when you were alone," I said. "For the time being, not even your husband can know that your father is alive."

"You think these people would do something to us?"

"If they think you know what your father knows."

"I don't know what to say or even how to feel," she said. "I'm so happy and grateful my father is alive and you're telling me nothing bad has happened to him. But now I'm afraid that something bad might still happen. If there are people out there who want to hurt him, he's still in jeopardy."

"The feds are pretty good at what they do," I said. "They need your father alive. They are gonna do all they can to make sure that happens."

She started crying again.

"I'm sorry," she said. "All of this is just too much for me right now. My emotions are everywhere. I don't know what to think or what to do."

"I know it's easier said than done, but you're gonna have to pretend like you don't know your father is alive," I said. "Whatever you've been doing the last couple weeks, keep doing it."

"How long do you think they will keep him in Puerto Rico?"

"I have no idea."

"How long do you think it will take for them to tell me he's alive?"

"I have no idea."

"So I'm supposed to go on with my life, pretending like nothing has happened and I don't know anything?"

"For the safety of your father and yourself, yes."

"What about you? Does this mean you're done with everything?"

"Just the opposite. I'm not done until I've finished what I started."

I SAT OUTSIDE OF JULIETA'S building, patiently waiting for her to come home. I had tried her buzzer, but there hadn't been an answer. Darkness had started to settle on the busy streets of Old Town as the millennial crowd began filing home from their busy days at their downtown firms. Parents arrived outside of their apartment buildings in rideshares, none too soon for the exhausted nannies desperate for relief.

After a couple hours of watching the front of her building, I caught her walking down the street. She carried an expensive tote bag with a bunch of shiny gold buckles and zippers. I got out of my car and hurried across the street to her building. She was startled when I stepped in front of her.

"No shopping today?" I said.

"I don't shop that much," she said, "and it's none of your business how I spend my time."

"Just figured you'd be out on the job hunt," I said.

"Is there anything else you want to say to me? Because I'm tired, and I'd like to go into my apartment and be left alone."

"Rio is dead."

The shock on her face was immediate and genuine.

"What did you just say?"

"Rio Vazquez is gone. Permanently."

"How? When?"

"He was killed in County yesterday. Someone decided to snap his neck while he was sleeping."

Tears welled in her emerald eyes, then started slowly leaking from the corners. She was the only person I had ever seen who looked more beautiful while crying.

"I don't understand any of this," she said.

"Which part? That he was killed? Or that maybe he died because you lied to the police about sleeping with him that night?"

"Who would want to kill Rio?"

"That's the question I wanted to ask you."

"How would I know?"

"I think you know a lot that you haven't been honest about. For starters, why are you living in an apartment owned by the alderman of the Fourteenth Ward?"

"Alderman? My apartment is owned by Liam."

"No, Liam works for the alderman who owns this apartment. Have you ever heard of Pat Flynn?"

"No. I don't follow politics."

"Small old guy who's worth a lot of money and has a lot of power. He doesn't just own your apartment; he owns the entire building."

"I thought Liam owned the apartment. That's what he told me."

"What else did he tell you?"

"I can't say."

"You won't or can't?"

"They're the same thing."

"Are you scared?"

She looked at me for a moment.

"No," she said. But I could see the fear in her eyes.

"I can help you," I said. "These are very dangerous men. I don't know what they've been telling you, but you're not safe, especially since Rio is now dead."

"I have nothing to do with him being dead."

"Au contraire," I said. "And I think you know that. And I think you're doing some quick calculations right now about which way you should go and whose side you should be on. You're confused."

She nibbled on her lower lip. The tears had slowed, but they were still coming. Her eyes sparkled under the streetlights. An old woman walking her dog looked at us momentarily, then pressed on. I kept scanning the area. After the bomb and the events of the other night, I wasn't comfortable standing out in the open like this.

"I don't believe Rio is dead," she said.

"You want me to take you to the morgue so you can see him on the table?" I said. "He's dead, and these guys you have an arrangement with, whatever it is, likely had something to do with it."

She considered my words. An ambulance passed on nearby Wells Street, siren blaring like the world was coming to an end. She waited for the ruckus to quiet down before saying, "What do you mean when you say you can help me?"

"I think you're vulnerable and in way over your head. These men are heartless killers. The minute they deem you useless or a liability, they will have no problem doing to you what they did to Rio. I can try to stop them."

"Just you? By yourself?"

"I have friends. One of them is very violent. It's always good to have him on your team. Not good if you're on the other side."

"They never told me he was going to get killed," she said.

"What did they tell you?"

"He'd be taught a lesson, and then he would leave me alone forever."

"Rio and I had already struck that deal. You didn't need to go and freelance on your own. Now you see how they teach lessons."

She looked down at the sidewalk. "I need to go and think about this," she said. "This is all too much right now."

"If I were you, I wouldn't spend the night here," I said. "You're vulnerable out in the open, just like we are right now standing here."

She looked up at the building contemplatively.

"A few days ago, someone blew up my car," I said. "Had it not been cold that day and had I not turned my car on remotely, I would've been splattered all over the concrete and the other cars in my garage. After that, three guys came for me after I finished working out at the gym. Luckily, I had my gun in my bag and that friend with me who I told you likes violence. You don't have time to go up there and think through things over tea and biscuits. You need to make a decision right now, right here."

Her head fell to her chest. She started crying, hard. I reached out and brought her to me. She rested her head on my shoulder. We stood like that for several seconds. I kept scanning to make sure no one was watching or coming. She separated from me and wiped the tears with the back of her hand.

"Do you have somewhere you can spend a couple nights where they won't know how to find you?" I said.

She nodded.

"Go upstairs, pack a bag, and I'll wait out here for you. I'll make sure you get to wherever you need to go safely."

38

After I dropped Julieta off, I went back to my office. Something she had said was bothering me, but I couldn't figure out what it was. I checked to make sure my front door was locked before unlocking it with my key and walking into the office. Someone had pushed a large, thin envelope just underneath the door. It was much too thin to contain an explosive device, so I picked it up and brought it to my desk. I opened it up and pulled out the stapled phone logs of Julieta Romero. Burke had come through right on time.

I went through my process of analyzing and charting the numbers. The logs went back three months. Over the next couple hours, I compared some of the numbers in her log to numbers I already recognized or had highlighted in Joaquin's logs. I recognized Carmen, Joaquin, and Smiley. There was another number that bothered me. She never called that number; rather, it was always an incoming call, and it only called in at night. Those calls never lasted more than fifteen or twenty seconds. I dialed the number. No one answered. I disconnected the line and went back to the logs.

My phone rang. It was Burke.

"You alright?" he said.

"I'm fine. In my office, looking over the logs you dropped off," I said.

"Are you in there alone?"

"Yes. Why?"

"Patrol spotted a suspicious car parked half a block away. Black Ford. A man and a woman. They arrived about an hour ago. They haven't moved."

"They run the tag?"

"Patrol can't see it from their vantage point. I told them to sit tight a little longer. You're inside. The Ford isn't moving. I don't want to make an approach if it isn't necessary."

"I'll be here about another hour before I call it quits."

"Call me before you leave. They'll keep an eye on the Ford."

I hung up and went back to the logs. Julieta didn't make as many calls as I'd expected she would, especially for a young, attractive girl. She must have done a lot of texting. I kept asking myself, *What do Flynn and Smiley want with her? They need her for something, but what? Are they connected to Rio in any way outside of Julieta?*

My phone rang. It was the number I had dialed a few minutes ago.

"Who is this?" a man's voice said.

I felt like I had heard it before, but I couldn't place it.

"I was going to ask the same question," I said.

He paused.

"You called me," he said.

"Do you know Julieta Romero?" I said.

"Who is this?"

"Ashe Cayne."

"Are you serious? This is Detective O'Halloran."

What was Julieta doing talking to O'Halloran?

"Is this your private cell?" I asked.

"It is," he said. "How did you get it?"

"Julieta."

He paused. He was thinking.

"She just gave you this number out of the blue?"

I wanted to ask him questions, but I wanted to do it in person.

I didn't want to just hear his answers. I also wanted to see how he responded.

"We haven't talked since your interview with Rio," I said, "who's now suspiciously dead. Let's connect. There are some things I've found out that might interest you."

"Let's meet tomorrow," he said, "after my shift. Call me in the morning, and we'll set a time and place."

I called Julieta. She said she was fine. I told her to call me if she heard from Smiley or O'Halloran. She wanted to make sure they couldn't physically get to her. I instructed her to stay put for a few days and avoid leaving the house or telling anyone, including Carmen, where she was staying.

Burke called back.

"They're gone," he said. "They just pulled off."

"They get a tag?"

"Partial. They're running it now."

I put the call logs back in order, then sat them on my desk.

"I just got off the phone with O'Halloran," I said. "Something is up. He was talking to Julieta Romero before and after Escobar was killed."

"What's his connection to the girl?"

"I don't know yet. I knew he'd called her to corroborate Rio's alibi, but I didn't know O'Halloran had called her several times before Escobar had been killed."

"How did he know her before he even got the Escobar case?"

"That's what I want to know."

"And why didn't he come clean that he had spoken to her before?"

"Something else I'd like to know."

"Did you ask the girl about this?"

"Not yet. She's scared. She definitely knows something, but she doesn't know if she should tell me yet."

"Where is she?"

"I had her move out of her apartment. She was a sitting duck over there."

"Two people behind this are already in the ground. But what is *this*?"

"That's what I'm trying to find out."

"They're still working on those three guys you and Mechanic shot up," he said. "They've got two of them identified. One lived in Hoboken; the other lived in Newark."

"They imported muscle all the way from New Jersey?"

"Seems that way. Third guy didn't have an ID on him, and they haven't gotten any hits on his fingerprints."

"Maybe they were extras from *The Sopranos*."

"Sopranos?"

"*The Sopranos*. Gandolfini. HBO. Wiseguy TV show based in Jersey. Don't you have a TV in your house?"

"I do, but the missus is always watching that Home and Garden TV channel. Everything is renovate this, renovate that. I know more about fabric swatches than any man who carries a gun should know."

"Don't say that too loudly," I said. "You might lose your tough-guy card."

O'HALLORAN AND I HAD AGREED to meet at Ferro's on Thirty-First Street, just blocks away from Rate Field on the South Side. The business had been in the same family's hands, serving beef, burgers, subs, hot dogs, and their famous Italian ice, since 1986. We were seated inside a small glass-enclosed area. I had a basket of fries and rib tips in front of me while O'Halloran was working his way through a beef brisket sandwich.

"What happened to that kid was wrong," I said. "He never should've been locked up."

"We had DNA, a verbal threat, and motivation," O'Halloran said. "And an alleged witness who would not corroborate his alibi."

"You forget that I once sat where you now sit," I said.

"What does that mean?"

"I know the kind of politics that go on behind the scenes."

O'Halloran took a healthy bite of his sandwich then wiped the corners of his mouth.

"At the very least, the kid should've been out on bond," I said.

"That wasn't my call. You know that."

"And you can sit here, look me in the eyes, and say you really believe he was the one who killed Escobar?"

"I didn't have any other suspects," O'Halloran said.

"Did you look?"

"I can't just make up suspects. If there's no one else to investigate, maybe that's because no one else needs to be investigated."

"Or maybe there's no one else to investigate because you can get the guy you wanted for it the entire time."

"What's your angle, Cayne?" O'Halloran said.

"I have a problem when powerful people take advantage of others who have less. And I hate bullies. They're nothing more than cowards preying on those they consider weak."

"Escobar is dead. There's nothing you can do now that will bring him back."

"And now Rio is dead, a guy someone set up to take the fall for Escobar."

"How can you explain the DNA?"

"I can't."

"Neither could Rio."

"Where are you getting your orders from?" I said.

"Orders?" O'Halloran said.

"C'mon, man. It's you and me here. You don't have to feed me the departmental bullshit. You know what I'm talking about. Just shoot straight."

O'Halloran looked at me for a long moment as he considered my words. He then nodded his head and said, "We're talking cop-to-cop."

I nodded.

"I'm the low man on the totem pole," he said. "You've been there before. You know how it works. I don't make these decisions. Word comes down from upstairs, I ask questions, and they give the answers they want to give me. It is what it is."

"You just leave it at that?"

He shrugged.

"How do you go to sleep at night knowing what you know?"

"Listen, man, I like what I do. I care about what I do. But at the end of the day, this is a job. I can't fight city hall."

"Does this go all the way up to Bailey?"

"Just a figure of speech. I don't know how far it goes up."

"So you're okay with just going along for the ride?"

"Sometimes that's part of the job. You know that. I don't want to be out looking for a new gig mid-career. I plan on retiring from the department. Voluntarily."

"Trust me, I'm not trying to disrupt your retirement plan," I said. "I just want anything you can give me so I can figure out what's really going on. Your name will never come up. I give you my word."

"I've read and heard enough about you to know you're a really smart guy. From what you've already said and the questions you've asked, it sounds like you have a bead on what's been happening."

"Was it your decision to make the arrest?"

"It was on paper."

"Did the orders go all the way back to headquarters?"

"Most orders like this do."

"You know who's involved?"

"I'm not in that loop."

"Someone had to give you the direct orders. Who did that?"

"My sergeant, but I know he was given orders from someone above him. I don't know who that person was. I didn't ask."

"I've seen the call logs. You talked to Julieta Romero several times before and after Escobar was killed."

"Is that a question, or are you just making a statement?"

"Both."

"I talk to witnesses all the time."

"She wasn't a witness before Escobar was killed and Rio was identified as a possible suspect."

"What's your point?"

"You know my point. You're not going to answer the question."

"I've answered enough questions. Like I said, you're a smart guy. You have enough to put some things together."

O'Halloran drained the last of his soda, got up, and walked away.

39

Early the next morning, I had Mechanic park outside Julieta's new, undisclosed location, then I jumped into the Mustang I had rented and headed southeast on the expressway toward Indiana. The air was cold and thick, and even the roads looked like they were preparing for the punishing winter ahead. I turned the radio to the classical station, climbed to a comfortable speed, then worked my way through the vast, empty farmland and into rural southern Michigan as it curved around the other side of the lake.

It had been a while since I had been in this area, the playground of Chicago's wealthy. Just a little over an hour's drive from the urban grit of Chicago, but it was as if you were hundreds of miles away in Maine or Vermont or the small beach towns along Cape Cod. Streetlights were rare. Crime was nonexistent. The trees were thirty and forty feet high, decades old, and still strong from all the fresh, unpolluted air and the warming sun.

Penny, of course, had a palatial estate of many acres sitting on a bluff overlooking the water. She had invited me to play her golf course there many years ago. In just a matter of minutes, I found myself turning off Red Arrow Highway onto a narrow road straddled by rows of impressive houses on both sides. However, those on the west side of the road, closer to the water, stood taller and more majestic than their still-respectable brethren across the street. I approached a wide-open lawn surrounded by a white pastoral post and rail fence. The gigantic colonial house sat far back from the road, at the end of a gray pebbled driveway that curved its way through the manicured lawn and dropped off visitors in a circular area in front of an audacious gabled portico.

I was about to turn into the driveway when I noticed a man riding a lawn mower at the end of the property closer to the road. I stuck my arm out and waved at him. He drove in my direction, pulled up beside me, and turned off the mower. He wore a wide-brimmed straw hat that shielded his deeply tanned, leathery skin. He was thin, but his hands were abnormally large for his frame and heavily calloused.

"A lot of grass to cut," I said, getting out of the car. Shaking his hand felt like rubbing sandpaper.

"Lucky we're near the end," he said. "Probably one more cut after this, and the cold weather will do the rest."

"Nice property," I said. "You take care of all this by yourself?"

"Only after the main season is over," he said. "This is way too much for one person. There's a whole team during the spring and summer."

I looked at the house and the attached garage. I didn't see any cars or activity.

"Anyone home?" I said.

"No, they won't be back for a couple weeks. You need something?"

"Actually, I wasn't looking for them. I was looking for a guy named Diego. Thought you might know him."

"No one by that name works here," the man said. "You sure you got the right address?"

"This is the Flynn property, right?"

"It is."

"I don't think he's a full-time employee or anything," I said. "I think he came to do some work back in April."

The man squeezed his chin in thought. I took out my phone, brought up the photo I had of Escobar, and showed it to him.

"Santana!" he said. "Of course. Yes, he came back in April. Good man. He hasn't been back in a while. I promised him I'd eventually make my way over to Chicago to see the city a little."

I didn't have the heart to tell him that he would never see Santana again.

"What kind of work did he do here?" I said.

"He had a big job, him and his boss. They installed three new furnaces and three air-condenser units. They did it start to finish in just a week."

"His boss?"

"Yup, the man who owned the company. Black guy. Really fit. He was a good man too. He was a navy vet. Had some really good stories."

"You sure Santana did the work with the owner?" I said.

"A hundred percent. Just the two of them. They worked first thing in the morning to late afternoon."

I pulled up a photo of Blackwell and showed it to him.

"That's him," the man said. "The guy was rock-solid."

"I know some of these big places usually have a property manager or someone who works in the house who organizes everything. Is there someone who does that here?"

"Nope. Mr. Flynn does it all himself. The missus helps out here and there, but he's in charge. Everyone reports to him."

"Was he here when Santana and his boss did the installation?"

The man nodded. "Oh, yeah. That was an important project. They wanted to have everything ready for the summer. He came out here and spent several nights making sure it went alright."

I had all I needed.

"When I catch up with Santana, I'll let him know I met you," I said. "What's your name?"

"Bruce Sheffield," he said, "but everyone calls me Shef."

We shook hands, and I got back into my car. I took one last look at Flynn's summer manse and wondered what his constituents back on the West Side who survived on WIC cards would think about their alderman, who liked to call himself a "man of the people."

Once I had pulled away from the property, I dialed Mrs. McCarley's number. She sounded tired when she answered. The stress of running the office alone was definitely getting to her.

"I need to ask you some specific questions," I said. "Your answers are extremely important, so I need you to be sure."

"This sounds serious," she said.

"It is."

"Okay, I'm ready."

"Did Blackwell work at any of his jobsites?"

"What do you mean, 'work'?"

"Did he still do the labor, like installation, servicing, helping the guys with any of the work out in the field?"

"Never. He stopped that about eight or nine years ago."

"You sure?"

"Positive. He hurt his back lifting something from one of the trucks, and he swore that day that he had done enough lifting and pulling. He moved into full managerial work. Visiting customers to write estimates or stopping by if the guys came across a problem they couldn't fix and needed his opinion. But he didn't do any more service calls or site work."

"Maybe he did small jobs occasionally for a friend or family member? Something quick that wasn't too intense?"

"No. He would have one of the guys do it. He might've stopped by to make sure everything was going alright, but as far as him getting his hands dirty? Absolutely not."

"I need you to pull up the calendar from April," I said.

"I know it's been a while, but I'm almost done pulling together that list that disappeared from the desk and my computer."

"I might not need that anymore," I said.

"Well, if you don't need it, let me know, because I could be spending my time on something else. Lord knows I don't have a second to waste around here."

"I will. Do you have April up yet?"

"Yes."

"Look at the week of April 7. What jobs are you seeing for that week?"

"We had eleven residential calls, and everything else was taken up by work over at the Obama Presidential Library."

"Where were the residential calls?"

"Hold on, I need to get into another screen."

I continued driving south on Red Arrow Highway. I drove toward Whistle Stop Grocery. Two cars were parked out front. One was a white MINI. The other was a black Ford with tinted windows. I had seen it before. I slowed down and turned into the lot. The taillights had white flashers inside them. The tag was Illinois. I committed the number to memory and quickly pulled out of the lot.

"I have the screen opened up."

"Were any of those jobs in Michigan?"

"Michigan? We don't do work in Michigan."

"Ever?"

"Not since I've been here."

"So all the addresses you're seeing are in Illinois?"

"And one in Hammond, Indiana."

"I need you to look at the bank account. Can you sign in online?"

"Give me a sec."

I looked out my rearview mirror to see if the black Ford had pulled out of the parking lot. It was still there. In fifty more feet, I'd be too far to see the store or the car.

"I'm in the account," Mrs. McCarley said.

"I need you to look up the April statement and check the payments you received that month."

"There are a lot of them," she said.

"Get a pen and write down these names. Pat Flynn. LuckyShamrock Enterprises. Green Dragon Real Estate Holdings."

"These names don't ring a bell. Well, Alderman Flynn I've obviously heard of, but the other names I've never seen before. But let me check."

"Have you ever done work for Flynn?"

"Never."

"Maybe work for his office on Fifty-First Street?"

"Never."

I got on the expressway heading toward Chicago. The black Ford wasn't behind me. I texted Burke the tag number.

"I'm not seeing any of these names on the checks received," Mrs. McCarley said, "or on any of the transfers. A lot of customers aren't even writing checks anymore. They pay through Zelle."

"I need you to look through May's statement and check for those names."

"Let me check."

Meanwhile, Burke texted me back.

That's the car that was outside your office building. It's FBI.

"Nothing for May," Mrs. McCarley said.

"June?" I said.

"I'm ahead of you," she said. "I'm into the second week of August. Nothing."

"What would be the cost of installing three new furnaces and three new air condensers?"

"That depends on the brand, size of the equipment, and where it's being installed. Some jobs can be more difficult because of physical obstructions or because they require additional manpower."

"Can you give me a range?"

"I'd say anywhere between fifteen thousand on the low end to over twenty-five thousand on the high end. But like I said, it really all depends. I can't give you exact numbers unless I know the job."

"Is it possible someone paid that kind of money, but their name wasn't attached to the payment?"

"Not possible," she said. "I keep the books. I know all the money that's coming and going. I wouldn't accept a payment for that kind of money without knowing where it's coming from."

And there it was. The oldest play in Chicago's thick, notorious book of dirty politics. Flynn took care of Blackwell getting all those lucrative contracts in his ward, and in return, Blackwell made sure Flynn's summer mansion was well heated in the winter and chilled appropriately during the summer. This wasn't the first time Flynn had done something like this, so why would he have felt the need to dispose of Joaquin Escobar? Chains made of the strongest metals were only as strong as their weakest link. Escobar was that link, and the FBI must've known that. They also must've known that Flynn's second weakest link was Blackwell, which was why he was absconded to the tropical island of Puerto Rico. They were going after Flynn, and they were going heavy.

40

In an hour, I was back on the crowded Dan Ryan Expressway in Chicago, heading to my office. I still had some unanswered questions, but I was certain Flynn had had Escobar killed in an attempt to eliminate a potential witness to his illegal kickback scheme. I was certain Flynn had entered into these kinds of arrangements hundreds of times while he was in office. What was it about this one that had him so nervous?

I thought about Shef and what he had said about Escobar being a good man. Then I looked out at the vast city and thought about all the good men who had been put into the ground by the murderous lot like Pat Flynn. The image of Shef flashed in my mind: his big hat, weather-beaten skin, and enormous hands. I couldn't stop thinking about how rough his hands were. His nails were chipped and caked with dirt and grime and who knew what else. Then it suddenly came to me. I swerved across traffic to the anger of the other drivers, who were flipping me the middle finger, and exited up the Garfield Boulevard ramp.

Burke called in.

"You have two more suits outside your office," he said.

"And I had two suits who followed me to Michigan," I said.

"What the hell were you doing in Michigan?"

"Admiring Flynn's waterfront manor."

"What for?"

I brought him up to speed on what I had learned from Shef and what I had pieced together from the absent payments in the bank statements.

"They've been trying to nail that motherfucker for years," Burke said. "They must finally have the noose around his neck."

"Which is why they suddenly swooped in and took Blackwell off the grid," I said. "With Rio gone, Blackwell would be next."

"You're gonna need to sit down and talk to the suits."

"I'm planning on it."

"When?"

"After I confirm one more piece of the puzzle."

"Keep me updated."

I disconnected the line and began racing west on Garfield. I was pissed at myself for not thinking of this earlier.

Mechanic called in.

"We have a problem," he said.

"What's going on?" I said.

"A black SUV just pulled up to the apartment building. Your friend Smiley jumped out and ran inside."

"Have you seen Julieta at all today?"

"Nope."

"I'm on my way to you. Ten minutes. I'm gonna call her."

"What do you want me to do?"

"Turn your car on and sit tight."

I dialed Julieta's number. It didn't ring. It went straight to voicemail. I dialed it a second time. Same thing.

My phone buzzed. It was Mechanic.

"I'm going as fast as I can," I said.

"Not fast enough," he said. "He came out holding her by the arm. He put her in the car, and now they're rolling."

"Are you on them?"

"Right behind."

"Which way are they heading?"

"South on Halsted."

I made a U-turn at the median and started to head toward Halsted.

"Have you crossed Garfield yet?" I said.

"A couple minutes ago. We're on Seventy-Third."

I was only eighteen blocks away. Not far, but the traffic lights weren't cooperating.

"I'm about to make the turn on Halsted," I said. "Stay close."

"What do you want me to do if he stops at a light?"

"Just hang with him until I get there. As long as they're driving, he's not gonna do anything to her. I'll stay on the phone."

I caught about ten blocks on Halsted before I came to a stop behind a city bus and a garbage truck. I tried to dip to the right of the bus, but there wasn't enough room between the bus and the row of parked cars. I waited for the light to turn green, and once there was enough space between the truck and the bus, I split them.

"They're taking a turn on Eighty-Seventh Street," Mechanic said.

"East or west?"

"West."

"Can you see into the car?"

"Nope. Windows are too dark."

I flew through a red light at Eighty-First Street, barely missing a car making a turn across my lane.

"We just went past Racine," Mechanic said.

"I'm turning onto Eighty-Seventh."

"Just hung a right on Ashland."

"I just passed May."

"He's pulling into a driveway. A small warehouse next to a used tire shop. East side of the street. What should I do?"

"Pull in nearby, but don't let him see you. Keep a visual on them."

I flew through the intersection of Racine and Eighty-Seventh. I was only a few blocks away from Ashland.

"I'm almost there," I said.

"He's getting out of the truck," Mechanic said. "He's walking around to her side. He just pulled her out. Shit."

"What?"

"He has a gun."

"Jesus Christ!"

"I can't just sit here," Mechanic said. "I'm getting out. They just went inside."

I pulled into the parking lot. I saw Mechanic's car, Smiley's SUV, and Mechanic walking calmly across the parking lot. He had his piece out and against his thigh.

"Here," I said.

Mechanic turned and looked at me, then motioned to indicate they had gone through the single door next to the closed metal rolling door. I cut across the parking lot behind him to the side of the building.

"I'm looking for any other access points," I said.

"Copy that," he said.

I walked along the side of the brick building. There were no doors or windows. The same when I got to the back of the building. However, on the other side, there were three large windows about eight feet off the ground.

"Three windows on the north side of the building," I said. "One fire escape at the northeast corner."

"Is it operational?" Mechanic said.

"It's old, but it looks like it works. Do you see any cameras?"

"One over the door where they entered," he said.

"Nothing back here or on either of the other sides," I said. "Meet me by the windows."

We met on the north side of the building.

"We have to move fast," I said. "I don't know what he'll do to her. I'm going on the roof to see if there's an entry point."

There was a rolling dumpster and two old metal garbage cans sitting in an open area about ten yards away from the building.

"Let's see if we can get the dumpster underneath the windows. If you can get on the dumpster, you'll be able to see inside. We have to find some way in."

We went over to the dumpster. The wheels were old and rusted, but with great effort, we were able to move it underneath the windows. I ran to the back of the building and climbed the rickety ladder to the roof. There were two large skylights. I walked as quietly as possible to the first window and called Mechanic.

"I'm on the roof," I said. "Two skylights. I'm at the first one. I looked through it. I don't see anything."

"I'm in the window. I don't see anything either. Open space. Some machines on a couple tables. They might be in a room or an office that I can't see from where I am."

I quietly walked over to the second skylight and looked through. Nothing.

"No visuals at the second skylight either," I said. "I'm going to try to draw him out."

"Wait," Mechanic said. "I see movement. She is walking slowly across the floor. Do you see that?"

I didn't see anything. I walked back to the other skylight, trying not to make any noise. Still nothing.

"They're outside my field of view," I said.

"He is pointing the gun at her."

"Do you have a clean shot?"

"Negative."

I looked around me and found a metal plate that had been attached to an air-condenser unit in the middle of the roof. I picked it up and went over to the skylight.

"I'm going to try to draw him away from her and out into the open," I said. "Once I do that, if you see an opening, take it. You'll probably have only one shot."

"It's me you're talking to," Mechanic said. "That's all I need."

I knelt next to the skylight, took the metal plate, and tapped it hard so that it could be heard below. I kept tapping slowly so Smiley would know it wasn't just an incidental noise. I wanted him to think it was intentional. Just as I was about to tap the plate for the eighth time, I heard a large explosion—a gunshot and shattered glass. I couldn't see what had happened.

Mechanic's voice came through my earbud.

"Bingo."

I raced down the ladder and around to the front of the building. As I arrived, the door flung open, and Julieta ran into my arms, crying and screaming.

"It's over," I said. "You're gonna be alright."

I walked her to my car while Mechanic went inside to gather Smiley.

"He's still breathing," Mechanic said.

Once she and I were in the car, I called and gave Burke our location.

"You set up Rio," I said.

She looked up at me, tears still streaming down her face.

"You went to his apartment that night with the intention of getting his DNA. You seduced him, because you knew he wouldn't be able to resist. In the middle of having sex, you scratched him. You left his apartment and met up with Smiley. He took the DNA from under your fingernails and transplanted it under Joaquin's fingernails."

"I had no idea that's what they were going to do," she said, crying. "They told me they had a way of convincing Rio to leave me alone. They told me they would take care of me while I got myself back on my feet. Not once did they say Joaquin was going to die or that they were going to frame Rio for a murder he didn't commit. You have to believe me."

Wailing sirens were quickly approaching us.

"I do," I said. "But I'm not the one you'll need to convince. Good luck."

I got out of the car and waited for the police to arrive.

"WE REALLY NEED YOU TO cease all activities related to Pat Flynn," Colangelo said. He was the FBI agent who had been the first out of the car when I arrived at my office. We now sat across from each other at my desk. Lundquist was the name of the female suit who sat in the chair next to Colangelo.

"I have enough to give to the police to have him arrested for conspiracy to commit at least two murders," I said. "Harrington can be flipped to testify against him."

"We understand that," Lundquist said. "We know you've put in a lot of work. But we are nearing the end of an operation that's been years in the making."

"And because you have three letters on the back of your jacket, your investigation supersedes my investigation," I said.

"That's not how we look at it," Colangelo said. "We'd like to think of this as a collective effort. We're on the same team here."

"You want what I have, but you won't give me what you have," I said. "You call that a collective effort?"

They looked at each other.

"Gentry has vouched for you," Colangelo said. "She said you can be trusted."

"I'm glad someone thinks that."

"We've been watching Flynn for a while," Lundquist said. "We have him on racketeering, bribery, and extortion. Fourteen counts total."

I whistled. "He'll die in prison if you can get a conviction on even just some of those charges."

"That's our intention," Colangelo said. "Which is why we're interested in what you know and what you have."

"What exactly do you have him for?"

They looked at each other again, then Lundquist said, "Some of what you've been working on and already figured out."

"Blackwell."

"He's been extorting Hank Blackwell for a number of years. Flynn's granted him city business and various permits in his ward in exchange for Blackwell hiring the services of Flynn's private law firm for some of his legal work. Flynn's also gotten favors from Blackwell and others in the form of free work."

"Like the work done to his summer house in Michigan," I said.

"Exactly," Lundquist said.

"Which is why he had Joaquin Escobar killed."

"Escobar was a threat to him."

"Why did he feel that way about Escobar and not others who could've blown the whistle on him?" I said.

"This has been a big operation," Colangelo said. "The longer these investigations go on, the greater the likelihood that there are leaks. Flynn found out we were looking at him, and he knew TNL Heating & Cooling was a big problem because it was a way for us to get in."

"So he removed the threat. If Escobar was key to your case, why didn't you protect him?"

"What happened to Mr. Escobar was unfortunate," Lundquist said. "We regret we couldn't save him, but at the time, we didn't know how much Flynn was aware of what was going on. When Mr. Escobar died, we knew there was a problem."

"Which is why you took Blackwell."

"We couldn't afford to lose both witnesses," Colangelo said.

"Where does Turner fit in all this?" I said.

"What do you know about Turner?" Lundquist said.

"She has bad taste in sandwiches."

They smiled.

"I saw photos of the handoffs," I said.

"How?" Colangelo said.

"Someone anonymously sent them to me."

"To our point about leaks," Colangelo said.

"Turner is working with us also," Lundquist said.

"Was she also extorting Blackwell?"

"We'd prefer not to get into that," Lundquist said. "Let's just say, she's been critical to the last stages of this investigation."

"I have enough to turn over to the police and have him arrested," I said.

"We've been working with CPD," Colangelo said.

"Which might be the reason why you've had leaks."

"We've considered that," he said, "but with an investigation of this size and scope, we need to partner with other agencies. There's a risk that comes with that. We try to minimize the risks, but sometimes they can't be avoided."

"What's next?" I said.

"We're going to indict him on those fourteen charges," Lundquist said.

"When?"

Colangelo looked down at his watch. "The US attorney for the Northern District of Illinois is in front of the grand jury as we speak. Flynn will be in custody before the start of the afternoon rush hour."

"Hell hath no fury like the prosecutorial arm of the US government."

41

One Month Later

"Will they get him?" Ivan asked.

Ivan and I were sitting in the clubhouse of Grove XXIII, Michael Jordan's private golf course in Hobe Sound, Florida, waiting for Penny Packer to arrive. Two US senators sat at the table next to us with a movie star and the CEO of a sneaker company. A Cy Young Award–winning pitcher for the Houston Astros sat at the bar, laughing it up with one of the anchors from a national morning news program.

"They raided all three of his offices," I said. "They intercepted more than nine thousand of his calls in one of the longest wiretaps in US history. I think they're going to get him."

"When is the trial?"

"Next year."

"What takes so long?"

"The wheels of justice grind slow but grind fine."

"What about the man who actually killed my uncle?"

"Smiley will never walk this earth again as a free man. It won't bring your uncle back, but it might bring your family some comfort knowing that his killer will only leave prison in a body bag."

Ivan nodded. "It helps," he said. "The thought of him getting away with Joaquin's murder would've haunted us forever."

"I heard Penny gave you the name of a great lawyer for your civil suit against him and Flynn."

"She did. He's already been in touch with their lawyers. I think they want to reach a settlement."

"That's good for your family. This could be a big help to your aunt and cousins."

I thought about Flynn's summer mansion in Michigan and wondered if there was a *FOR SALE* sign out front on that freshly painted white fence. Just that image alone would be poetic justice.

"What about that girl he was seeing?" Ivan said.

"Julieta," I said. "She's probably going to plea out. Depends on the state attorney, but she might get some time, or they'll give her a long probation."

"How can people sleep with someone, be in a relationship and be in love with them, then turn around and be part of a plan to kill them?"

"Happens all the time. Unfortunately. The heart is one of the most complicated organs in the body. I don't think anyone will ever fully understand it. I stopped trying a long time ago."

Penny emerged from the locker room looking like a billion dollars. The owner of the New York Yankees stopped to give her a kiss as she made her way across the room. A former president stopped and hugged her.

"Are you ready to go, men?" she said.

Ivan and I stood, and we each gave her a kiss.

"What did he say to you?" I said, pointing to the former president.

"He asked to join our threesome," she said.

"What did you say?"

"Never in a million years."

Ivan was in disbelief. "You turned down a former US president?" he said.

"Without even thinking about it," Penny said.

"Why?"

"Because he's a known cheater. And I could never sit back and let anyone cheat me. Not even a guy who was once the most powerful man in the world."

We walked out of the dining room and through the dark glass doors that led to the course. Our caddies were patiently standing by our golf carts, at the ready. Ivan looked around and took it all in, the sun warming our faces as those back in Chicago were bundled up against the bitter cold.

"I really want to thank you for helping my family," he said. "I knew deep down in my heart that he didn't die by accident, like they said he did. But I never thought anyone would be able to find out what really happened to him."

We shook hands and embraced.

"There's something my grandfather told me as a little boy that I will never forget," I said. "Even to this day, it still motivates me."

"What's that?" Ivan said.

"'Three things cannot be long hidden: the sun, the moon, and the truth.'"

Acknowledgments

In the course of writing the Ashe Cayne series, I rely on a plethora of experts and professionals to give me the details on procedures, justifications, history, and other details that I try my best to accurately reflect. I am especially grateful to my now-retired friend the inimitable Detective Socrates Mabry as well as other extremely generous members of the Chicago Police Department who have tolerated my incessant and detailed questioning. Any procedural mistakes I have made are not to be attributed to them but to me. I also want to acknowledge the many readers of the series who send me emails and messages on social media, expressing their love for Ashe Cayne and encouraging me to write faster. Damian Cherry is at the top of that list. I hear and see you, and appreciate your support!

About the Author

Ian K. Smith is a #1 *New York Times* bestselling author. His Chicago-based Ashe Cayne series is currently in development to become a streaming TV series, and his novel *The Ancient Nine* has been optioned to become a motion picture. His acclaimed novel *The Blackbird Papers* was a Black Caucus of the American Library Association fiction honor award recipient. Many of his books have been number one bestsellers and have been translated into more than ten languages. He remains a health and fitness enthusiast, and rarely turns down a round of golf or a good workout. He is a graduate of Harvard and Columbia, and did his first two years of medical school at Dartmouth, finishing his medical degree at the University of Chicago.

For more information, you can visit:
www.doctoriansmith.com
Instagram: doctoriansmith
TikTok: theofficialdrian
Facebook: IanSmithMD
X: @DrIanSmith